THE DEMONS OF JAITRAYA

Shubira Prasad

Vitasta

Published by
Renu Kaul Verma
Vitasta Publishing Pvt Ltd
2/15, Ansari Road, Daryaganj
New Delhi - 110 002
info@vitastapublishing.com

ISBN: 978-93-86473-90-5

First Edition 2020
Second Reprint 2021
MRP ₹ 350

Edited by Veena Batra
Typeset & Cover Design by Somesh Kumar Mishra
Printed by Vikas Computer and Printers

Dedicated to my father (Late) Shri Anant Swarup
from whom I inherited my extreme
love for reading.

Contents

Acknowledgements

There have been many people who have been directly or indirectly involved in the formation of this book. Lipika Bhushan of Market My Book was the one who kickstarted the whole thing and introduced me to many people in the literary circle. My publisher Renu Kaul Verma with whom I had an immediate rapport. My editor Veena Batra who guided me every step of the way. Somesh, who has so beautifully designed my book. And of course all the people in Vitasta who helped in turning my manuscript "The Demons of Jaitraya" into a book.

My sons Saurabh and Sarvesh along with their wives Shubhra and Deepika who gave me excellent suggestions from time to time. Aaroh and Myra with their endless curiosity compelled me to do more research. Above all the encouragement of my husband Arun, a history and current affairs buff, who is not much into fiction but who never failed to surprise me with his ideas on how to tackle demons.

Prologue

Circa 6300 Bc

The sound was deafening. He tried in vain to open his eyes. They were sealed with his own dried and caked blood. He tried to wipe the blood with his hands but he could not move his fingers. Every part of his body seemed to be broken. He could not move. He was covered with mud. Pebbles, stones, rocks and boulders from all sides smothered him. He was buried alive miles deep inside the Earth. His whole world seemed to be this utter darkness. He could smell the Earth everywhere but not the plants or the greenery; it seemed as if there had never been any plant life or the universe was like this only, a dark cavernous cave which held one in shackles. Was this death? he wondered. Did it matter? he thought in his apathy. Nothing was important—life, death or pain.

As consciousness came to him, he remembered how he came to be in this condition. He was struck by lightning. He tried to brace himself as he fell on the ground but the ground opened up like an unending chasm and he fell into it. He was in a tomb-like environment. He could not move and the pain was excruciating. Apart from being shot in the air by bolts of lightning and falling down, he could not remember anything. How long he had lain there he did not know. The air was thick with dirt. He was thankful that there was some air in the tomb that he was enshrined in. He learned that if he did not move at all, the pain would be just a bit less. But his restiveness only helped in increasing the pain manifold. Each and every sense of his was being decimated gradually. At a loss to know what to do, he almost gave up though he did try to keep himself awake, to what purpose he did not know. He tried to sleep while he waited for death. But this was death only, probably much worse. As the air diminished he began forgetting everything about his life and also his will power to live.

A long time back he had been cursed by a sage that he would keep on forgetting about his strength and prowess. He had the power and strength to break the moulds that had entombed him, but because of the curse he did not know that he had the power to break himself free. He did not remember anything. He would remember this only after somebody reminded him. That is why ordinary humans prayed to him and reminded him of his great powers. But here, there was nobody to remind him.

It was not in his nature to wait for outside help. Rather it was always the other way around. After ages, he thought he heard a sound through the deafening silence in his ears.

"Hanuman!"

He was on the verge of entering his last and ultimate sleep. He was in too much pain and agony to respond to the sound. After some time he heard the sound again. It was as if somebody was calling him. He ignored it again.

"Hanuman! Hanuman!"

The call persisted and was sounding desperate to seek a response. He knew it was just a figment of his imagination. No sound could penetrate the thick layers of rock and slag that engulfed him. But as the sound continued he realised that it was not coming from outside his body but from inside it. The sound was in his mind and in his heart and it went on and on now almost lamenting and in tears. Suddenly everything was clear. It was as if loads of adrenaline had been injected in his veins. His heart pounded with only one thought in his mind. He sat up and opened his eyes and saw everything. Except that he couldn't open his eyes and there was no question of shifting in this necropolis of earth and stones. Rejuvenated he sat up in excitement except that he couldn't even move. Pain lashed his body in enormous colourful waves. He despaired, '*Prabhu*, (Master), I hear you but I am unable to come to you,' he cried in his thoughts in despair not knowing whether his prabhu would hear him or not.

"Hanuman, I can hear you," came the desperate and exultant reply, "Where are you?"

"I don't know Prabhu, I am trapped under the Earth, I cannot move or see," he replied telepathically.

"Oh! Okay Hanuman, I am coming to you," replied Bhagwan Ram.

"Yes, Prabhu," Hanuman replied joyfully and tearfully. A

few tears trickled from his eyes loosening them of the encrusted blood. He still could not open them. But he was happy now, his pain almost forgotten. Instead of him going to the rescue of his prabhu, it was his prabhu coming to rescue him.

There was not much time to think after that. Suddenly the ground above him crumbled and was blown away. Drops of muddy rain fell on his face. He took a deep shuddering breath. Slowly he felt his face. Yes, he could move! He rubbed his eyes gingerly washing away the blood. He could now see the inky blue sky, the stars twinkling like pink, red and white jewels. He realised that he was watching the sky through his bloodstained eyes. *Jai Shri Ram!* His prabhu had found him and saved him! Despite his discomfort, Hanuman's thought was only of his prabhu and how he had failed him.

Jai Shri Ram, he mentally chanted his miraculous mantra. With great effort, he flew out of the cavernous hole. It looked as if a huge mountain was thrusting out of the Earth with Hanuman at its helm. Hanuman bolted in the air with the rocks and boulders following him for some time then falling down on the ground and rolling far and wide concordant to their sizes. Hanuman fell down sobbing at Shri Ram's feet. Shri Ram tenderly and carefully picked him up as if he was a small child and placed his head on his lap.

They were in a small clearing in a jungle, though now the clearing was covered with flora and fauna and boulders and stones which had been pulled out from their roots when Hanuman flew out of the bottomless crevasse. It was almost night. But there was enough light for Ram to assess Hanuman's condition. Soldiers with torchlights had made a tight circle around them. In the dusk, the shadows of the trees and the soldiers with their torches had started dancing around Hanuman. He felt no pain and no trauma. He was in his *Prabhu's* arms. He was ecstatic.

"Laxman!" ordered Shri Ram, "Get Vaidyaji quickly. Hanuman needs immediate attention."

"Yes bhaiya." Laxman rushed away. Ram took Hanuman in his lap. Hanuman closed his eyes and sighed. He had come home. Laxman rushed back with Vaidyaji on his toes and his huge bag of medicines, herbs and other medical paraphernalia. In this vicious and incredible war, Vaidyaji and his assistants were fully prepared for such contingencies. Shri Ram himself was in tears seeing the condition of his beloved Hanuman whom he never considered as his attendant, rather more as a friend and helper. But Hanuman was unconcerned with all this. He was reunited with his prabhu and that was all that mattered.

It took Hanuman a couple of days to recover fully. He was still covered with the herbal bandages Vaidyaji had put on him from head to feet—the bandages soaked with various healing herbs. But it was his own superhuman immune system which was healing him so fast. He fretted and fumed. The guilt that he nursed in his heart would just not go away. He was supposed to get rid of the extraneous forces of the demon king Ravan's army, but they had outsmarted him. He would have destroyed them; there was no doubt about that. Nobody, absolutely nobody could ever thwart the great and mighty Hanuman. But the cunning demons had anticipated their annihilation and that of the demon king Ravan and his army of demons, so some of them had silently planned their escape. They knew exactly when and where Hanuman would come after them. He would kill and destroy them without any effort and mercy. Therefore they planned to buy some time for themselves. They placed hurdles in his path, minuscule for Hanuman but giving them enough time to fly or burrow and hide in different places, change their shapes and go into deep and long hibernation for centuries. These demons now would not leave anything to chance. *Yugas* would pass before they came out. Now they would come out only in Kalyug when human civilization would itself be at its lowest zenith, where human beings would themselves behave like demons and vampires. In this scenario, it would become extremely difficult to sort out the demons from the demoniac humans.

A few days had passed. Hanuman walked towards Ram who was sitting on a hillock in a pensive mood. Hanuman quietly sat down at Shri Ram's feet and waited. The battle was over. Shri Ram was the king of Ayodhya now. The mood was sombre; even the wind hesitated in blowing fast. The trees were quiet; the birds and the sky waited in animated suspense. The hills rolled around them like impatient, angry waves. The dark sky hung low giving a claustrophobic feeling. Hanuman could gauge his master's frame of mind. He knew that his prabhu was upset. He also knew that it was not because of Sita *maiya* but something totally different which had to do with him. He sat there patiently.

After a while, Shri Ram spoke, "Hanuman I know you are upset and rightly so, but they have got away. Though no mission is impossible for you, this is going to be a very long wait and extremely tedious. Very soon the fourth Yug will begin. This will be the Kalyug; it will be a future devoid of any hope; it will be an unprecedented road. Scholars and thinkers will know that goodness is being erased; greed and wealth will become the synonyms for success. Might is right will be cherished. Human beings will become demons along with the real demons who will emerge from their dormancy. Life will be an unending dystopian nightmare from which there will be no awakening. Despair, corruption, and pollution will be as ubiquitous as air and water. The simple and weak-willed human beings shall be forced by the emerging demons to unwillingly become like them. It will become impossible to segregate human beings from the demons, males as well as females. There will be *rakshasas, bhoots, praits, dakinis, shakinis* and so many other kinds of demons. We have to counter these in the most forceful manner possible. We have to gather a new set of committed warriors who will impart their training along with their divine weapons to their descendants. Their progeny will have these capabilities along with the scientific developments of their own era. From now itself you will begin the training of warriors to find and destroy the leftover demons. Initially, you will train warriors in the Himalayas, later they can form groups and come down and spread all over the Earth. They, in turn, will train other warriors. You will control everything though from a distance when Kalyug comes."

"Yes Prabhu." Hanuman understood immediately though he still hankered after the lost opportunity.

"And Hanuman, very soon I shall be going back to

Vaikunth; you will stay back till the end of Kalyug to oversee all this and spread the message of *Ramayana* in your way. There is nobody more qualified than you to be my emissary of *Ramayana* and the destruction of the rest of the demons."

For a moment Hanuman did not grasp what his prabhu had just conveyed. He understood about the training of warriors and destroying the demons. But when he inferred the full gist of his master's order, he was devastated. His Lord and master was leaving this world without taking him! How could this be possible? Death would be preferable to living without his master. He fell at Shri Ram's feet. There was a gasp from Mother Earth and the nature around them. There were mixed feelings. The sadness that Shri Ram would leave them but the reassurance that Hanuman would be there to protect them.

"Prabhu," Hanuman sobbed, "You cannot leave me here. I am your servant. My life is nothing without you. My very existence is because of you. Prabhu, I implore you, take me with you or don't go—stay here on Earth to guide us and love us. All the wrongdoings on Mother Earth will be healed by you. We cannot come to you in Vaikunth, it is forbidden, and yet staying away from you is unsurpassed pain. Your absence will only bring me sorrow, for my heart will be with you in Vaikunth and my mind and body will be here on Earth. How can this be possible Prabhu?" Hanuman was heartbroken.

"Hanuman you are *Chiranjeevi* (immortal). You will stay here till the end of time. It will be your duty to protect all the devotees from the demons both inside and outside this world. The cruel and fierce Kalyug is on its way. You will help in establishing Dharma in this Kalyug. You know I cannot stay here, but I'll keep on coming here at predestined times in various avatars to guide the people. But it is my blessing to you to be here on this Earth to spread goodness everywhere, righting the wrongs done to human beings by the demons and by other human beings. In addition, you will also spread the word of the *Ramayana* and teach the people about righteousness, honesty, truthfulness, caring and loving. Your trainees will destroy the absconding and the leftover demons."

This was said in a very neutral tone but Hanuman knew that it was a command. He kept his head down. His lord's wish was his command.

Bhagwan Ram continued, "Hanuman, to maintain the balance of this Earth, good and evil will have to coexist albeit on parallel lines. We have to fight our inner demons as well as demons on the outside. We can reach the highest levels of our efficacy by fighting these demons, whether small or big. We will always be there to guide human beings to be good and get rid of evil. This whole world is Maya or illusion. We have to guide the people of the Earth to open their eyes and see the truth. You have been blessed by Brahmaji with so many boons. You will be immune to weapons, you will be able to change into any form that you desire and you will be able to travel anywhere at any speed. These are just a few of your powers. Who better than you to lead and look after the world?"

Hanuman heard his prabhu loud and clear and understood everything. But the despair in his heart was too great. His very life was leaving him till eternity and there were no elixir vitae to solve this problem. It was his prabhu's desire.

"When will you take me with you Prabhu?" he asked in

anguish. This was the mighty Hanuman who did not allow even Yam Devta or the God of Death to come near his prabhu, who now had no choice but to adhere to these directives.

"At the end of Kalyug, Hanuman, when I shall come in my Kalki avatar. I will bring righteousness and happiness again to this earth. At that time you will leave with me," Bhagwan Ram answered.

Hanuman bowed his head. The decree was announced. The *Panchtattwas* or the five elements of Earth, Water, Fire, Air and Space also bowed down to God's proclamation and set to work.

Early Twentieth Century
Aishani

Aishani was not a classic beauty. She was of average height and somewhat good looking too. She was fair and had regular features. To an ordinary viewer at first glance, she looked like an average girl, but a second look gave her away. Her eyes had a tendency to change their colour according to the atmosphere around her. In quiet times, her eyes were blue or hazel; when she was disturbed they turned yellowish brown and when she was angry they turned reddish brown. But generally, they were dark brown in colour. She had artistically long and softly tapering fingers. Though they looked soft they were very strong, capable of lifting heavy weights and crushing herbs with pestle and mortar and equally soft when putting them around a sick patient or child. The positive aura which radiated from within her struck everybody. Everybody wanted to be her friend, be it boys or girls, young or old. She had an unusual aura.

She was in the last year of her graduation pursuing Psychology as her major subject. She had a keen interest in the human psyche, and with her astute understanding of human nature she was able to excel in her chosen subject. Like any modern girl, she was smartly dressed and carried herself with utmost grace. Her father, Pandit Ram Sharan, was a pandit and an Ayurvedic doctor. She had a younger brother Jayant who was in senior school and her mother, Madhu, was a homemaker. Theirs was a normal middle-class family which led a normal life doing all the mundane things that an average ordinary family does.

However, there was much beyond the ordinariness that the family showcased. Along with their usual school and college, Aishani and her brother Jayant attended another school which had different subjects and different kinds of training. This was an Ashram or Gurukul which was known as the School of Ancient Warfare. Here they were taught ancient methods of fighting in a war with enemies who were other entities apart from human beings. These were known to be creatures which had escaped from the great war of the *Ramayana*. These creatures were expected to attack the Earth and its inhabitants in myriad evil and cruel ways.

Despite her unwillingness to miss any of her college studies, Aishani had to miss quite a lot of her classes because of her training at home and in the Martial Arts Academy. Many times she had to miss her classes at home because her father Pandit Ram Sharan was not available. He was also her teacher who taught her Ayurveda and all esoteric subjects. She had a very good knowledge of Ayurveda and always suggested herbs and special spices to patients who suffered from mild illnesses. She was at her best helping people and animals, birds and even insects. Her kind nature and inner beauty shone like the sun but it was her simplicity that immediately made the people around her very comfortable and relaxed, especially her father's patients who were happy whenever she was there to look after them in his absence. Her mere presence provided them solace and they felt special.

Her hair was like molten chocolate cascading over her shoulders. Sometimes, when she was very moved by a happening or somebody's plight, her hair helped in hiding her face and thus her emotions too. The aura that emanated from her made her look much taller than she was and made people want to look up to her. There were no pretensions about her; she was what she was, in and out, and people around her knew it and were reassured by it. They trusted her knowing that their trust would never be betrayed.

Pandit Ram Sharan owned a sprawling house almost on the outskirts of the town. The two front rooms of the house were turned into his Ayurvedic and puja shops. One room held Ayurvedic herbs and medicines and the other had a collection of puja items along with yantras, talismans and religious books. Beyond these two rooms was a huge library which housed a large number of books on almost every subject but mostly esoteric in nature. There was a large covered verandah in front of the two rooms. Comfortable cane chairs were scattered on the verandah. It was where Panditji would sit and read the newspaper or his books. Sometimes Madhu would also sit there to cut vegetables or knit a sweater.

The rambling huge house had an open square space in the middle and several rooms around the square. There was a Tulsi plant in the centre of the square and several flowering potted plants also. Aishani's mother kept a herb garden here growing herbs like coriander, mint, dill, etc. There was a garden in front of the house and there was a huge backyard too. The back garden was where Aishani and her brother Jayant had grown up. There were fruit trees all around. There were two mango trees, the branches of one grew horizontally and they were always lush with leaves. It was a huge tree almost fifty years old. The other mango tree grew vertically. Aishani and her friend Ruby would climb on the larger tree with horizontal branches, and spend most of their time there talking or reading. The other mango tree which grew vertically almost always housed a nest of one bird or another.

Both the girls watched in fascination when a cuckoo would lay her eggs in the crow's nest and the crow would sit on the eggs and rear the baby cuckoos as its own. That was the law of nature and they were fascinated by it. There were other fruit and flowering trees also—*jamun, shahtoot*, guava, *phalsa*, and pomegranate. Of course, a grove of banana trees was also there. Colourful bougainvilleas lined the boundary wall of the backyard beginning with white, yellow, and then finally red flowers. Pandit Ram Sharan was very fond of roses. He had planted various species of roses in the front garden along with dahlias and petunias in the winters. In winters his garden was a blaze of colours and the admiration and envy of his visitors and patients. The summers would be a blaze of sunflowers and the bushy kochias and the hardy zinnias. There was a special bed for marigolds. Aishani's parents liked to offer these flowers to their deities in their puja room. They offered white and yellow flowers to Saraswati, pink and red to Laxmi and red to Durga. If these colours were not available then the ubiquitous and auspicious marigold was always there.

Aishani and her mother had placed birdhouses and birdbaths in both the front and the backyard. She and her mother would feed *satnaja* or seven grains to the birds. As a result, there were all kinds of birds in their gardens throughout the day from the smallest sparrow to larger ones like Neelkanth. Different species of birds came for their food and bath at different times of the day. If one chose to see this aspect of nature with patience and serenity, then Pandit Ram Sharan's house was a delight and haven for bird watchers. Aishani would get up early in the morning, complete her ablutions, change into comfortable clothing, go the balcony outside her room, lay her yoga mat on the floor and do her Surya Namaskars. Her balcony faced two trees, one large and one slightly smaller. The big one was a mango tree and smaller one a guava tree. She would stand on her balco sometime inhaling the sweet, clean, slightly scented the air around her. The birds would also begin the song and chatter by this time. After that, she di of yoga, then went down and changed for th to their shop on the ground floor and ther

The early morning hours were he day. The shop would still be closed f pujas and meditations took a long time so she had the shop and the adjoining library all to herself. Of course, her mother would be busy in the kitchen and her brother Jayant had no interest in the shop or the library. After quickly cleaning and dusting everything including the books and the artifacts, she would do *aarti* of the three Goddesses—Durga, Lakshmi and Saraswati, light *diyas* and Guggul dhoop; then she would sit down with the books she had selected the previous night to be read this morning. There would be absolute silence in the shop. There would be peace and quiet outside too except for the warbling and singing of the birds who flitted happily across the windows and in and out of the trees.

The early quiet mornings were her most cherished times for reading and studying. Complete silence, no customers or patients to disturb her thoughts. She could literally hear her thoughts and talk to herself and have a conversation with herself. Her father would enter the shop at around 10:30 so she had almost three hours to herself to read all the valuable books that were there in her father's library. These were the great books on Ayurveda, Astrology, Astronomy, the Bhagavad Gita, the Vedas, the Puranas, the Upanishads and so much more! For her studying these books was such stimulated reading. It was almost as if she had an affinity to the knowledge contained in these books. When she read some of the chapters, there seemed to be a sense of déjà vu in her. But what kind of déjà vu could she have on reading the ncient texts? When she thought about it the familiar feeling uld just fade away. She was so interested in the star systems, lanets, the *Nakshatras* and what they entailed; the *tantra* and the *mantras*—what they meant and where they could be applied, how and when they could be chanted and how they were pronounced along with different materials—all this was very fascinating for her. She always felt that she was so lucky to be born at this time and place with such enlightening and magical things around her which at the moment were mainly books. She was quite adept in these subjects too, her teacher and her guru being her father.

Pandit Ram Sharan was a renowned pandit who was more of a scholar and an academician than a pandit. He was of medium height, very fair with a balding head and penetrating eyes. He could read a person by only glancing at him or her. He always wore very white and very clean clothes. His wife Madhu made sure that his dhoti and kurta were always ready, lightly starched and properly pressed. Pandit Ram Sharan was much more than what he claimed to be or what people thought of him. He almost did not belong to this world; rather he was not of this time.

He had always been Aishani's teacher right from the beginning of time, in one form or other. His relationship with Aishani panned many generations but it was always the same, that of teacher and student. Sometimes in more lucid births they just picked up and continued from their last births with Aishani always wondering how she and her teacher could relate to so many things without knowing each other.

Her father had been teaching Aishani right from the time she was a toddler. She could recite the gayatri mantra from the age of three ever since she had started speaking. And now, at the age of eighteen, she knew all the main shlokas; she knew all about the yantras that were in the shop and how to activate them. She knew quite a lot about tantra too but her father forbade her to use it or advise any customer on it. Tantra vidya involves very ritualistic incantations and objects, sometimes parts of animals and birds. It is a very secretive ceremony and very effective too. If not performed meticulously it can give adverse and disastrous results. Theirs was purely a Vedic shop which sold only Vedic items.

Her mother did not allow her to do any household chores; it was as if Madhu instinctively knew that her Aishani was meant for much higher things which were not related to household duties, though Aishani could make good tea the way her parents liked with lots of milk and ginger and sometimes jaggery also. Without even her husband telling her Madhu knew that her daughter was meant for much higher things and that her husband was training her for these things.

She also knew that there were others also involved in training her daughter. All these thoughts scared her so much that she had stopped thinking about them. She knew that there was going to be violence in Aishani's life; she knew that Aishani's destiny was to get rid of as much of the evil forces as was possible. Madhu also knew that there were other such people also who were getting rid of evil, and others who were born to destroy these evil forces just like Aishani was. She feared for her daughter's life. Pandit Ram Sharan also had tied a *tabeej* around Aishani's left arm to protect her from negative forces. But he knew very well that much more than a *tabeej* was required to protect his sweet innocent daughter.

Her parents were very proud of Aishani. They were a bit

concerned for her brother Jayant, though they hid their feelings quite well. Jayant did not show any inclination towards his father's profession. The library left him cold. He grudgingly went to procure the Ayurvedic herbs from the bylanes of the city and sometimes from outside it also. He knew everybody and everybody knew him. Both brother and sister were sunny in nature always looking at the brighter side of things. But whereas Jayant was merely a happy go lucky boy, Aishani was all that and more—she was serious, hardworking and very focused.

Jayant and Aishani were two opposites. Where Aishani was sober, focused and soft-spoken, Jayant was just the opposite. He was of middling height and slim with a mop of curly hair. Always on the go, he had a horde of 'best friends'. He was always laughing, cracking jokes and spreading laughter around. He was the apple of his mother's eye and he was everybody's favourite too. Like Aishani he was also enrolled in the Warfare College or Gurukul or the Ashram and he too used to go there for his training along with Aishani. But unlike Aishani he did not excel in any subject and it was known to his teachers and parents that he was not interested.

He was not a failure in any subject; it was just that these subjects did not inspire him. Nor was he looking for any inspiration. His mother was just too happy that this child of hers was going to lead a normal human life. Jayant was two years younger than Aishani. There were not many things common between brother and sister but the invisible bond between them was so strong that once in a while their parents felt that they could communicate mentally without talking or even looking at each other. So much so that Pandit Ram

Sharan and his wife were absolutely reassured that not a hair on Aishani's head would be harmed if Jayant was around or even if he wasn't there, they were so attuned to each other. Like Aishani, the studies and the training at the Gurukul came easily to Jayant but whereas Aishani took everything very seriously and her shoulders already seemed to be weighed by an unknown dark destiny, Jayant took everything lightly and laughed at the slightest provocation.

It did not disturb him at all when he did not do well in some of his tests. He would do well in the next ones. There had been occasions when he had not attended a few classes which was a very serious matter in the Gurukul. Such truancy had to be reported immediately to Guruji, the head of the institution. In a few instances, a couple of students had even been thrown out of the Gurukul. Jayant would go sheepishly into Guruji's cottage.

Everybody—his colleagues and even the teachers would await with bated breath to hear the outcome of the drubbing which Jayant must surely be getting at the hands of Guruji. Their breathing would become normal with relief when Jayant would come out of the cottage with a sheepish smile on his face and join his comrades.

He never told anyone what conspired inside Guruji's cottage, no matter how often anyone asked him. For one, he could not tell them that his presence in the Gurukul was mandatory and that his antics, which of course he enjoyed very much, were a subterfuge to distract attention from his sister so that she could continue with her training uninterrupted. When he went to Guruji, Guruji would reiterate his responsibilities regarding Aishani and that would be all.

Nobody could guess that behind his playful and happy façade was a razor-sharp mind which could think ahead and all around his sister Aishani. He could think of her present and visualise and plan for her future too. As of now, of all the people around them, it was only Jayant who knew how important Aishani's mission in this life was. Millennia had passed; everybody had forgotten something or the other, the demons as well as the keepers of peace on the Earth—the peace which would be led by Aishani and her partner. In fact, Aishani wasn't even aware of the fact that she had a partner in the scheme of her life. It was the childlike Jayant who was aware of most of the facts of their past births and their place in the context of the present century.

He knew that the reality was far away from his projected image. He knew that there were other people also out there who were Aishani's protectors. But probably none of them knew about each other. Jayant was aware of this fact that there was a definite hierarchy in his sister's bodyguards of which one would be her protector, partner, and husband too. He was aware that Aishani would be at her destructive best in annihilating the demons only with her partner's energy, help and support.

He also knew that the real fireworks would begin only when Aishani's partner would enter the scene. Whether this person was in their vicinity or not, he did not know. He could be anywhere—in the Ashram, or in their college or somewhere else. At the moment everybody or whoever was in Aishani's vicinity just had this primeval instinct to protect her. They did not know about their own reasons for wanting to protect her or how she was going to lead them. This was a fact of which even Aishani was not aware.

These were the four primary inhabitants of Pandit Ram Sharan's house. Apart from these four, there were other people also, mainly the two servants—a male servant, and a female servant. The male servant was Chhedi and the name of the female servant was Deepa. Deepa used to stay with them while Chhedi used to come from a nearby village. They had been very well trained by Aishani's mother Madhu, so much so that their household always ran on smoothly oiled hinges.

There was another member of this household, a very integral part of it without whom the house wouldn't be a house at all. This member was the house itself. Pandit Ram Sharan's family had been living in this house for generations. So many generations had lived and gone in this house. It was not only a structure with four walls. There was a history to each and every room and wall of the house. It had seen so many ups and down that it had become an entity in itself. Its presence was felt by only the four people in the family. Any other person saw it just as a beautiful structure. There were ways of the house speaking to them in a language which only they understood.

Aishani could spend her whole life in what she called her father's magic shop. It wasn't a magic shop per se, it was just that the unconventional solutions he or sometimes Aishani gave to people, helped them so much in their problems that they started calling it the magic shop. Many people had so much faith in Pandit Ram Sharan and Aishani that they would come only to them for any problem, physical or emotional. All

Aishani wanted was to learn from her father about the great books which were in the library which adjoined the shop—books on Vedas, Puranas, mythology, the Gita, books on Ayurveda and of course books on Tantric Vidya—the list was endless. She was almost always drowned in these books, but her mother wanted her to attend regular school and college. Her father had reluctantly agreed. It would have never crossed Aishani's mind to reject her mother's desires. Ma's wishes were her wishes, there were no two ways about it, but it was her father she looked up to. Her father was her mentor, her friend, guide and philosopher, above all her fun-loving friend. She always depended on him to involve her in some fun activity whether it was a delightful conversation or gifting her an invisibility cloak for her twelfth birthday.

Aahh! Yes, Aishani's twelfth birthday was a memorable one. After the party was over and all the guests had gone and all the gifts were opened, everybody was very tired. Her mother, after winding up everything, told the children to complete their school homework. Jayant went to his room, her mother went up to her room and her father went to the library. The birthday girl too went to her room and completed her homework. It was quite late and she was tired and sleepy after all the excitement. But there was still one exciting experience left. This was a gift from her father on her birthday. He always gave her his gift at the end of the party after all the excitement of the party and the gifts was over. The gift was always special and she would happily wait for another whole year for his special gift.

As was her habit after completing her homework she would go to her father's study or library where he would teach other subjects not related to the mundane syllabi of her school. She would listen wide-eyed to her father's teachings. She knew and understood that there was much more to these teachings. It would be just a matter of time when her father would tell her all about it, but he would do it slowly and gradually so that she could assimilate all the information.

When she went inside her father's study, he was writing something, but she knew that he was waiting for her. Pandit Ram Shankar stopped his writing as soon as he saw Aishani standing inside the door. "Come beta," he said, "I have a wonderful gift for you."

Aishani kept quiet and waited expectantly. Her father's gifts were always wonderful even without his saying so. She loved his gifts. She had a feeling that this time her father's gift would surpass all his other gifts.

"Sit beta," he said and turned towards his cupboard. This was one cupboard which no one was ever allowed to touch or open. Pandit Ram Sharan kept it under lock and key and kept the key with himself. Even if anybody got hold of the key and resorted to opening it they would have been unable to open it because Pandit Ram Sharan had sealed it with some special mantras which only he knew.

It was a very casual thing in this household. Everyone knew that if Pandit Ram Sharan had kept it under lock and key then it was for a special purpose and for their own good. Panditji took out something like a shawl from the cupboard. A shawl! For a moment Aishani could not believe it! Baba was giving her a shawl! She took it in her hands. It was the softest piece of cloth that she had ever seen or felt. On closer look it wasn't a shawl, it was more of a cloak with a hood. Aishani held it in her hands. It was so soft and delicate and light. Had she not been looking at it she wouldn't have felt it also. But still, it was a shawl or cape—whatever!

"Thank you, baba, it's beautiful," she smiled demurely.

"I'll show you beta, it has to be worn in a special way along with a special mantra."

"You teach me the mantra baba, I'll wear the cape." Though disappointed, Aishani always spoke respectfully to her father. Her father smiled. He could make out the disappointment on Aishani's face though she tried to hide it. She wore the cape around her. It completely enveloped her, its gossamer threads twinkling like little stars. Her father had finished reciting the mantra. Nothing happened. She waited patiently.

"Come here beta," he said softly gently leading her towards the long mirror which was hanging on one of the walls. Mirrors increase the number of books hence knowledge, her father used to say. She stood in front of the mirror and gasped, "Baba," she almost screamed then lowered her tone in case anybody got up. There was nothing to be seen in the mirror and she was standing bang in front of it. Baba had not let her down at all! She had known that such things existed but never that she would have it as a gift, Oh! It was superb! She looked at her father, who was smiling indulgently.

"Baba, it's awesome, I don't know what to say," she twirled this way and that taking her hand out of the cape and looked at the mirror. Sure enough, her hand was reflected in the mirror.

"Oh baba, I'm so happy, thank you for giving me the best gift ever!" She ran and hugged him. "Wait till I show

Ruby," she laughed excitedly and ran back to the mirror again.

"Baba I'll be able to see and do so many things now and nobody will be able to see me."

Panditji let his daughter run about excitedly in the room and watched her dance in front of the mirror. She even took off the cape and draped it carefully over a chair. The chair disappeared. Pandit Ram Sharan just sat there and watched his daughter and her happiness. God knows how much she needed these small nuggets of happiness. He sighed and waited for her to cool down a bit. Finally, Aishani, with a big sigh of contentment, came and sat beside him.

"Do you know baba, it senses that you are wearing it and camouflages even if you haven't covered yourself fully with it! Of course, you know that baba, tell me more about its abilities," she requested.

"Ash," he said softly as soon as he thought that she would listen to him now. "Beta now pay attention," he said seriously. Aishani looked at him and immediately knew that he was going to say something important. She became serious herself.

"Ash you are growing up now. This cloak has to be taken seriously. It cannot be played around with. Its powers are not very strong. You can play with it and use it when you want some peace and quiet to do your work or sometimes just for fun but use it judiciously. Don't go to places where we tell you not to go. Though it hides you it is not so strong that malefic people will not be able to see through it. I have given it to you to play around with it. By all means, share it with Ruby but nobody else. And do not tell anybody also."

"Yes baba," Ash said equally seriously. Though she did

not fully comprehend the import of her father's words she was mature enough to understand his fears.

"Goodnight beta, now go and sleep, you can play with it tomorrow."

"Yes baba," she tiptoed and kissed him. "Thank you, baba," she smiled and ran off to her room with her cape. Back in her room, she sat down on her bed. Sleep had long evaded her due to the excitement brimming in her heart. There was calm and quiet everywhere. It was a dark night but the stars were shining brightly; they were as big as marbles and of different shining colours. No, no, that was not possible; stars could not be of different colours. She peered at the stars again; they became their normal silver colour.

She knew this was happening because she was so happy and excited. She wore the cape again and stood in front of the mirror. There was no reflection there; she looked some more and sure enough there was a part of her foot peeping out. Giggling she covered her foot and it was gone. She wanted to show it to Ruby immediately.

Instinctively she knew that it would be wrong to go to Ruby's house now. It was almost midnight. Ruby had been there with them in the evening for her birthday. Aishani sighed. She had to wait until the next morning. The next morning when as usual Ruby went to Aishani's room she was not there. Ruby waited for her but Aishani did not come. Ruby heard a familiar sound. It sounded like Aishani but when she turned Ash was not there.

"Ash where are you?" she called out. In reply, she heard a soft giggle. Thoroughly mystified, Ruby looked for her at all their usual hiding places in her room. Ruby was sharp enough to realise that Ash was up to some mischief which she could not pinpoint as yet.

So she did the next best thing. She took out her book and started reading without paying any attention to Ash's giggling. After five minutes of silence when she looked up there was Ash standing right in front of her! Ruby started, "Ash! Where did you come from? Where were you?"

Ruby could not believe her eyes and ears when Ash told her about her birthday gift. They wore the gown together and preened in front of the mirror turning this way and that even without seeing anything, both whispering and giggling. Very soon they slipped out of the house without anybody being the wiser. Oh! What fun they had! They learnt a few more things about the cape, that they could not hide from animals and that sounds intensified when they were inside the cape. But these things were not enough to dampen their enthusiasm. They were so excited that they hardly paid any attention to these shortcomings.

The Present
Dreams and Gurukul

Aishani knew that she was destined to learn so much more, an inkling of which she had when her father had taken her to the School of Warfare. She was around sixteen or seventeen years of age when she experienced violent dreams, dreams where she was either chasing someone or being chased. In her dreams, she would be absolutely calm and cold-blooded even though she would be seething from inside. Most of the times, she would be chasing and killing the monsters, but sometimes she would be racing away from them. She would wake up with her heart palpitating. Often there would be a blurred figure of a man beside her imparting mental and physical strength and succor to her. She would be aware of him yet not aware of him. Once, in one of these dreams, this shadowy figure was not there. She had felt as if she had less than half of her strength and hence she could not annihilate all the creatures. She woke up in great terror and sadness as if she had lost the most precious thing of her life. Aishani could not behave normally for a couple of days after these dreams. She would remain listless for days. Sometimes she would confide in Jayant about these dreams. He often gave a humorous explanation for her dreams which would lift her mood gradually. Though he did not confide in her, deep down he knew that the hazy man was Aishani's partner from her previous births and they had always won every battle when they were together.

It was the killings which disturbed her so much. So many times she thought that she was chasing some beastly creatures who were screaming horrendously and trying to outrun her. They would be covered with blood; sometimes their arms or legs would be ripped or slashed and they would be begging her for mercy. And Aishani would be in such a rage that she would just hack through them and kill them. She would wake up covered in sweat and shivering with shock.

It would take her some time to get over the feeling of revulsion at the killings and the rivers of flowing blood and then realising that it was just a dream. Though in hindsight she never remembered the clothes she was wearing in these chases, she was pretty sure that they were not clothes of contemporary times. Sometimes she would wake up in the middle of the night with a jolt, her heart thudding, her body shaking and her teeth chattering. She had to get up to drink water as if she had actually run for miles. The dreams rapidly became a routine affair. Sometimes she saw the creatures getting the better of her and killing her instead. Many times Aishani was scared to go to sleep as she was positive that she would get the same disturbing and frightening dreams again. One night, after yet another horrendous dream, she went and sat on the verandah with a glass of water. Sleep was out of the question now. She just sat there, mutely staring at the grass and the tall dark trees with their long shadows.

"Ash!" It was her father. "Why are you sitting here beta, why aren't you sleeping?"

She looked up. She knew that sometimes her father took a night stroll around their garden, so it was no surprise that he was there.

"Nothing baba, I couldn't sleep," she shook her head clearly disturbed. There were tears in her eyes.

"Ash beta, what happened?"

"I don't know baba, it's these dreams I have every night. I just cannot sleep after that."

"What kind of dreams beta?" Pandit Ram Sharan asked her softly. He had an inkling of the kind of dreams Aishani was having. In fact, he had even been waiting for these dreams to take place. It was time.

"Oh baba," Aishani was almost sobbing now, "Baba I see myself in a sort of jungle and I am chasing somebody with all intentions of killing it or him. Then baba, sometimes I see that somebody is laughing maniacally and chasing me, and though I am not afraid I want to escape very badly."

"Is it always the jungle beta? Do you remember the thing which you had been chasing or the thing that chases you? Try to remember."

Aishani tried hard to remember, "Not really baba, but it did seem to be a big and grotesque creature. Sometimes the creature and I would be fighting in the air and sometimes in the water. I always become breathless in the water in the dream as if, as if I will swallow water and drown! Baba how can I get rid of these dreams?" she asked, her eyes welling up with tears again.

"Go back to sleep beta, you will not get the dreams again," her father put his hands over her head and recited some mantras silently and then blew on her forehead. "Get a good night's sleep. Sleep late if you want. Tomorrow your mother and I will sit together with you and talk."

"Yes baba," she said then turned, "Why baba, is it very important?" Aishani's mother never interfered in her father's teachings. There had been only a couple of instances when both her father and mother had sat down together to seriously talk to their children. Her parents had such a bond that they instinctively knew and supported each other. Moreover, her mother was most of the time busy with the household chores.

"We will talk in the morning. You go and sleep comfortably now," Pandit Ram Sharan said tenderly. After she left, Pandit Ram Sharan sat down for some serious thinking.

On the one hand, he was elated. These dreams meant that Aishani was being reminded about her past births in bits and pieces. It also meant that she was now ready to be admitted in the College of Warfare otherwise known as Gurukul. But it was no ordinary school like in ancient times. It was that and much more. There were no Gurukuls in India now and the few that were there were so secretively hidden that no one knew about them. Only a handful of the lineage of great pundits and scholars and warriors knew about them. Such people were so committed to their cause and destiny that there was no question of any of them divulging anything about these Gurukuls.

On the other hand, Pandit Ram Sharan was feeling a deep sense of loss and heartache that his sweet and innocent daughter would now learn and perform the acts which were against her very basic human nature of this birth. He also had no doubt that gradually she would remember quite a lot of her previous births, though not all, but enough to understand and recognise her destiny and be captivated by it. There would be no greater achievement for her than the destruction of the demons who had so cunningly and intelligently managed to escape their destruction in the great war between Bhagwan Ram and the king of demons Ravan. This was the sign that the whole of Gurukul was waiting for, these dreams of Aishani. These dreams meant that Aishani was now ready to face her past births and hence her future.

The next day they woke up very early. It was still dark. Aishani sat opposite her father and mother at the table in the library. There was nobody in the house. The puja shop would be opened later in the day. Jayant had gone on one of his school excursions. Aishani knew that something very important was going to be told to her as her father and her mother had never chosen this time for discussions.

"Ash beta we will begin with those strange dreams of yours. These dreams of yours are not merely dreams, rather they are reminders of your past births."

Aishani was puzzled. She looked quizzically at her mother. Her mother nodded. Now Aishani was shocked. Amma knew! But what?

"Beta you come from a long line of warriors. You have been a warrior from the time of *Ramayana* and much before that also."

"But baba I am yours and amma's daughter. Warriors are Kshatriyas and we are Brahmins. How can I be a warrior?"

"Ash beta, now listen carefully. Of course, you are our daughter and born to your mother. But by nature, you are a Kshatriya. In every birth a set of parents are chosen for your soul so that you can do your work effectively without hindrances." He looked at his wife. A message passed between them and he seemed satisfied.

"In this birth, it is our honour that you have been born to us and that we have to raise you with all the right values and awareness, and make you conscious of your past *sanchit* or amassed karmas which will be helpful in accelerating your education and training."

"Baba, Ma, what are you talking about?" bewildered, Aishani was in tears. Her head was spinning. She looked at her mother, mutely imploring her to be more helpful. Lovingly, her mother Madhu took Ash's hands in her own, "Hush baby, take a deep breath. You are our daughter and ours only, our biological daughter, who comes from a long lineage of warriors. You will gradually understand everything beta. Give yourself some time to let this whole thing sink in. But first, you have to go with your baba to the Gurukul or the College of Warfare and Magic. Though there is no magic, things happen in such a way that they seem to be magical. Here you will be taught that magic is nothing but a very advanced stage of science. We call magic what we cannot comprehend with our limited knowledge and awareness."

Aishani looked at her father. "Yes beta, you will slowly remember and understand everything, but we have to begin with your training first. We will go there now. There is no time to waste. Pack a few necessary items, not much, and a couple of your favourite books. You will be staying there for some time. Go and get dressed."

Aishani had no choice but to agree. She went to her room to get dressed. Her head was spinning. There were a million questions she wanted to ask but she knew that even if all her questions were answered she wouldn't be able to assimilate them in one go. Before leaving, her mother did her *aarti* and put a vermillion *tika* on her forehead thereby sealing the fact that she was really going for something momentous.

Aishani followed her father as he walked towards the marketplace. Soon they reached the Community Center. Here quite a number of meetings were held regarding the town and its upkeep. Pandit Ram Sharan used to give his discourses here very regularly.

Aishani had also been here many times with her father not because she was asked to do so but because she liked to hear her father's teachings and the teachings of the other scholars also. She was puzzled now. Her father had told her that he would take her to be admitted in a Gurukul or in a school of ancient warfare. But this was the community hall. How could warfare be taught here? She looked questioningly her father but he just gestured her to follow him.

They went to a small room adjacent to the hall. It was a room with no furniture and had plain walls. Pandit Ram Sharan went towards one of the walls, stood in front of it and chanted some mantras. He then touched the wall with the tips of his fingers and chanted a few more mantras. Amazed, Aishani watched the wall as it changed colour and started shimmering. Very soon the wall disappeared and it became an entrance of sorts. He gestured to her to follow him.

As soon as they crossed the threshold the wall closed behind them and there was a huge forest in front of them and behind them also. She looked at her father with questions bubbling inside her but he seemed to be in no mood to answer her. Quietly she followed her father. She looked around. It was a very dense jungle with thick foliage and huge trees and broken branches and twigs. She could hear the beginnings of the sounds of birds and animals everywhere. Aishani was not scared because her father was with her but because it was not in her nature to be scared of anything. There were long twisting paths all around the ancient and gnarled trees whose roots were crisscrossing each other.

They had left their house almost at dawn. It was an autumn morning and the sun had just started peeping through the dense foliage of the perennials; the dry brown leaves which had fallen on the jungle floor made a crunching sound with every step of theirs. The reddish glow of the sunrays falling on the green and brown leaves and the twisted ancient roots provided a kaleidoscope of colourful pictures which took away Aishani's breath. The fauna of the forest had just begun stirring and she could make out the sounds of some soft movements nearby. Some insects and birds had just got up from their sleep and were clearing their throats for their chirping and warbling and calling out to each other. Somewhere nearby she could hear the gurgling and the tinkling sound of a stream. It was all so pleasant, beautiful and soothing that Aishani felt that she was watching a movie.

"Baba, it's all so beautiful!" she exclaimed.

"Yes beta, so it is. Remember this also that, beauty lies in the eyes of the beholder. Today you see divine beauty around you, tomorrow if you are disturbed the same forest may look ugly to you."

She gave her father a puzzled look. It was not like Baba to speak negatively about anything. She sighed. Things were not going normally for her and her parents since the last few days. Maybe Baba was anxious about leaving her here in this forest. But for the moment, she was going to absorb herself in the beauty of this forest. Baba would look after the rest, she thought with conviction.

After some time they reached a clearing and Aishani's eyes opened wide. It was a huge place with wildflowers and young and ancient trees everywhere. In between, there were many huge clearings and what seemed to Aishani, many cottages and many open-air classrooms. There was a huge structure where she presumed a *havan* was regularly held. She could see a huge *havan kund* made of mud and mortar and beautifully decorated too.

There was a huge stack of mango wood and branches there, presumably for the *havan*. The mango wood was cut into neat logs and stacked properly. Pandit Ram Sharan took her towards one of the larger cottages. They took off their shoes in front of the cottage and went inside.

A very imposing old man was sitting on an *asana* made of tiger skin. Her father told her that he was Guruji or Swami Ramanuj, the head of the Ashram. Hardly anybody knew his real name. He was just called Guruji by everybody. Guruji was a majestic and noble figure. His age could be anything from sixty years onwards. The rumour was that Guruji was hundreds of years old but there was nobody to ask and nobody to tell. It was also rumoured that he was Lord Hanuman's representative here on this Earth. Hanumanji was said to be the only living deity on the Earth left here by Bhagwan Ram himself, to annihilate and destroy the leftover demons in the world. Lord Hanuman was said to be residing in Gandmadana Mountain near Rameshwaram in Tamil Nadu and sending his representatives to all the parts of the world in order to form Gurukuls and train warriors to destroy the demons.

Guruji had a great personality with white hair and a long flowing white beard. The white hair on his head was tied up in a knot on top of his head the way Brahmins tied their hair with the rest of the hair hanging like a ponytail from the knot. He had a silver-white mustache and a long, equally silvery white beard. He had many lines on his face especially the cheeks and forehead. But he looked surprisingly fresh, very active, and he had a twinkle in his eyes. He was sitting on an *asana* and there were two more *asanas* laid out for his guests. Both father and daughter touched Guruji's feet and Guruji blessed them. It seemed that he was waiting for them. Both Guruji and Aishani looked at each other and something struck Aishani straight in her heart. It was a sense of déjà vu as if she had been here earlier and that she knew Guruji from some past birth. Guruji's eyes were twinkling. Inadvertently, Aishani smiled back. And then tears came to her eyes and she started crying. She was shocked at her response to Guruji. His eyes had also become moist. He patted her hand and said, "You can cry as much as you want beta, we are meeting after such a long time."

Surprised, Aishani looked up at him.

"Yes beta, we have known each other through the ages. I have remained the same but you have had to change into different people in your births throughout the ages."

Aishani kept quiet. She was getting an inkling of what was and what had been.

"You come from a race of female warriors from the time of the *Ramayana*. You and your tribe have been specially blessed by Maa Durga and Maa Sita to fight and destroy the demonic forces of this world and beyond too. In this birth, Pandit Ram Sharan and his wife Madhu are your parents. They have been specially chosen so that in this Kalyug, proper *sanskars* and education could be given to you along with your war schooling. You will always have a team of people working for you. They will be totally loyal to you. You will have a partner also who will be your equal if not more, in everything that you will be directed to undertake."

Guruji waited for Aishani to assimilate the information. As for Pandit Ram Sharan, he lowered his head and eyes so that Guruji could not see the sadness in them, the sadness of losing his most precious possession. But Guruji knew and understood a father's pain at voluntarily sending his most beloved daughter to the most gruelling period and challenges of her life even though he knew these challenges would be more than fulfilling.

For Aishani not everything sounded alien, a few things seemed quite familiar too. She did not ask any questions. She knew that she would eventually understand everything. A few things were coming back in her consciousness.

Guruji was looking at her kindly and affectionately as if he was looking at a long lost daughter. He carried on, "Beta, in course of time, you will remember many things, people and happenings from your past which will help in guiding you towards your goal in this birth." Aishani knew that Guruji was talking about her past births. Till now, she had vaguely believed in past births and reincarnations. Now with her father and Guruji reiterating the fact, she knew that it was so. There was something which Guruji had said that struck a chord in her, but there were so many revelations going on that she could not pinpoint it.

"At the moment it is almost impossible for you to assimilate so much at one go. Give it time and take it slowly," Guruji's eyes twinkled as if he had known her all her life, which indeed he had.

"In the course of your duties, you will come across many individuals, some familiar and some not so familiar. They will become part of your team. You will have to sift through them to find out who your real well-wishers are and who are your enemies. But enough of these epiphanies. Plenty of time for them." He called out to someone who must have been waiting just outside the cottage. He came inside and bowed respectfully to Guruji and nodded to Paṇḍit Ram Sharan.

"Manohar, you know Pandit Ram Sharan and this is his daughter Aishani. This is Manohar, one of the instructors here.

Manohar knows each and everything about this Gurukul. There is nothing here that he does not know. He will be your guide for the next couple of weeks till the time you settle down completely."

Manohar bowed to Guruji and to Pandit Ram Sharan and looked at Aishani. Aishani folded her hands in a namaste. Manohar returned her namaste and then his eyes widened. He looked at Aishani again then turned and looked at Guruji. A message passed between them and Guruji nodded. Manohar's whole demeanor changed immediately. From a strict, distant and cold looking instructor Manohar almost instantly changed into a hand wringing and simpering person. His sidelong glances towards Aishani were making her very uncomfortable.

"Manohar," Guruji said a bit sternly, "Aishani does not remember much of her past as of now. With our guidance, she will remember very many things about her life. We have to help her by not barraging her with our emotions. That will not be helpful. Take her around to the places that were once familiar to her. She will arrive at her own conclusions herself."

"Yes Guruji," a chastened Manohar whispered then turned towards Pandit Ram Sharan and Aishani and gestured to them to follow him.

He took them around everywhere and showed them the most relevant places. The Gurukul was so huge that it could not be covered in a day or even days and weeks. Everything was so beautiful, so green. It was a lush forest albeit without the muck and debris of leaves and branches and animal droppings. In short, it was a beautiful man-made forest. Manohar showed her the places where the classes would be held. These were:-

1. Agni Sthana—this was the place where prayers would be held and *havans* would be performed. This was an everyday routine in the Ashram. Every morning very early, students, as well as teachers, would congregate together for the *havans*. They would assemble around several *Havan* Kunds. Wood would be lit in the *havan kunds* and everybody would pray.

2. Brahma Sthan—This was the place where the *Vedas* and *Puranas* and *Upanishads* were taught. The *Puranas* were added much after the *Vedas*. Aishani was familiar with these ancient texts. There were various versions and interpretations of these texts in her father's library and she had read quite a bit of these sacred scriptures.

3. Vishnu Sthana—Raja Niti was taught here. This was one of the most important places in the Gurukul. Administration was taught here along with politics. Aishani knew that she did not have much interest in this particular subject.

4. Mahendra Sthana—Military Training. She knew instinctively that this part of training would be most crucial for her. She again had a sense of déjà vu when they came to this part of the Gurukul. It was as if she had already been here. There was a vision of her having a sword fight with another person. She shook her head to have a better view of her memory, but as usual, it was just a flash of memory which just would not come back.

5. Vivasvata Sthana—Astronomy was taught here. Her favourite subject. On clear nights she would gaze at the sky for hours as her father taught her about the various stars and constellations. She knew that she would be repeatedly coming here.

6. Soma Sthana—Department of Botany and the study of

herbs, fruits, flowers, trees, etc. This was also a familiar subject as her father had taught her quite a lot about Ayurveda of which Botany was a major part.

7. Garuda Sthana—Department of teaching the various modes of Transport and conveyance. This was where they would be made familiar with the numerous modes of transportation right from the time of Satyug when the Pushpak Viman was used. This was named after the God of birds, Garuda Devta.

8. Kartikeya Sthana—This was the department which taught military intelligence and organisation for e.g. how to organise patrols and be part of battalions, etc.

"There are many other departments," Manohar informed them, then turning to Aishani's father he said, "Panditji, you know every inch of the Gurukul like the back of your hand. It's quite embarrassing for me to be your guide and show you places which you know better than me. How can I show you anything different?"

"That's right, Manohar, but Guruji wants Aishani to see the Gurukul with neutral eyes and arrive at her own conclusions. If I show her around she may get a biased view."

Manohar nodded his head in assent. They continued on their journey.

"The Gurukul is as huge as a mid-level city, maybe even bigger. It almost touches three states; we don't find it so huge mainly because it is situated in a forest interspersed with two meandering tributaries of the Ganga and several streams and lakes. There are very few man-made structures which have been constructed only on the most compelling proviso."

Aishani was paying full attention to Manohar. Once in a

while, she did get the strange feeling that she had seen some of these things earlier and experienced them too. When she thought about it nothing came to her mind, but she was not summarily going to dismiss her thoughts. She deduced that some of her feelings may be true also.

"This is admittedly such a huge place. Then why is there only one entrance to the Gurukul and that in the heart of the city from a room in the Community Centre?" Aishani was genuinely puzzled.

"Well, that is not entirely so," Manohar said smugly. Though his veiled reverence of Aishani was still there, he did feel a bit important in apprising her about the salient features of the Gurukul.

"There are many invisible entrances to the Gurukul all around it. Depending on one's physical proximity to the Gurukul or the Ashram, people can enter it. In fact, even that is not necessary. The whole of Gurukul is surrounded by an invisible boundary wall, something akin to electrically wired boundary walls. Senior instructors and even senior deserving and chosen students like you can come and go from wherever they want to," Manohar simpered again and Aishani flushed and looked at her father for help. Pandit Ram Sharan mutely signalled her to ignore Manohar's fawning.

"As for one of the entrances being in the main town it's because demons and their ilk will not be so prone to visit a human infested place so frequently. New pupils are trained to use these gateways so that even if they make a mistake, it might be overlooked by a demon, simply because of the presence of other humans."

Hundreds of questions were ready to come out of her

mouth, but her father stopped her with a gesture. There was plenty of time to ask questions later on. They carried on with Aishani catching a few things and not catching many other things. Her training would begin after a few days when she had acclimatised herself to the new environment. Her father left her in charge of a lady instructor who took her towards the female pupils' quarters. These were a set of spartan huts, providing just the minimum basic needs. Pandit Ram Sharan said goodbye to his daughter. Father and daughter hugged each other. She noticed that her father's eyes were moist. She herself had started feeling alone but she was excited also. There were so many things to explore and discover.

"There is a surprise for you beta," Pandit Ram Sharan informed her.

"What baba?" What could be more surprising and strange than all this!

"You will have a roommate also beta," her father smiled.

"Who baba?" she asked curiously. He kept quiet and smiled mysteriously. Aishani waited, then squealed with delight.

"Ruby, tell me that it's Ruby."

"It's Ruby."

"Oh baba, I can't believe it!" Aishani clapped her hands in delight.

"She will join you in a day or two."

Gurukul and Adheesh

Unlike the ancient times, pupils at the Gurukul were now allowed to go home on weekends; sometimes they could go to the Gurukul daily too. The forest where the Gurukul was situated was not far away from the town where Aishani lived with her parents. But as her father explained to her she could not just walk into the Gurukul. Of course, they could, but that would come at a much later stage. At the moment there would be too many explanations to be given to the 'normal' people. In fact, nobody was allowed to have a glimpse of the forest. It was only when one was inside the forest and the Gurukul that one marvelled at the enormity of the whole place.

There were only two more students whom she knew who would be going to the Gurukul along with her. One was her best friend Ruby and the other was Ruby's elder brother Uday.

Ruby had another younger brother Tejas. Aishani's younger brother Jayant was also there. Pandit Ram Sharan informed Aishani that these two boys would be joining the Gurukul after some time, only after they were made to understand and assimilate their roles in the scheme of things, which was to destroy the demons and protect Aishani. Aishani was herself grappling with all the new revelations in her life. As of now, she had least knowledge of her actual role in this birth let alone people protecting her from all sides. She sighed. Like Guruji said, she had to learn to be patient. Past memories could not be rushed.

Things started moving when Ruby came to join her after a couple of days. Aishani had felt quite lonely these last two days. Her classes were yet to start. Presumably, the students were left alone to their own devices to acclimatise themselves to their new surroundings. She was not a very gregarious girl by nature. She liked to stay alone with her books. The only time she became a bit chirpy was when she talked to her father's patients who many times came only to talk to her and unburden themselves. A mere touch or a soft answer from her could automatically solve many of their problems. Her father knew about this gift of hers and unless the disease was severe he preferred her talking to the patients.

Her homesickness ebbed a bit when Ruby came to the college. Ruby, with her sunny, beautiful and positive personality transformed Aishani's outlook about the whole place. Aishani being sober wanted to begin her studies immediately, but they were left on their own for some time. Though Ruby also did not complain about the austere arrangement of their rooms as they were used to living almost like that, still even a cup of tea or keeping a book in their rooms was not allowed. Since there seemed to be plenty of time, both of them went exploring around the premises. The Gurukul was one of the largest institutions they had ever seen; it came with its wonderment and bewilderment too. Apart from their living quarters, almost everything was in the open. The classes were held in the open and if it was very hot or it rained they were going to be held under thatched roofs. It was all so very archaic and endearing.

"Everything is so very old here," Ruby mused, "If we are going to be trained for killing the demons of the world then we should have had better surroundings and infrastructure and weapons. What do you say, Ash?"

Aishani kept quiet. She knew better than to question all this. If Baba and now Guruji wanted them all to be trained here then there had to be something much more than what they were witnessing. During this conversation, they were walking in the most charming part of the forest. In fact, it looked more like a garden than a forest. There was beauty everywhere; it was the most tranquil place they had ever seen. Suddenly Aishani straightened up.

"Shh! Can you hear something?" she asked Ruby.

Ruby strained her ears, "No Ash I can't hear anything, must be a squirrel or a bird."

"No Ruby, I can hear the clanging of weapons, there is definitely some kind of fight or practice going on."

Ruby always took Ash very seriously.

"Let us go towards the sound," she whispered.

Both of them turned towards the sound though Ruby still

could not hear anything. Suddenly they were transported to a clearing where many students were jousting. But how did they land here? Both of them were walking in the most peaceful surroundings, then suddenly this! How was this possible? They stood there bewildered and none the wiser. Nobody paid them any attention. Both Ruby and Aishani were rooted to the spot not knowing what to do or how to retrieve their steps.

"Hello girls, I see you are on an exploring trip." This was Manohar, their friendly guide and one of the faculty members. They folded their hands in namaste and wished him. They kept quiet not knowing what to say, but Manohar could read the confusion on their faces.

"I see you have discovered this place by mistake. But this is no mistake. The whole of Gurukul is full of such training places. These can be seen only by those students who pass one exam and go to the next level. There is no secrecy. It's just the way things work here. There are too many layers of training here not visible to the layman or our enemies which are too many to control."

Ruby blurted out, "Then how did we come across this place? We are novices here."

Manohar smiled, "Nobody is a novice here. In your case, it was Aishani who could hear the sounds and arrive here. It's because she is Aishani, the chosen one; everything is visible to her." He then turned towards Ruby, "Gradually you will also begin to see places and hear sounds like any other disciple, but it will take time. These two free weeks have been given to you to discover things on your own. Once your classes begin you will not have time for even the most mundane things." Then turning towards Aishani he gave an almost small bow as if he couldn't help it, and then turned abruptly towards the other students leaving the girls stunned by surprise.

The next few days were spent in discovering more places and things. They also found that the forest changed colours according to its moods, sometimes its own internal moods and sometimes as a reaction to the outside stimuli. These were fun halcyon days without knowing that they were being closely observed by Guruji and her father, Pandit Ram Sharan. They were waiting for Aishani to remember as much as she could.

When the classes began, Aishani had to attend all the classes but she knew instinctively that she would be attending the Mahendra Sthan, the Karthikeya Sthan and the Garuda Sthan more than the other departments. The first two departments dealt with war and fighting and the various components of war and battle. Slowly Aishani would arrive at the assumption that she was meant to train for fighting and destruction. In this context, whenever she saw herself as a destroyer she became very disturbed but gradually she would come to an understanding that her whole being was being geared to destroy evil on this Earth and beyond it too.

The Garuda Sthan was perhaps one of the most important departments in the Ashram. It taught how to reach from one place to another in so many ways—on the surface, in the air, in the water and even inside the Earth's core, besides time travel also. There were mantras to make oneself invisible inside any vehicle or make one too small or too large. The syllabus was too huge. Some of the vehicles were literal armories but invisible. Guruji in his own way had also expressed his desire to everybody that Aishani had to be given top priority in these classes.

Within a short span of six months, Aishani outshone everybody in her class and the next class too. There were other very brilliant students also both amongst her seniors as well as her juniors. But Aishani was oblivious of all this. From the time she entered the Gurukul, she was sincerely going through each and every point of her present curriculum. While she periodically still got a sense of déjà vu whenever she accidentally entered a new place in the Gurukul, the dreams, rather the nightmares, had stopped.

She went home most of the weekends. She was so full of her studies that she couldn't wait to tell her parents about them. While both her parents shared and understood her excitement, her mother did not actively participate in the conversations. Sometimes there would be tears in her eyes which she tried to wipe ineffectually, but Aishani had noticed the tears. However, she kept quiet. Her mother would leave after some time on the pretext of cooking Aishani's favourite foods.

"Baba, why is ma so upset? Both of you sent me for the training, not you alone."

"Yes beta, Madhu knew exactly where we were sending you. Your mother is human. At times she is only aware that you are our daughter and all her love and protective feelings for you come to the fore. She foresees a very arduous and dangerous future for you. She also knows that there is no other future for you. You will choose this and this life only. You have been designated by God himself to rid this Earth of demons and you have been blessed by Maa Durga herself. Maa Durga is Shakti or power in its purest form. In your case, a minuscule part of her powers has been passed on to you. This is why you are known as the chosen one. No one can surpass you in fighting the demons. Because you are human you will always have doubts. This is why you are being sent to the Gurukul to remember your powers and shed your doubts. What greater glory can there be to follow Prabhu's wish and help mankind. It is this love and her maternal feelings which your mother can't get rid of."

Aishani paused. She could understand her mother's feelings. She would go to Ma in the evening and sit with her and talk to her. Maybe that would lessen her pain. But right now she had to sit with Baba and sort out some of the problems that she was facing in a couple of her classes.

The days, weeks, and months were just a blur for her. She was so captivated and engrossed in her training that she never let any other thought enter her mind. She did not notice the admiring glances of her colleagues or even the jealousy of some of her less capable classmates. She never noticed her teachers being surprised and amazed by her prowess. There was just one thing in her mind, which was to focus fully on learning as much as she could in the shortest possible time. The training came almost effortlessly to her. It was as if she just had to awaken long forgotten memories and polish them.

The only time she would become somewhat aware of her surroundings and the people around her was during the *havans* which she had to attend every alternate day. The *havan* was a very integral part of the many disciplines of their syllabi. It was performed every morning to clear the Gurukul of any negativity that might have cropped up during the day or night.

The chanting and the offerings in the sacred fire cleaned them internally too and made them stronger. The teachers and the students would chant mantras and add small amounts of the *havan samagri* and ghee into the sacred fire. Aishani would be totally engrossed in the process.

All of them would be sitting together. Sometimes their hands or bodies would touch while throwing the *havan* samagri into the fire. It was a very natural and common thing to happen. But it would happen once in a while that whenever Aishani's hand touched one particular student's hand, some sort of small sparks flew from her hands.

At first, Aishani was startled. The other student shifted a little away from her but not before she noticed one of the teachers observing this. The instructor's eyes opened wide in amazement. Confused, Aishani too shifted away somewhat. This happened a bit regularly now much to her discomfiture. She started becoming careful during the *havans*. All the students had to sit together to put the *samagri* in the fire. So a little touching and shuffling was to be expected. In Aishani's case sometimes the sparks would fly and sometimes they wouldn't.

Gradually she became aware that the sparks would fly only when one of the boys was near her. She also became aware of the uncomfortable fact that whenever there was a *havan*, she and that boy would imperceptibly be made to sit near each other or maybe it just happened and then the sparks would fly. Probably because they were the top graders in the class. Apart from getting amazed and curious smiles from the other students, Aishani was now aware of the connection. This was so embarrassing for her that she became extra careful by making sure that she was nowhere near that boy when they were performing the *havans*. She became inquisitive and wanted to know who was the boy and why was such a thing happening whenever they were near each other? She was so engrossed in her training that she did not know anybody in her class. Sure she knew all of them but only in a cursory manner. She knew what they were studying and sometimes in what subject they were specialising.

Her weekdays were spent in the Gurukul and weekends at home. Apart from this, she had no other life. She had never felt the need for any other hobby or diversion. But now it was somehow becoming a bit difficult to ignore these events.

She could not share her embarrassment and disconcertment with her parents, but she had become very curious about this bizarre phenomenon, and of course about the boy. When the earlier sparks had started happening, she had started noticing the boy. He was a smart handsome boy who also seemed to be equally startled by these incidents.

"Ash, what is wrong with you? Why don't you talk to me anymore?" This was her best friend Ruby.

"Nothing," Ash said casually but her cheeks turned pink with embarrassment.

"Oh come on Ash, you cannot hide anything from your agony aunt Ruby. Hurry up now and tell me what is it that you're hiding."

Aishani sighed. It was hopeless to hide anything from Ruby. Sooner or later she would pry the truth from her. Might as well tell her now.

"It's nothing Ruby. Remember the times when we perform the *havans*."

Ruby narrowed her eyes, "Yes, what of it, did you make any mistake, no wait—you of all the people cannot make any mistake in the *havan*. There can be no faux pas there. There must be something else. Was the *havan samagri* wet or was something wrong with the mango firewood?"

"Ruby wait," Aishani said exasperatedly. Now that she wanted to tell, Ruby wasn't letting her talk, "It's none of those things Ruby."

Ruby stopped midway. She looked at Ash closely. Ash's colour had heightened and she seemed to be in a tether. Ruby took Ash's hands in hers and asked softly, "What is it Ash?"

"Oh Ruby, I don't know but when I throw the *samagri* in the *Havan* Kund sometimes my arms brush against the other pupils who are also doing the same thing," Aishani stopped.

"Go on," Ruby prompted her.

Ash looked here and there feeling trapped. Ruby waited, she had a gut feeling that this was going to be a big revelation.

"Whenever my arm has brushed against one particular boy, sparks fly and they last for about ten seconds or so. Oh Ruby, it's so embarrassing!" Aishani blurted out.

Ruby heard and was speechless for some time. She knew that Ash was not making it up; Ash did not have that kind of flighty imagination.

"What kind of sparks Ash? As in electrical sparks? Do you get hurt or burnt? Ash, does it happen with other people also?"

"No only when he is near me," Ash answered breathlessly.

"Is he aware of it?"

"Yes, he also seems to be equally startled. Ruby, I can't change my position in the *havan* rotation as Guruji wants me to head the *havan* but he has shifted away a bit though. It seems that his position is also fixed, so he cannot shift much. And the worst part Ruby…" Aishani's words were tumbling out now. It was such a relief to tell someone.

Ruby's eyes were excited, "Ash what is the worst part?"

"The *havan* Guruji has noticed these sparks."

"Oh, and has he said anything? Ash, you've been caught!" Ruby declared loftily.

"Ruby! How can I be caught when I didn't do anything? Anyway, that is not all that important now."

"Oh, then what is important Ash?"

"Guruji was smiling both times as if he knew about the sparks!"

"And how did you feel Ash? Did the sparks hurt you?"

Ash blushed, her cheeks suddenly looked pink as a winter blooming rose. How could she describe her feeling to Ruby? She could not begin to describe it to herself. It felt as if she had been transported somewhere else. There had been such utter euphoria in those shocking moments. It was as if a kaleidoscope of memories was opening up and she could see and feel so many things. But all this stopped the moment the sparks died. All that remained was a memory of pure love and a gamut of emotions.

"No Ruby, they did not hurt me nor were they like electrical currents as we know. They were just there as if trying to remind me of some long forgotten beautiful things."

"Or," Ruby smiled mischievously, "Maybe you've met your prince charming and so sparks flew."

Aishani blushed again, "I knew you were going to say this, that is why I wasn't telling you," she said in mock anger.

"Oh okay, Ash I'll tell you what we'll do. Next time when we perform the *havan*, point out this boy to me. I'll find out everything about him."

"Ok," Ash said dubiously. She did not feel over-enthusiastic about Ruby's approach. Ruby had a very straightforward approach towards most of the things in life. She would either bulldoze to get her own way or tell her story to many people to arrive at a conclusion. Ash did not want any of these methods to be used. She did not want any nudge or wink glances to come her way.

"Oh Ruby," she said hesitantly, "Be discreet, I don't want anybody to know about it. It'll be too embarrassing for me."

"I know dear, don't worry I'll do my research as quietly as a church mouse," she smiled encouragingly.

Ash left it at that. She did not want to give too much importance to the matter in front of Ruby even though Ruby was her best friend. She just wanted this to be as much of a secret as possible. How could she explain the euphoric and the sudden joyous feeling whenever her arms touched his arms and the sparks flew! This was no coincidence. This was real and she had to know why this was happening and why without knowing him, how was she so attracted to this boy. A few days later on a weekend Ash was in her father's library when she saw Ruby rushing towards their house.

"Ash, where are you?" Ruby almost screamed in excitement even though she knew where to find Ash who would inevitably be in the library. Instinctively Ash knew that Ruby had found out something about the boy. She rushed out of the library in haste lest somebody heard Ruby's excitement and started asking questions. Holding her by the arms she dragged her inside the library and shushed her. She herself was trying to hold her excitement.

"Oh Ash, I've found out who he is!

"Shh!" Ash was excited herself but she didn't want the whole world to know. Ruby's excitement was so palpable that somebody was bound to notice. She pulled Ruby into her room and closed the door.

"Now tell," she said imperatively. Ruby's eyes were dancing impishly. She wanted to play hard to get but she knew she couldn't be so cruel to Ash, her sweet, naïve best friend.

Ruby began, "Well Ash his name is Adheesh; his father is Shri Vidyadhar Mishra the great industrialist. They have many hotels and hospitals apart from other businesses. Theirs is a joint family. He has two uncles. I haven't been able to find out if he has any siblings. All in good time. At least his parents know of his special capabilities, that is why he is in our college of warfare. Oh, Ash! Isn't it great?" Ruby was feeling very proud of herself.

Ash was skeptical, "Wonderful Ruby, you've done a great job but…"

Ruby looked at Ash closely and understood. "I know," she was a little crestfallen, "It doesn't solve the spark issue," she smiled and Aishani blushed again.

"Yes Ruby, that too, but who is he? I mean we now know that he comes from this great family. All that is good, but who specifically is he? And why do sparks fly when he is near me? Why do the *Havan* Gurus smile when this happens? Does Guruji also know? O my God! Everybody knows! I'll never be able to show my face again," Aishani covered her face with her hands almost crying with mortification.

Ruby pushed on, "Forget about it for some time, Ash. Only a couple of people have noticed it. I think only you two and the teachers. And do you honestly think that anything can be hidden from Guruji in this Ashram? I am also very curious. Just wait, you'll know everything at the right time."

"That's a most wonderful idea. Why only forget about the sparks let's forget about the person himself. I don't want to have any stress in the Gurukul," Aishani said firmly.

Ruby looked at her friend closely. She wasn't going to be fooled so easily. Aishani had mindfully closed the topic. Ruby knew that Aishani would not talk about the incident or the boy again but she also knew that Aishani would not be able to stop thinking about Adheesh either. In the short span of time Ruby had tried to study Adheesh closely. She had to concur that there was some special charisma and magnetism in Adheesh. These qualities did not come to the fore in front of a layman, but Ruby was different. Seemingly indifferent without a care in the world Ruby was actually a very sensitive girl, especially where Aishani was concerned. That there was a connection between Aishani and Adheesh, this fact was established but what kind of connection?

But Ruby needn't have worried too much. It seemed Adheesh himself had become very conscious of the intermittent sparks and the feelings that they evoked in him. Without telling anyone he did his own research on the girl and found out a bit about her. But he wasn't really interested in this research. The only worthwhile thing he considered was that her name was Aishani. He knew that they somehow knew each other and also meant a lot to each other.

Adheesh was one of the most handsome young men in the Gurukul. He had a fully toned body with a well-chiselled angular face and tousled but straight hair with a shy smile. He was tall. His eyes reflected his brown hair. They were speckled with gold which became more prominent when he paid extra attention to anything. But that was not as important as the intensity that shone through them. There was honesty and gentleness in his eyes which also reflected his great spirit, his focus, and his manliness.

He was lion-hearted. But in contrast, he was also as gentle as a flower. At the moment his eyes reflected confusion and the golden flecks in his eyes became more pronounced. He knew that he had some kind of relationship with Aishani from their past births. The surge of happiness which shot through him whenever their arms touched during the *havan* pointed to a sweet story. There were the sparks too as if they were urging him to remember. But remember what, when and how! He wracked his brains and tried to remember but nothing came to him. He also knew that there was only one person who could answer his burning queries. For once Adheesh was stumped.

He did not want to go to Guruji but nobody else would have the answer, he was sure of that. Whenever he saw Aishani (he had made sure that he saw her once a day at least), his heart would spring up strange but very pleasant feelings. These feelings ranged from pleasure to extremely protective emotions. He had become so enamoured of her that she was in his thoughts every second of the day. After two weeks he was no nearer to the truth. He had to give up his indecision and hesitation. Once he had made up his mind he went straight to Guruji. There were only a handful of chosen people who could approach Guruji any time of the day. Adheesh was one of them. That was also one of the reasons why he did not want to breach this protocol for a personal query. But there was a big surprise waiting for him when he met Guruji.

"Come Adheesh I have been waiting for you," Guruji laughed when he saw Adheesh's surprised expression, "It's taken you longer than usual." Adheesh folded his hands and touched Guruji's feet. Guruji blessed him. Then seeing Adheesh's bewildered expression Guruji became serious, "I shall come straight to the point Adheesh. Whatever has happened between you and Aishani had to happen; you two are old soul partners from the time of *Ramayana*. You do not remember this as yet. It will all come back to both of you. Whatever has been happening between the two of you is just the beginning. Gradually both of you will remember everything," Guruji paused.

Adheesh was thunderstruck. He had presumed that the sparks were his closely guarded secret. He started blushing. Then other thoughts rushed into his consciousness.

Partners, soulmates, what was Guruji talking about? Adheesh could not even hide his shock and confusion.

Guruji carried on as if nothing had happened, "You will remember everything. It will come to you on its own but you have to nudge yourself and Aishani also has to do the same thing. You have to be near each other to remember."

"How Guruji? We are not even acquaintances. We do not even know each other."

"Her father has a huge library with very precious books. He has an Ayurvedic shop also. Go and join the library as a member. Aishani also works there. Go and meet her on weekends."

"Yes Guruji," Adheesh said meekly and took his leave. He knew that Guruji had told him more than enough. Now he had to go to her house. His head was reeling with the information. He wanted to go to her house. He wanted to meet with her.

Shakini, Ruby

Aishani could never describe her friendship with Ruby. They had gone to the same school and now the same college too. They were going to the same martial arts school too. Ruby's parents, Badrinathji and her mother Ajita, her brothers Uday and Tejas were always there. They were so close that they were family or so it seemed to Aishani. It seemed that Ruby and her family were kind of protecting her, not that she required any protection. She had sometimes seen her father and Badrinath uncle discussing something seriously but stopped immediately the moment they saw her. Once she heard Badrinath uncle folding his hands in obeisance to her father and saying, "It will be done as you say bhaiyaji, no harm will come to Aishani." Aishani looked at her father questioningly. Pandit Ram Sharan just waved away her mute query She just could not understand why everybody wanted to protect her. She was just a normal college going girl who was very much interested in the esoteric arts and in helping people.

"No Ash you are not normal," Ruby told her exasperated but affectionately, "You are super normal. Look at you, you treat people as if you're a doctor, you really care; in fact, so many people have more faith in you than in doctors. Your remedies are so sought after. And your *totkas* are so simple yet so effective. But best of all are your fighting skills—is there a greater warrior than you!" Ruby was referring to their martial classes. Ruby and her brothers also went to these classes though they were in different batches. Needless to say, Aishani was at the top of all the classes. These classes besides teaching the martial arts also taught focus, strengthening of the pineal glands(so that they could anticipate the others' move and thought process before the other person could think of it), cleansing of the body, mind, and emotions so that one could fully focus on the task ahead.

"Why do they want to protect me so much, I am not in any danger as you know very well. Or do you know something that I don't know?" Aishani asked suspiciously.

"Well Ash, I don't know anything but I do know this that we are not undertaking these classes just for the sake of taking these classes. You especially are meant for greater things. We are all subsidiaries in the greater picture where you and some others are playing primary roles."

"Others? What do you mean? And what primary and subsidiary roles? What are you talking about Ruby?"

"Ash what I know is that you are somewhat like a queen

bee who has this great responsibility of looking after this Earth and beyond also, and we are your helpers looking after you and doing your bidding. By subservient I mean that we are here to look after you and do all the legwork so that you can focus on the main task and perform it flawlessly."

"Ruby, what are you talking about? My head is spinning,what task do I have to perform? How are you all subservient to me? There are other men and women like me? What is so special about me? The only difference between the others and me is the training that I am undergoing, but you are also undergoing that training, then how come you are subservient to me? How can that even be possible?"

They sat quietly for a long time. Aishani looked up and sighed, "I suppose there is some truth in what you are saying though what I don't know. How do we find out Ruby? If Baba had wanted to tell me he would have told me a long time back."

Ruby looked at Aishani pensively, "Ash maybe now is not the time for you to know everything. See, you and I and Jayant and my brothers have been training for the martial classes. We and the others also have never questioned them because we instinctively felt that we are being trained for something special. It never crossed our mind to question that, otherwise who goes into a special jungle through a wall in a room? We have been honed for some very specific works to be headed by you and a few other persons."

"Who are these other persons? Where are they?"

Ruby smiled, "Well I don't know about all of them but I can guess about one of them."

"You do?" Aishani exclaimed excitedly but then stopped

suddenly when she saw the impish smile on Ruby's face. She went red and her heart started thudding.

Ruby looked at her and laughed, "Oh then I don't have to tell you who that person is. It seems you already know."

"Stop it, Ruby," Aishani said fiercely, "Be serious now."

Ruby became serious. "Ash we have to find out what this is all about. The whole thing is probably too big for us to be told and who will tell us." They thought for some time but no answers came to them. Ruby slowly pondered as if collecting her thoughts, "I think your father will be the best person to tell us." She looked at Aishani, "Will you be able to ask him, Ash?"

"I don't know," she said slowly, "There are things I know that Baba will not be comfortable answering. Let me think of a way to approach him."

Ruby was an epitome of grace and beauty. She had a curvaceous body, wavy light brown hair that fell to her hips, naturally pink lips and features that outshone any other girl. She had a languorous air and was seemingly not bothered about the people around her. She had a playful and mischievous look. She was so immune to her own charms that she treated everybody equally and in the friendliest possible manner. Her beauty and her style made her the most sought after girl in the whole campus of their college. Aishani could do so many important things behind Ruby's cover. By the time people realised what was happening, the deed was already done with none being any wiser. They knew that many things that they did together could not have been done without Ruby's femme fatale demeanor. They were so attuned to working together like this that they did not give it any further thought.

Pandit Ram Sharan could foresee the future of these two girls to a certain extent and he was very disturbed by it. They were all tiny minuscule parts of a macro plan of which the main roles would be played by Aishani and Adheesh. Panditji did not see a very gratifying role for Ruby but he was secretly relieved that Ruby's sunny disposition would see her through all the travails and turbulence in the girls' lives. He knew that nothing was too lofty or too low for Ruby in order to protect and help her friend Aishani. He also knew that whenever Ruby would compromise to help her friend, Aishani would feel extremely guilty and not forgive herself. He had to instigate his own daughter and her friend to kill, plunder and destroy. But there was no other solution. Their paths had already been chosen and laid out for them.

What only Pandit Ram Sharan and Guruji of the ashram knew about Ruby was that Ruby was someone else, not a human being. This was a fact that nobody else knew, not even her own parents or even Ruby herself. Ruby came from a line of Apsaras or heavenly beings. Apsaras are celestial nymphs or fairies. They are beautiful and sensuous. Physically they are so beautiful that their bodies seem to be transparent and luminous. They have long lustrous flowing hair which they like to keep open all the time. They shine in their clothes. They are sweet natured and like other celestial beings, they can take the shape of other beings also. Apsaras are very enlightened, cultured and knowledgeable. They are ruled by the ruler of heaven, Indra devta. Folklore says that whenever Lord Indra felt threatened by the *tapa* or meditations of great sages, he would send an apsara to break the *tapa* of the sage.

Tapa in the Hindu tradition is a form of deep strong meditation. It is enabled by a state of brahmacharya which includes *tapas* such as *vrata* or fasting, *shrams* or hard physical work, silence and asceticism which is bare minimum living devoid of physical comforts. Tapa is also enabled by the state of brahmacharya or sexual abstinence. The goal of tapa is to attain the final Nirvana, to be one with God. One of the corollaries of great tapa was ascending the throne of Swargalok. (heaven). It is said that some of the ancient sages were so strong that their Tapa had reached this stage of Nirvana. Indra devta, the ruler of *Swargalok,* would invariably send these apsaras to break the tapa of these sages so that his throne would be protected.

The apsaras were so beautiful that even the great sages could not resist them. Once a sage got entangled in the viles of the apsara, his tapa would be broken and thus he would no more be a threat to Indra's throne.

Ruby was one such apsara albeit in a human body. She was the direct descendent of one of the chief Apsaras of *Swargalok*—Menaka. Ruby herself did not know that she was an apsara. All she did know was that Aishani was her best friend and had to be protected at all costs. As of now both Ruby and Aishani were blissfully unaware of the fact that Aishani needed to be protected and from what.

Ruby's powers would come to light very soon. Lord Hanuman, the only living deity on Earth, had many representatives in the world that had their own Gurukuls or Ashrams. These Gurululs taught and trained warriors to annihilate and destroy demons which were left over from the time of the Great War between Bhagwan Ram and the demon king Ravan. Hanumanji himself resided in the Gandmadana Mountain near Rameshwaram in Tamil Nadu in the South of India. Everything was above board in these Gurukuls,—exemplary teachers, exemplary students and their heads known as Gurujis were specially chosen by Hanuman himself to run these institutions smoothly without any glitches. This blueprint had been carrying on successfully for ages. Some Gurukuls had something extra while others had something else. Needless to say, they ran almost on parallel lines most of the times. Their main task was to ferret out the demons from the darkest corners of the universe and destroy them.

All these Gurukuls were in communication with each other; their heads and some senior gurus were regularly in touch and helped each other whenever required. Sometimes there was an exchange of students. But human nature is the same everywhere. There was one-upmanship here too. Every Gurukul wanted to be the best in everything which sometimes could not be possible. Aishani and Adheesh were being trained in the best Gurukul. Very few people knew about Aishani's prowess, but the handful who knew this knew that Aishani and Adheesh would be the pride of any Gurukul or rather the world too. Adheesh would naturally follow Aishani anywhere. Having Aishani in any Gurukul would be a feather in the cap of any head of any Gurukul.

It was with this thought in mind that Swami Seemanand came to this Ashram presumably on a goodwill visit. All the heads of Gurukuls were personally chosen by Lord Hanuman. They lived the lives of strict ascetics. They lived very austere lives, were brahmcharis and did not have any contact with the opposite sex. If at all such a thing happened then such a person was removed to undergo strict penance for years.

Swami Seemanand would have been successful too in poaching Aishani had it not been for Ruby. Ruby came from the great line of apsaras who apart from being divinely beautiful were intellectuals also. They were fully aware individuals who could talk to any person for hours on his or her favourite topic. They could change their appearance also according to the likes and dislikes of the other person, for example, if the individual whom they had been instructed to ensnare happened to be a demon then that apsara could change her appearance and become a beautiful she-demon.

Swami Seemanand was born in a very pious Brahmin household. His entire life had been full of austerities and meditation; he led a pure and exemplary life. If there was one vice he had, it was to follow the divinity of his lord and master, Hanuman ji, and seek his blessings. He was always hungry to meet his master and sought different means to impress him.

There was a catch, however. Swami Ramanuj or the head of this Ashram or Guruji had deep and strong intuitions. He was hundreds of generations older than Swami Seemanand. He had had direct contact with Lord Hanuman from time immemorial and had been regularly blessed by his God. Besides, Swami Ramanuj was a very diplomatic person. He knew the reason for Swami Seemanand being in his Ashram. Guruji's ashram was the top-notch Ashram in the whole universe not because of its geographical location or the students or the teachers. All that was also there, but it was because of his intelligent and clever administration and of course his vast hands-on experience of everything. He knew how to utilise the right people at the right time and was thoroughly ruthless when it came to protecting his ashram and its inhabitants and in annihilating the demons. There was no need for Guruji to give any special instructions to Ruby. Ruby knew her job. Just a glance from Guruji towards Swami Seemanand was enough for her.

From then on Ruby became almost a shadow of Swami Seemanand. She was in every satsang that he gave. She was in every practice session that he undertook. She made sure that she asked very pertinent questions to Swamiji. Sometimes she had to be physically near him if she had to properly understand anything. These were the times that a special smell came from her which only Swami Seemanand could sense and smell. Imperceptibly, Swami Seemanand began waiting for Ruby to begin his classes. He found it easier to conduct his classes after taking a whiff of Ruby's perfume. It may just have been Ruby's special smell rather than her perfume. It worked as an aphrodisiac for Swami Seemanand. When his focus shifted from Aishani to Ruby he could not tell. Things came to a head when he offered to teach the higher forms of Kundali meditation.

Ruby started visiting him every morning at dawn when there was nobody around. Sometimes they would sit cross legged inside his hut and meditate on a particular kundali. While Ruby caught things immediately, Swami Seemanand found that he could not concentrate enough. Ruby's transparent beauty, her thin clothes under which he could see everything and her musky smell maddened him. Ultimately one day he could not stop himself and took her in his arms.

Ruby was waiting for him. She too put her arms around him.

When Swami Seemanand woke up later in the day, all was lost. He sat up; Ruby was still lying beside him sleeping. He looked at Ruby closely and understood. His tapa was broken and now he would have to undergo long years of penance to return to the Guru fold. He knew that Swami Ramanuj knew everything. Without waiting for anyone and without saying goodbye, Swami Seemanand took up his satchel and left. He would go to any secluded place in the Himalayan region and begin his penance.

Things went on as usual in the Ashram. Nobody paid much heed to the abrupt departure of Swami Seemanand. Many venerable Gurus came to the ashram, gave their lectures and their specific training and left. This was an ongoing process and nothing was amiss. If there were any changes they were noticed only by the main protagonists of the whole operation that is Guruji and Ruby. Even Aishani was not aware of Ruby's secret trysts with Swami Seemanand. Ruby and Aishani continued their studies and training.

In the beginning, Ruby was shocked when she literally saw the sparks fly between Adheesh and Aishani. This was the first time she saw Aishani being attracted to any boy. That Adheesh was attracted to her was not in doubt at all, but Aishani too! Ruby prepared her arsenal and waited for Guruji's command which did not come. Rather, the fledgling romance seemed to be obliquely encouraged by some of the faculty members too.

What a nice pair they make, Ruby thought guiltily, then shook her head. Like the others before him would she have to entice Adheesh as well? The earlier boys were no competition at all. But this would be different. For the first time, she had seen Ash getting attracted to anybody. And Adheesh was too serious a person to be attracted to any other girl easily. Ruby could feel some sort of divine attraction between the two; it was like two magnets attracting each other. Then there were the sparks. Who could deny this chemistry! Did Aishani really need any protection from this kind of chemistry? Would Adheesh's presence in Aishani's life really harm Aishani? For the first time, she also did not want to entice Adheesh and divert his attention from Aishani. There was such sincerity in Adheesh's eyes whenever she saw him looking at Aishani. But what if she got instructions from Guruji? She waited with bated breath for Guruji's instructions for a job she did not want to do. The instructions did not come. Ruby was getting perplexed now. She knew that Ash had to be protected from any distractions at any cost and that Ruby was the first medium to get rid of any distractions in the form of male attention. Ruby was now getting desperate. She was waiting for the unpleasant execution of a job. This waiting was getting on her nerves.

She sat under a tree in a clearing in that part of the Gurukul which was not frequently visited by people. She sat there, closed her eyes and mentally chanted Maa Durga's mantra. Every day, she sat under this tree and meditated and at the end of her meditation she would ask to meet Guruji. Nothing happened.

Quite disappointed, Ruby decided to continue with her prayers. On the fifth day, she met Guruji while he was on his rounds in the Gurukul. Ruby was practising her archery. She had chosen a corner for herself where she practised. She knew that she would never be good at it as it went against her very nature but she was enrolled in the college of warfare where she had to learn the basics of being a warrior. She did not notice Guruji coming up to her. For a moment she was startled when she saw him beside her. Putting her bow and arrow on the ground Ruby folded her hands in namaste. Guruji blessed her.

"Aishani and Adheesh are born soulmates," Guruji came to the point straightway. "After the initial training they have to be together. Everyone in this ashram is in his or her own way associated with the destruction of demons in this world. Out of the present group, Aishani and Adheesh are the main protagonists for annihilating them. But some demons are much greater in strength and valour than either Adheesh or Aishani. Hence they both have to become one to fight these demons."

Ruby gasped. This was revelation indeed! She knew about Ash but she had no inkling about Adheesh.

"They will first complete their training, only then will they come together to make our earth demon free. All of you around them are their most loyal servers though many don't know this as yet. Till then undergo your training and your work and help and encourage them in any way possible. Do not ask too many questions."

"Yes Guruji," Ruby bent and folded her hands in acquiescence. Did she see a shadow on the ground or what is just her imagination? Guruji blessed her again and went on his way.

Ruby was ecstatic, not merely because of Adheesh and Aishani but because Guruji had heard her silent call. God had opened another chapter in her learning. For the next week, Ruby was on cloud nine; she was happy that her role had been somewhat refined, she was happy for her friend Aishani and she was happy for Adheesh too. Though she was not sure Ruby had a flash of a memory in which she was beside Aishani fighting some shrieking creatures.

It was evening when Aishani left Ruby's house to go back home; she promised herself that she would ask her father after dinner. The sky was getting darker as if ready for rain. She heard distant rumblings of thunder. Pulling her scarf around her, Aishani started walking faster. As she walked, the hedges and shrubbery sang. They sang every time Aishani passed them; it was a sort of a happy lisping song flowing through the leaves of the hedges. The small green leaves of the shrubbery were covered with tiny red, white and orange flowers. This was a sound that always made her happy. This fifteen-minute walk from Ruby's house to her own was always invigorating for her. Today more so as the harsh rays of the sun were obliterated by the dark clouds and there was a light sprinkling of rain too. In this heat what could be better than this! She paused. Something was not right, it was the same sweet sound but it did not sound so happy today. In fact, there wasn't too much of song and sound also. Though some of the birds were still chattering, their happy evening warbling sounds were missing. Probably because of the rain, she thought. She tried to pinpoint the difference.

After a minute she found the reason for this. In fact, it was downright sad! Many birds were silent. It was the silence of these birds that drew her attention; the wind was singing but its lilt was not there. She rubbed her arms, it was getting cold. Better hurry up, she thought and put her right foot forward. She stumbled. Straightening, she tried to walk forward but stumbled again. The song of the wind through the leaves again became the sweetest song that she had ever heard. It was especially sweet. Aishani could not place the kind of bird from which the melodious song came. She was familiar with most of the birds of that region and their sounds. But this sound was very different and quite exotic too, and with that came an insatiable urge to go inside the bushes and see what kind of bird was singing this song. She fumbled again.

She got up and tried to balance herself by holding a branch of the bush but fell headlong into the bush. As soon as she touched the bush, grief and despondency surged through her. She, who was smiling and humming along with the birds a moment ago, was crying. After some time she started sobbing hysterically. She didn't know why it did not cross her mind to question her own behaviour. It was as if the entire world's anguish and despair had fallen on her and were connected to her and crying seemed to be her only mission. The more she cried the more miserable she felt. Faintly, she heard someone calling out to her. Two arms were trying to pull her out of the bushes but Ash was so absorbed in crying that she did not pay any attention to these overtures. Finally, after what seemed ages, her sobbing slowed down to hiccups. She still could not see anybody, had no desire to see anybody. Her world had crashed around her and everybody was responsible for it including herself. From crying, she went into massive melancholia. Without analysing the situation she slipped into this coma-like depression. Aishani just sat there like a statue in her own morbid thoughts oblivious to her surroundings. She wasn't aware that Ruby had sensed that something was wrong and that Aishani needed help.

Ruby had just gone inside her house when the eerie feeling struck her. It was an emergency! But where? She looked at herself carefully. No, it was not her! Then who? Without understanding, Ruby's antennae were working double time. There was such urgency in her rushing thoughts. But what, where? She knew that someone very close to her was in danger and she also knew instinctively that it was her job to save that person! But who? Suddenly Aishani's face flashed in front of her. She could see Aishani crying hysterically.

"Uday! Tejas!" desperately calling out to her brothers and without waiting for an instant Ruby flew out of her house and was by Aishani's side in less than a minute. To her horror, Aishani was sitting hunched up inside a bush and crying uncontrollably. She didn't know whether her brothers had heard. The sky had darkened and it was raining persistently.

"Hush, Ash, hush," Ruby put her arms around and tried to pull her out of the bush, but Ash would not budge from that place. No matter how hard Ruby tried, Ash was glued to that place. Ruby was in a fix—if she left Ash to get help, Aishani might hurt herself more. Gritting her teeth Ruby put her hands on Ash's arms and with all her strength pulled her outside the bush. Ash came out. Her crying had turned into soft hiccups. Hearing some sounds Ruby looked up. Thank God! Both Uday and Tejas were there. Brothers and sister looked at each other and instantly sized up the situation.

"Shakini!" Ruby whispered.

"Yes," Uday whispered. Turning to the younger Tejas he said: "Go get Gangajal and *Gomutra* and rush back immediately."

"Yes bhaiya," Tejas knew what was to be done. He ran towards their home. In times of emergency, there was nobody faster than Tejas. Uday sat down with Ruby who was trying to control Aishani. Aishani was now sobbing quietly but desperately. Her eyes had frozen like ice sans their warm and bubbly glow. Aishani was looking at her and not looking at her—she was looking through her. Ruby knew that she was there somewhere inside in the coldest place imaginable. She wanted to reach out to her and reassure her and rekindle her warmth but she knew that would be met only with cold frozen tears and dark pain. It was the cry of a person who has been drained of all hope. It was a kind of desolate sobbing. Her face and body had also undergone extreme changes. Her almost pink healthy skin had become a pallid grey, her hair which had become entangled in the bushes when Ruby had pulled her out looked like broken pieces of a broom. Ruby's soothing words made no difference. Aishani was beyond all natural reason and calming.

Uday and Ruby looked at each other, "How could this happen, Uday?" An unspoken communication passed between them lest the evil spirits heard them. By that they meant Shakini an evil spirit who seemed to have invaded Aishani's body and mind. Though Uday and Ruby did not know why, they knew perfectly well that Aishani was a rare and prized catch for all evil spirits. They had not been told the reason for it as yet, though they always wanted to protect her not because she was weak but because she was so strong. Impatiently they waited for Tejas to return. Just like Ruby, her brothers were also undergoing training in the martial arts and they were also proficient in the esoteric arts. It was because of the vigorous studies that they knew that Aishani had been struck by Shakini who had the power to change a person's psyche in the most negative manner. They were like femme fatales who would ensnare unsuspecting males in lonely places, make them fall in lust with them. Then after using up all their energies, would eventually kill them.

Shakinis normally entered only the body of physically and mentally weak people, especially males, but Aishani was neither male nor weak either physically or mentally. Ruby and Uday had no answer to this neither were they looking for an answer. They just wanted to help their friend by all means. Suddenly Uday felt a tug on his hand. He looked down. Aishani was looking up at him in a different way. He caught his breath. He had never seen Aishani like this. In one instance she was crying and writhing in pain; at the same time she was giving him come hither looks. She looked so beautiful and innocent and frail. No, this could not be happening; Aishani was just not this type of girl nor had she ever given him any indication that she was attracted to him. He glanced surreptitiously at Ruby. She did not seem to have noticed anything. There was another tug, this time near his thigh. A shiver ran through his body. This was just not the time for such things and even in his wildest imagination would Aishani do such a thing; Nevertheless, he did feel a bit elated. His dark side threatened to take over. Aishani wanted him to help her. This time Ruby did notice. Her eyes widened.

"Uday," she said urgently, "The Shakini is taking its hold on Ash. It's trying to turn Ash into itself, that is into an energy and vigour sucking parasite. You know once these beings suck the vitality out of a person by enjoying its body, they kill it."

Uday heard his sister without paying much heed. But he understood that it was not Aishani who was giving him such looks, rather it was Shakini who was making her do this. The real Aishani was the one who was crying in pain and depression.

Recently a very gruelling training had begun for only Aishani. This was not a normal training which all of them were undergoing; it was a training which they would probably not undergo at all because it was so rigorous and because Aishani was the chosen one. Only a handful of them were personally chosen by Guruji. They did not even know who else was in the exclusive group. They only knew Aishani and Adheesh were part of it. At this juncture, they did not even care. Their only worry was Aishani who was slipping into a coma like trance.

"Here bhaiya," Tejas panted and handed the bottle of Gangajal and *gomutra* (cow urine) to Uday. Uday shook his head to clear it of the unwanted thoughts. He opened the bottle, poured the whole bottle of Gangajal on Aishani and made a circle with the holy water around her. Aishani shuddered and started shaking.

Next Uday sprinkled *gomutra* over Aishani all the time incanting some mantras. Aishani started shrieking. She caught hold of Uday. It was as if someone was tearing her from limb to limb or as if she was being ripped by a shard of glass. She screamed again. This time it was not any creature but Aishani screaming.

"Ruby," she babbled, "What is Uday doing? Tell him to stop hurting me! My skin is burning."

Ruby's heart thudded. Was her Ash coming back, had the creature left her? But the next minute the blood drained from Aishani's face and the inhuman screams started again.

A very distressed Ruby turned to Uday and said, "Uday, she won't be able to bear so much pain. Don't sprinkle any more *gomutra* on her." She tried to take the bottle from Uday. Uday let her take the bottle and looked at Aishani. Aishani was whimpering now.

"We have to take her home." Fortunately for them, Uday's syllabi in the martial arts college had one stream on getting rid of Dakini and Shakini, the female demons. These were two kinds of spirits—the good ones and the bad ones. The good ones helped mankind to achieve salvation while the evil ones entered the body and mind of a person and endlessly tortured him, mainly sexually, eventually ending in that person going mad or dying. Both Ruby and her brothers could vaguely sense that such a thing could happen to Aishani if serious exorcism of the Shakini was not done immediately. In Aishani's case, it seemed that more than one entity had entered and entrapped her mind and body so that they could turn Aishani into a Shakini herself. Combined with Aishani's powers the Shakini would become the most powerful creature on Earth.

Nobody had instructed Ruby and Uday to be with Aishani all the time, but now they knew that that was what the elders would have wanted. Quickly Uday picked her up like a rag doll with Aishani fighting and resisting all the time. Once she whimpered and tried to put her arms around his neck in a seductive gesture. But Uday had made himself immune to her wiles now. Ruby and Tejas hovered around them nervously. They half dragged, half carried the crying and screaming Aishani to her house. Hearing the commotion her mother Madhu came out. Seeing Aishani like that she cried out, "Ash what happened?" She looked at Ruby questioningly but did not waste any time. She flew inside the house straight into her husband's library.

Pandit Ram Sharan was immersed in one of his books. Hearing the commotion he looked up. His wife Madhu was there looking at him speechlessly. He got up and looked behind her. What he saw took his breath away. He had visualised this situation many times and was prepared for it also. But he was not prepared for the stabs of pain which shot through his body and heart when he saw his daughter in that helpless state. She was like a wet rag with dark streaks of tears running down her face and neck. His Ash, his brave, strong, bold Ash whom nothing could disturb! Pandit Ram Sharan knew that something like this was bound to happen but so soon! They were all caught unawares. This meant that the *asuras* (demons) had come out earlier from their hibernation, zeroed onto their enemies and started attacking them in different forms. This attack on Aishani was not going to stop here. The Shakini or may be more than one Shakini had entered her body and imprisoned her soul and no way was she going to come out unless very drastic measures were taken.

He had already prepared the Shakini Yantra and kept it safely hidden in his almirah. He used to take it out every day and pray to it in order to keep it activated. He knew such things were bound to happen, there was no escaping them. He brusquely instructed Ruby and her brothers to take Ash to the annexure and make her sit on the ground there. This was a plain bare room with just a couple of *durries* thrown here and there. There was a mud stove in the middle of the room. There was only one door from which they had entered and a small window in the south wall of the room. Pandit Ram Sharan's wife had deliberately removed herself from this tense and urgent scene as she knew that the Shakini would sense her agitation and become stronger. This could permanently harm Aishani and weaken her husband's exorcism too.

"Uday, Tejas, stand on either side of the door, guard it and make sure that nobody comes inside."

"Yes Panditji," they both said in unison. All of them were very badly shaken. Nobody was taking any chances now. Pandit Ram Sharan was now quiet and steady. He looked for his wife who was already in the other room. Ruby would have to be there to assist him as he wanted her to witness what he was doing and learn from him.

He went to the almirah which was kept near the south west side of the wall and took out two plain white papers, red ink, a few barks of the pipal tree, *Shankhapushpi,* half a litre of water and small pieces of acacia wood. Placing the acacia wood in the mud stove, he lighted it. Then he put the mud bowl on the fire and poured water into it. He then put the Shankhpushpi (an ayurvedic herb) and the pipal bark in the water. While the water was heating he took the white paper and started writing the Shakini mantra with the red ink.

The room became very still. Though there was electricity

Pandit Ram Sharan had lit a few earthenware lamps which were filled with mustard oil. Whatever natural light was there was coming through the small window on the southern side of the room. It was already dusk and raining so the light was not much. Suddenly the room turned very dark and Aishani started retching. Ruby placed a hand on her shoulder to soothe her but Pandit Ram Sharan waved her hand away. Aishani was howling with misery again. Her pain was coming in waves, broken only by the shuddering need to breathe. The sharp pain was lancing through her mind and body. The pain was so acute that colourful spots danced in front of her eyes. She desperately wanted her body to be purged of the Shakini. Apart from the pain, the Shakini was playing havoc with her mind and emotions too. In desperation, Aishani caught a corner of Ruby's dupatta and tugged at it desperately. Ruby gulped and looked at Pandit Ram Sharan who was engrossed in making the concoction.

"Baba don't do it. It's paining," Aishani gasped. Ruby drew in her breath but Pandit Ram Sharan did not pay any attention to her entreaties and continued writing and chanting the Shakini mantra. Aishani started wailing, imploring her father to stop writing but he calmly continued. There was raw pain in her screams. Ruby closed her eyes and ears. She knew better than to entreat Panditji to stop his chantings. Aishani's mother had already closed her door. Uday and Tejas looked at each other with deadpan expressions. All this while Aishani kept on screaming because of the pain caused by her father's chanting of specific Shakini mantras. He checked the cauldron of water in which he had put Shankhpushpi and small barks of pipal tree. The water had been boiling for some time and now it had churned into a simmering reddish brown concoction. Panditji finished writing the yantra and waited for it to dry.

Ruby could not really concentrate on what Pandit Ram Sharan was doing; she was so distracted by Aishani's crying, and ranting. She was in so much pain that she was speaking gibberish now. Very calmly Panditji took out a cup of the concoction from the boiling pot and sprinkled it over Aishani all the time chanting the Shakini mantra. As soon as the water touched Aishani she started howling again. Her screams were so ear piercing that Ruby could not bear it anymore. Heart palpitating with distress and sympathy Ruby quietly slipped out of the room. Madhu was sitting in the next room her whole body turned to stone. She was staring into space her lips silently chanting some prayers. The moment her eyes fell on Ruby she gestured frantically for her to go back to where Aishani was. Ruby meekly went back inside the room. Aishani's screams were making her blood run cold. Instinct was telling her to run away from this hell of a room and not return, but instinct was also telling her to remain here and be a witness to everything in order to help her friend. Aishani was screaming in terror now.

On instructions from Panditji, Ruby had kept the window fully opened and removed the curtains also. Aishani was shaking uncontrollably now. Pandit Ram Sharan instructed Ruby to hold her tightly. Ruby was very agitated. This was not her friend Aishani. In a span of an hour Aishani's whole demeanor, even her physical appearance had changed. This was another person. Aishani always brought happiness and sunshine with her. This was a disconsolate, despondent hag who brought extreme sadness and melancholy and anxiety to the atmosphere. Panditji kept on sprinkling the concoction over Aishani and she kept on screeching. By now Ruby had understood that she was not Aishani but the Shakini who did not want to leave her body but was being forced to, and that too very strongly.

Aishani would have either fallen on the ground or run away from the room had Ruby not held her in a vice-like grip. Aishani's howls of misery were worsening. Ruby was crying along with her, her lashes blinking heavily with her tears. The raw pain inside Aishani was getting too much for her, her spirit screaming for its release from her own body. Searing fiery bursts of pain and sorrow pulsated from her body. She howled and blubbered whenever the concoction touched her. Between the two sprinklings of the concoction, she would feel black mists swirling in her mind taking her towards sleep and sweet oblivion. But this relief was not going to be granted to her. The sprinkling would begin again and so would her pain and she was becoming weaker. She now started looking for ways to escape this painful trauma.

All of a sudden, she started retching. She retched and retched until there was nothing inside her. She still kept heaving and then a wave of heavy dark grey smoke came out of her mouth and nostrils. For a moment it stayed put as if deciding where to go. Panditji kept on chanting and sprinkling the brew. With a surreal scream, the dark smoke turned into a beautiful woman. She folded her hands and entreated Pandit Ram Sharan to leave her. She had the most melodious and sweet voice that Ruby had ever heard.

"Panditji please have pity on me. I have nowhere to go. Just give me one day's time, I will myself leave after one day, I promise," implored the beauty.

Perhaps it was all a misunderstanding, thought Ruby, maybe she really needed a place to stay. Ruby looked at Pandit Ram Sharan in hope and anticipation. But the beautiful woman's entreaties had fallen on deaf ears. Pandit Ram Sharan continued chanting and sprinkling the brew over Aishani and the beautiful smoky woman. Now the woman was howling too. She changed her form and turned into an old bony hag then turned back into black smoke again. Suddenly the dark acrid smoke billowed out of the window and disappeared. Aishani stopped screaming and fell to the ground wearily in a stupor. Ruby also relaxed. Aishani would be alright now. But Panditji kept on chanting the Shakini mantra and sprinkling the medicated water over her. Panditji gestured to Ruby to bring *gomutra* and sprinkle it in the room and on its walls also. He conveyed all this silently as he was still chanting. Ruby did as she was told.

Very soon Aishani started crying and screaming and shaking again. Ruby was shocked. She had just witnessed the Shakini leaving Ash's body in the form of the dark smelly smoke. So why was Ash screeching and jerking again? She looked at Panditji. He again gestured to her to sprinkle the *gomutra*. Some more black smoke came out of Aishani's mouth, nose and eyes, hovered over her for a minute and then whooshed out of the window and dissipated in the air. This went on twice then stopped. Pandit Ram Sharan continued his process for some more time till he was absolutely sure that

Aishani was free of the malefic entity. As for Ruby, she was shocked. She now understood that there was more than one Shakini in Ash's body and Panditji knew about it. That is why it took such a long time to purge Aishani of all the Shakinis, though her total purification would still take a few more days.

For the next one week, Aishani sat with her father in that secluded room where he chanted the Shakini mantra and periodically sprinkled *gomutra* over her. Gradually her ashen hue began fading; her pink glow returned and she started smiling again.

"Baba, can I continue with my training now?" this was after a week of her treatment. Even Pandit Ram Sharan was satisfied by her progress.

"I don't see why not, beta, you have recovered very well. You have been fully exorcised of the Shakini. You have become so strong now that they will never bother you again."

"Is it so Baba? One fine day they might decide to conquer me again," she shuddered at the memory.

"They will not now beta. You now have the Shakini purge inside you. They can smell and see this in you for miles around. Forget about Shakini now; all such beings will stay away from you. They will sense your mastery over the Shakini and your capability of destroying it hence will always give you a wide berth."

"But Baba I didn't get rid of the Shakinis, you did everything. I was just suffering from them permeating my body."

"Ash, a normal human being would have either died or gone mad by a Shakini entering his or her body. It was you and your mental strength which managed to get rid of them. I was just a medium in hastening the process."

"Oh Baba, don't be so modest," Aishani protested, "You did everything. You had the power and the knowledge to get rid of her. Baba, I'm so proud of you."

Father and daughter smiled at each other.

Uday and Tejas

Uday was Ruby's elder brother. For Uday, it was a happy household with everybody having a positive attitude towards life. Being the eldest, Uday's responsibility was to look after his siblings and when he grew up a little, to look after his home also. Their father had a grocery shop. His parents were busy, he didn't know with what nor did it cross his mind to ask them. His younger brother Tejas was like a young puppy always following either him or his sister Ruby. Uday also knew that they were somehow different from the other normal people. Though all three siblings were getting regular education, they were full-fledged students of the martial arts college. There was quite a lot of juggling for them between the two different kinds of schools, but then they were not ordinary people.

Uday was very proud of his lineage which he knew dated

centuries back. He was a tall, strapping, muscular young man who looked and was very strong also. Apart from this he had hidden strengths, some of which even he was not aware of. His father Badrinathji had hinted at his hidden strengths. In the martial arts college, Uday was one of the finest students excelling in almost every subject. He had a solid fan following in the martial arts college and in the regular college also. His arrogance, his jeering remarks and his tendency to gang up on others made his presence quite negative. The people around him could sense his cruelty lying just below the surface and could sense some missing emotion in him.

He could hike for miles with huge rocks in his backpack without any effort. Once, when they were hiking in the jungle a huge snake fell on him. It was a python. It wrapped itself around him before Uday had a chance to throw his backpack down. While the other boys panicked, Uday calmly caught hold of the python's thick tail and squeezed it. His eyes had turned totally black and he seemed to be very angry. He kept on pressing the python's tail and kept on inching up his grip. Very soon he had reached the middle of the snake's body.

The other boys watched in complete horror while Uday mercilessly and with great strength kept on squeezing the snake. Finally, the snake could not keep his hold on Uday's body. It tried to slither to the ground but Uday kept on choking it. There was a deflating sound as if the air was being squeezed out of something. The snake loosened its grip, fell down and died. Uday contemptuously threw it on the ground and stamped on it three times for good measure. Then adjusting his backpack he started walking on the mud path as if nothing had happened.

His eyes had turned back to their normal dark brown again. A couple of boys had seen his dark brown eyes turning totally black when he was angry or excited. But they had brushed their fears aside and thought that it was a figment of their imagination.

Nevertheless, they did not take any chances with Uday again nor did they go near him after these incidents. Ruby was younger to him by two years and was very dear to him. Uday had very successfully hidden this aspect of his personality from everybody or so he thought. It was hidden from outsiders but his family did know about it even though they never let him know that they knew, especially Ruby. She knew that something was not right with her brother. Sometimes, he seemed to her to be crueller than any person she had ever known.

Ruby had mulled about this aspect of Uday's personality and she did arrive at some conclusions. It seemed to her that the absence of feelings added to his cruelty and malevolence. Of course, no one could ever guess that Uday would ever portray such qualities, but Ruby knew that below the surface was a bubbling cauldron of sheer ruthlessness just waiting for a chance to come out. It was easy for him to hide his fatal flaws. Recently Ruby had noticed another alarming thing about Uday. A few times she thought that she saw him looking at Aishani in a different way for a longer time. She had shuddered and brushed away the thought. She did not know the meaning of Uday's glances but they did not bode well for everybody around them. As for Aishani she just considered Uday as Ruby's elder brother and a friend and colleague. Ruby also knew of Aishani and Adheesh's attraction towards each other and she was scared of Uday's reaction.

Uday excelled in all the courses of the Gurukul. Nobody could point a finger at him for anything. He was disciplined and immaculate in everything. But instead of becoming everybody's favourite, people kept themselves at arm's length. For some inexplicable reason, people avoided him in general. One of the reasons was that he was never anybody's buddy. He never shared anything with anybody least of all his feelings. That is what made people uneasy. That and the turning of his eyes coal black at critical times without showing any other emotion. People were wary of him; they were scared of him without knowing why. It was not only Ruby who had noticed his interest in Aishani. There were other people also who had noticed it, though Uday had been very careful in hiding his feelings.

But this was the Gurukul where intuition and the supernatural were taught amongst other things. There were sanyasis and sanyasins who besides being teachers were themselves taught to keep a strict eye on these students. Each and every student was to play a pivotal role in killing demons. They also had to be on the lookout for any cunning and super intelligent demon disguising himself as one of the students. Among their other duties, the teachers were masters in recognising the emotions of each student in the Ashram.

Very soon the news reached Guruji. Guruji became pensive after hearing the news. Uday was not a student to be trifled with. He had a very major role in eliminating the demons. Before this actually became a reality in Uday's mind and heart, the very core of his attraction towards Aishani had to be nipped in the bud.

Like any other Principal of any school, Guruji was in the habit of going on rounds of the classes. Sometimes he himself took one of the classes. This gave him the opportunity of interacting with the students on a one-to-one basis. Taking his decision Guruji went towards the classes. Today, he went to the class where Uday was training. The class was about to end. Nobody found it strange when Guruji asked Uday to go around with him. This was a very commonplace happening, that of Guruji walking with any student.

"Hmm," said Guruji, "You seem to be doing quite well in your training, better than last year."

Uday smiled and nodded.

"All of you are here for a purpose, you know that. You are almost in the last semester of your training. You are a very worthy senior. You head several important portfolios of the college. It's because you have proved yourself worthy of those titles and the work involved in them. I am proud of you my boy."

Uday smiled and waited. Guruji was not walking with him for mere chit-chat. There was more to come. To the average individual, Guruji was the portly jovial head of the institution always ready to share everybody's problems and dilemmas with a twinkle in his eyes. Not so to the people who knew him from close. Guruji firmly endorsed the Guru Shishya relationship and he always kept a distance between himself and the other instructors and students of the school.

"Next year you will go out into the world and face reality with all this knowledge at your disposal. Though you will be working in a team you will have additional responsibilities too," Guruji paused then continued, "Your main responsibility will be to ensure the total safety and security of your team members. Only after you ensure each and every member's safety will you go ahead to destroy the demons. You will have one of the most important roles in the greatest team that this college has ever produced. As such your role becomes all the more crucial."

Guruji continued, "Your team will have two leaders, a man and a woman. They will be equal in their powers but in most of the cases, it will be the woman who will execute most of the annihilations. She is especially blessed by Maa Durga . It is only when extra strength and power is required that the man will join her and together they will become the most powerful pair in this universe. The man will provide her with all mental, emotional and physical sustenance and support. They have been partners from time immemorial and will remain so. It has been so ordained by the Almighty himself."

A dim flicker of understanding was entering Uday's mind now. Guruji was warning him about something of which he himself had not become fully aware till now. He folded his hands in respect and asked, "Which people does this team comprise of Guruji? When will I be introduced to them? I am eager to meet them."

Guruji peered intently at Uday for some time, then seemed to be satisfied.

"All in good time son. The others are also in the final stages of their preparations for their exams. You know almost everyone in your team barring a few new faces. Introductions might not be a very good idea at this time. Everybody will become conscious and this will hamper their studies. I had to tell you because you will be holding one of the most important positions in the team. Never let any personal feelings or emotions come in your primary job of protecting your team especially the two leaders of your team."

Uday touched Guruji's feet. Guruji blessed him and the impromptu talk ended. Back in his room Uday took his bath and went for a walk. He was agitated. Guruji had very tactfully and in a very straightforward manner told him to lay off Aishani. In fact, he didn't even know that he was attracted to her. It was only later that he had started thinking of her and started looking at her differently. It was after the incident with the Shakini when Aishani had caught hold of his hand and given him a sensuous look. While he knew that it was the Shakini inside Aishani who was making her do this, nevertheless his feelings for her came to the fore. His feelings for her as a woman were at a very nascent stage. His eyes had turned black again though nobody saw them which did not mean that he was not dangerous now.

He ran and ran, for how long he did not know; it could be an hour or it could be a day. A huge wild boar charged at him. Without pausing and without batting an eyelid, Uday caught it by its hind legs and threw it on the ground. The boar did not have a chance to squeal also, it died so suddenly. By the time Uday returned he had knowingly or unknowingly killed eight animals whose only fault was to come in front of him. The jungle became very quiet wherever he ran.

When he finally returned he was covered with blood and gore. A few of the disciples saw him, but nobody had the temerity to cross and ask him, so scared were they of him. By the time he went to his room and had his bath, he had totally calmed down. His eyes had returned to their normal brown colour and he had forgotten about Aishani the girl.

In sharp contrast to the sober, almost dangerous Uday, was

Tejas, Ruby's younger brother. Tejas was true to his name—as fast as a deer or maybe as fast as a tiger, though this fact was never put to test. He could outrun anybody anywhere on any terrain at any time of day or night. He was of a very small built almost like a dwarf. As far as his father and Guruji were concerned they knew that this was no stroke of luck, it was as God wished. Aishani had to be covered from all sides with people of different calibres and strengths. Tejas was one of them.

He did not have the physical or the mental strength of Adheesh or the cruel killer instinct of his elder brother Uday, he was just fast and his loyalty, of course, was beyond question. Sometimes it seemed that he was faster than lightning. Why the Dakini and Shakini could not fully inhabit Aishani's body and permanently damage her was because of Tejas' swiftness. Even before the Dakini could fully penetrate Aishani's brain and body, Tejas was there with the *Gomutra* and the other *aushadhis* (medicines) so that some of them had to flee to the jungle screaming and screeching with their boils and pains. Another super ability of Tejas was that he could stretch his body to a great length, although this capability till date had not really been tried and tested fully.

Tejas was very fair with a head full of curly hair, very good looking and very sweet. Nobody took him seriously and he did not mind it. His happiness wasn't a reaction to the outside world; rather it came from inside him from his heart. Just having him around made a person light-hearted and made them forget their worries and tensions. His giggles, his gales of laughter, the impish eyes that made light of any incident were more than enough to make people want to be near him.

Uday did not have much time for Tejas and was most of the time impatient with him, but with Uday around nobody messed with Tejas either. Tejas was also somewhat intimidated by his elder brother whose lack of emotions always fascinated him. Ruby was another matter altogether. She always had a treat ready for him whether it was his favourite snack or a movie or a cricket match ticket. She even did his homework while he just ran here and there. Ruby's best friend, Aishani, was also his favourite though he was just a bit wary of her, she was so serious. She was also the best in everything—in her studies, in the martial arts, in creating magic. The other students, his friends, were also in awe of Aishani. They all knew that she was the favourite of all the teachers in the Gurukul mostly because of her hard work, sincerity and total focus on the tasks assigned to her.

Like everyone around Aishani, Tejas had also been reared with the subconscious knowledge that Aishani had to be protected no matter what. So be it. It never entered his mind to question this diktat. No one had specifically told him to look after Aishani, but he knew instinctively that if the occasion arose he would unhesitatingly protect her even at the cost of his own life. Both Aishani and Tejas were not aware of this decree which seemed to have been written by the Gods themselves. Guruji and most of the adults were aware of this fact though nobody ever said anything about it.

There was a time when all the youngsters realised how his petite size had been useful to them. All of them were playing in the jungle behind Aishani's house. It was more of an undergrowth than a jungle though they liked to call it a jungle. It was full of trees and shrubs with small hillocks here and there. There were small caves and underground tunnels also. To complete the picture there was a narrow stream also. So many times Aishani would just curl up under a tree with a book and become oblivious to the whole world. Ruby and Jayant could banter on any point for hours; Uday would target birds and small animals while Tejas would just run and jump around aimlessly laughing at nothing in particular. Aishani, Jayant, Ruby, Uday, and Tejas were just having fun running, talking and giggling. Uday stood a little bit apart trying hard to show that he was not enjoying, but nobody paid any attention to him. They were used to his dark, sombre moods. Today they were all sitting together huddled over something which Jayant had in his hands. They were huddled under a tree with luxuriant leaves so that they were partially hidden from any prying eyes. Jayant had a square piece of transparent stone in his hands. Uday was standing on the periphery of the circle but he was also peering intently at the stone.

"What is this Jayant? What is so special about it? It's just a pretty transparent stone," Ruby said disdainfully.

"Don't be so unbelieving Ruby," Jayant said. He had just come out of the stream from where he had fished out the stone.

"I have been trying to find this stone for a very long time. I finally got it today," he said triumphantly.

Even Aishani looked up from her book now. She knew that Jayant was not joking. As for Tejas, he was just hovering around.

"Tejas come here," Jayant called. Tejas excitedly pushed Ruby out of the way and went and stood in front of him. Jayant held the stone between his thumb and forefinger and showed it all around, "See it's transparent. Here Tejas you hold it now. Gingerly Tejas held the stone in his hands. Everyone waited with bated breath. They expected some fireworks, but nothing happened. A bit disappointed they looked at Jayant.

"Shh, don't make any movement, be still and look at the stone," he said. They looked. The stone was slowly taking on colour. It turned a pale green and then slowly turned bright shining green. All of them gasped.

"Oh! so it turns green from transparent," Tejas said in a tone of hushed wonder.

"That's not all, it changes colour according to the mood and personality of a person."

That had really caught their attention.

"That's not all," Jayant explained importantly, "It changes colour according to the present mood of a person, so if you are angry it will turn red in your hands and later when you become calm it may turn light blue or light green."

Now everybody wanted to hold the stone in his or her hands. In Aishani's hand, it turned pale pink, in Ruby's hand it turned a dark pink, in Uday's hands it turned a dark blue, in Jayant's hand it was yellow and in Tejas' hand it alternated between green and yellow. Everyone wanted to hold the stone so there was a bit of pushing and pulling also. To their chagrin, in this hubbub, the stone fell down from their hands and went into a hole in the ground. They were so familiar with this part of the jungle that they knew exactly which was a snake's burrow was and which was a rabbit's burrow. They all knew that this was a snake's burrow and a very long and deep one. They also had a rough idea that the inhabitant of this burrow was not a very poisonous snake; nevertheless, they never tested this theory and gave this burrow a long leeway. They were aghast when the stone fell into the burrow. It was so precious and they had just lost it! It was simply not possible to get it back. Suddenly without any warning, Tejas joined both his hands above his head like an arrow and dived into the burrow. He was so swift that nothing registered for a few moments. Jayant was the first to cry out, "Tejas you'll get stuck there! The snake might be inside!"

But Tejas was too far inside to hear any words of warning that the others were now screaming. His body was now almost two thirds inside the snake's burrow. It was as if some supernatural force and strength had entered his body and heart. At the back of his mind, Tejas was holding himself responsible for the stone being dropped in the burrow. His legs were urgently pushing him inside the hole, his fingers fervently moving, scratching at the soft crumbly mud trying to find the stone. And he was stuck. It was a very narrow burrow. No human hand could go inside it let alone a full body but Tejas was like a soul possessed.

His slender body had stretched like elastic and gone inside nimbly and feverishly removing the dirt searching for the stone but he could not find it. Suddenly his fingers touched something hard. His heart raced. Could it be the stone? Tejas turned it around between his forefingers. Yes, he was now sure, it was the stone. He gripped it tightly in his hands and started to turn back but to his horror there was no turning back. The hole was too narrow for him to turn back. He was so tightly jammed in the hole that he could not breathe or move. He could barely move his feet which were above the ground. He could not hear the panic shouts from above. He also could not tell them that he had retrieved the stone. His heart was now bursting from lack of oxygen. Above the ground it was only the detached Uday who could make out that there was still some strength left in Tejas.

There was still some feeble movement in Teja's feet. In a flash, Uday understood that Tejas was stuck and he wouldn't be able to come out easily even with help. Uday's forehead began glistening with cold sweat. He controlled himself. He clasped Teja's ankles his knuckles tightly weaving into each other. Then without waiting he grabbed Teja's feet in his strong arms and started pulling him out. But Tejas was by now fully submerged and stuck in the mud in the hole. The others stared at Uday incredulously but only for a moment. They immediately grasped that Uday in spite of his immense strength and power, could not pull out Tejas. With a cry of consternation and urgency, Jayant grasped Uday by the waist and started pulling him back. The girls also immediately understood. Both of them clutched Jayant. All of them started pulling Uday who in turn was pulling Tejas out of the snake hole.

But by now Tejas was so badly stuck that any more pressure and he would have broken in two. The unflappable Uday was also getting perturbed. His superhuman strength would only harm his young brother. His eyes became black and watery. All sorts of emotions passed through Uday's heart and soul. He wasn't aware that he loved his baby brother so much. In his desperation he was ready to do anything for Tejas but what? He tried to pull him out again this time a bit slowly with love and care, willing Tejas with all his heart to slide back slowly. Gradually, a dim realisation came to Uday's mind that Tejas had, in fact, started moving. He shifted his eyes towards the lower part of Tejas' body and couldn't believe his eyes! With all the pulling and pushing Tejas' body seemed to have become elongated and thin. In his excitement, Uday tried to pull him out some more without really expecting any results. But with his thinning body, Tejas did come out a little. Encouraged, Uday pulled him a little more. Tejas came out further, his body thinning and stretching out.

Uday was now very careful. He did not know what was happening and the others could not see. They just sensed that the mud was loosening and Tejas was coming out albeit slowly. After what seemed ages but were only a few minutes Uday felt the mud loosening up and he could yank Tejas a few inches out of the hole. The others could also now sense Uday's excitement.

They pulled Uday harder and suddenly Tejas was out of the hole. But they were shocked by what they saw. The middle part of Tejas' body had stretched to more than a foot and had become very long and thin and he was absolutely still. His midriff was like a thick rope covered with slimy wet mud. They gathered around him in horror. Tejas' whole body and especially his face were fully coated with mud. His nose, ears, eyes were caked with sludge. Whatever they could see of his face was ashen and his lips were blue. All of them were frozen in shock for a few moments. Suddenly his eyes opened and he stared at nothing and no one in particular. Then his limbs started shaking uncontrollably. Aishani was the first to come to her senses. She had helped her father with many trauma patients.

"Get the water bottles," she shouted hoarsely. The mud had to be cleaned. Nobody wanted to acknowledge the weird phenomenon they were seeing. They just wanted to see Tejas breathing. Both Jayant and Ruby rushed to where they had kept their water bottles. Uday made him sit up while they poured water over his face especially his nose. They did it very carefully ensuring that the mud did not go inside his nasal canal. Tears were rolling down Ruby's and Aishani's eyes. They were so scared and were almost giving up hope. As a last resort, Uday softly thumped. Tejas on his throat and on his back because there wasn't much of a throat and back left. Tejas, in any case, was a slim boy and now he had stretched so much in length. But even the soft thumping helped. He coughed and a small stone flew out of his mouth and he coughed again. "Water," he croaked. Tremulously Ruby made him drink water from the thermos. He drank thankfully, closed his eyes and leaned against the tree where Uday had propped him.

They waited around him with bated breath. They were totally clueless as to what to do now. Tejas seemed to be sleeping peacefully. After some time both Ruby and Aishani also lay down beside him and dozed off. Jayant too sat on a rock and nodded off. Only Uday sat ramrod stiff beside Tejas and observed him without batting an eyelid. Every five minutes Tejas would sleepily ask for water and drink it with his eyes closed. It was after the fifth drink that Uday began noticing that Tejas was shrinking a little. He kept on feeding Tejas small sips of water and Tejas kept on shrinking in size till the time he reached his original size. Uday stared at him then slowly relaxed. Tejas was becoming normal, the colour was returning to his face but he still slept. The others were also more or less half asleep and half awake. Only Uday was sharply observant of the changes taking place in Tejas' body.

It was late afternoon. Very soon it would get dark and they had to reach home or there would be too many questions to answer. Tejas was now waking up and so were the others. Immediately they sprang towards him. The girls started fussing over him while Uday and Jayant just looked on.

"Tejas!"Ruby squealed, "You've come back to your original size! How did this happen?"

"What do you mean? What happened? Why are you all sitting here like this? Look I'm sorry I dropped the stone but see I got it back also. No harm has come to it. See." He held out his hand with the magical stone.

The others looked at him in amazement. In the entire melee, they had totally forgotten about the stone. They looked at the stone. It was shining brightly. They looked at each other and began laughing. Tejas tried to get up but sat down.

"I have this pain in my back and waist," he groaned.

"Don't get up yourself, we'll carry you. Baba will give you some ointment and medicine and you'll be alright in no time," said Aishani.

Unknown to them as yet, Tejas' destiny had already been written as was all of theirs. There was a meaning to his being given a small size. Tejas' size and speed would make him a perfect sniper for killing and injuring demons, thus making way for Aishani's and Adheesh's perfect kills.

Getting to Know Each Other

Armed with his new knowledge and helpful guidance from Guruji, Adheesh started thinking of ways of meeting Aishani. Though he liked and admired girls, till date he had never thought of any girl seriously. Trust Guruji to throw a bomb on him like this, he thought wryly. In truth, he had never wanted to meet anyone more than Aishani. But the thought of going to her house was making him nervous. But he had to go, there was no choice; moreover, he wanted to meet her. There was no question of meeting her anywhere in the Gurukul. He knew that the minutest interest would blow up into a torrid love affair in the eyes and ears of every student in the Gurukul.

The coming weekend Adheesh went towards her house. There seemed to be a clinic of some sort on one side of the house. The main entrance had a welcoming air.

A man was sitting in the verandah wearing gold-rimmed glasses reading a manuscript. He looked up when he saw Adheesh approaching. He got up and waited for Adheesh to come up. Adheesh looked at him. He was wearing a spotless white dhoti and a white kurta. On his shoulder was a checkered red and white *gamcha.* He was of middling height and bald with an inch of grey hair around his baldness. He was the most distinguished person Adheesh had ever seen. Adheesh folded his hands in a namaste. The elderly man replied in affirmative.

"Have you come for medicines? The clinic is there on the right side," he said gravely and kindly and waved towards the clinic. "You go there, I'll be there in five minutes." He turned towards his manuscript probably to bookmark it.

"No sir, I have not come for the medicines. Guruji recommended your library to me. I have come to join your library if you allow me to."

Pandit Ram Sharan was puzzled. Why had Guruji recommended his library to this young man? What was so special about this man?

"Of course, of course, Guruji's wish is my command. Come and sit here beta. What is your name and where are you coming from?" Panditji gestured to an armchair in front of him.

"Thank you, sir, my name is Adheesh. My father's name is Shri Vidyadhar. He is a businessman. I am in the fourth year of training in the Gurukul."

Pandit Ram Sharan nodded amicably. Though it was a bit unprecedented for Guruji to send any person to use his library, it wasn't all that surprising. Pandit Ram Sharan was used to Guruji sending people to his Ayurvedic clinic. Guruji would also sometimes send people to him for some specific puja. Pandit Ram Sharan had always felt honoured whenever Guruji sent someone to him for his expertise and knowledge.

"That's nice, though my library is small as compared to the Gurukul's library; still there are some very rare manuscripts which you may find interesting."

"Oh, I'm sure sir, Guruji was all praise for your collection of books," Adheesh smiled, though he felt quite nervous.

"The library is just beside the Puja room. You go there; I shall come to you in a few minutes. I have to complete this chapter," Pandit Ram Sharan said pointing to his book.

"Yes sir," Adheesh walked towards the library.

Pandit Ram Sharan sat down, just a little puzzled. Why would Guruji send this young man to him to use his library? Was there another reason for sending this young man to him? Apparently clueless, Pandit Ram Sharan sat down to think. Guruji never did anything without any reason. Then it suddenly dawned on him. The thought came to him so suddenly that he almost staggered. He was the one! Recently Pandit Ram Sharan had started waiting for any sign from Guruji to inform him that the chosen one for his Aishani had arrived. He knew that Aishani was getting geared up and trained to face her destiny of destroying the demons and that in most cases she would achieve her full powers only with her partner. What he didn't know was that this partner was in the Gurukul itself and a sort of partnership had been acknowledged by both of them. Pandit Ram Sharan was not aware of the sparks that flew between Aishani and Adheesh or the feelings that those sparks evoked. He followed Adheesh to the library, where he was slowly walking along the shelves of books looking at them closely. Sometimes he would take out a book and turn its pages.

Pandit Ram Sharan looked at Adheesh closely. He stared for so long that Adheesh began to feel uncomfortable. He knew that there would be no similarities in Adheesh's features from any of his past births as his biological parents were different in this birth. But there was something in his personality which Pandit Ram Sharan recognised. That was his serious stance and his penetrating and patient gaze. He was satisfied and elated. So that is why Guruji had sent him to his library. He asked a few perfunctory questions about the Vedas and some more questions on martial arts, and in turn, was more than totally satisfied.

"Ok beta let me show you some more books on the interpretations of the Vedas and Upanishads."

Adheesh followed him. His heart thudded when he caught a glimpse of Aishani in the clinic. She was talking to one of her father's patients. She did not notice them. Adheesh was not to know that Pandit Ram Sharan was more on tenterhooks than him on more fronts than one. Guruji sending Adheesh to him meant that it was time for Aishani and Adheesh to reconnect with their past births. It also meant that some of the demons were coming out of their hibernation, hence had to be destroyed within a short span of time.

Everyone had to be put on alert! Most of all, Aishani had to be made aware of her powers and remember the varied and rich experiences of her past births. Pandit Ram Sharan did not know how much Adheesh knew or how much he remembered. He probably did not remember much as of now. They would remember everything when they were together and when they acknowledged each other, he thought.

They went towards a particular bookcase; Adheesh following Panditji. He was amazed at the size of the library and the number of books and manuscripts it contained. It was a connoisseur's delight. For a moment he forgot everything on seeing the rare authentic manuscripts on the shelves.

"Make yourself comfortable beta. Take your time, and you can also borrow a couple of books to read at leisure."

"Thank you, sir, that won't be necessary as there is absolutely no time after the training and regular college. You have such a wonderful library; I have yet to see a better one."

"All God's blessing," Panditji brushed away the compliment.

Hearing sounds in the library, Aishani came to check and stood stock-still when she saw Adheesh. A wave of emotions engulfed her, a sense of déjà vu, extreme happiness and of course surprise. She didn't know how to react.

"Ash beta come," Panditji beckoned her, "This is Adheesh. He is also from the Ashram and one year senior to you. You must have seen him there. Guruji has sent him here to use the library." Seeing Aishani's telltale blush he knew that they had already met or at least seen each other. But it had to be seen how much they knew each other.

Aishani smiled tremulously. They greeted each other shyly, then Aishani went back to the clinic. Her heart was thudding as she sat gingerly on the chair. He was here! He was here! Oh, what was she going to do! She wrung her hands in confusion at her mixed feelings. This had never happened to her. Well, lately so many things that she had never thought about had happened to her. She wanted to rush back to the library to be with him. She felt so shy that she wanted to sit glued to her chair. Oh! What was she going to do!

Aishani generally liked to be left alone. She was not lonely, she just liked to be with herself—with her books, read about Ayurveda and Naturopathy. In fact, she was never alone for a long time as people would come to her from faraway places to find cures for their problems. This was her father's forte, but her father had to go to many places for long periods and he would leave the shop in Aishani's capable hands. He could leave the shop with his son Jayant also, but Jayant did not show any particular interest. He preferred going to various places to buy astrological items and herbs for his father. So it was Aishani who did everything in the shop and the shop-cum-library adjacent to it. She did such a good job that many people came to meet Aishani only.

"Aishani dear, this cough of mine has literally become a pain in the neck. It's been almost a year now. Whenever I take antibiotics it disappears but resurfaces again after a week. Do something dear."

"Uncle, you start drinking *kadha* three times a day. Take four cups of water, add eleven peppercorns, one teaspoon of grated ginger and eleven *tulsi* leaves. Boil and then simmer the concoction for some time till it is reduced to three cups. Let it cool, then strain it. Add honey or salt and drink one cup thrice a day. And eat a few tulsi leaves also. Don't chew the leaves but swallow them; do this for about a week then let me know, and uncle, it would do you good to meditate for some time. Begin for five minutes then go up to twenty. I think you are taking too much of unwanted stress. Let go uncle."

It was such pieces of advice that people liked. Her compassionate and soothing voice cured half of their problems. Though they did not know it their subconscious mind told them that she actually heard and understood their problems and she knew how to cure these ailments naturally. It was as if she instinctively knew what even they did not know about themselves.

"Burn some bay leaves and let the smoke spread in all the rooms of your house. Do this every day for two weeks. You'll start calming down; the negative energies around you will start to dissipate and your anxiety will end," she would tell this to an anxious wife or mother who was worried about her unemployed husband or son who did not study.

"Here, wear this Ram Raksha strotra yantra. Your business rivals will leave you alone and your business will flourish. In the morning finish your ablutions, sit in front of your *temple*, chant the mantra which I am giving you, then wear this *tabeej* either on your forearm or around your neck strung in a silver chain. Chant this mantra daily and see your life improving," she would say this with so much conviction that the other person believed it immediately. With this kind of faith in her, the life of the people who came to her would naturally start healing. They knew that she would never forsake them. If one *totka* (remedy) did not work she would give them another and another till they actually improved.

Very soon it became a regular affair for Adheesh to come to their library. Sometimes he would sit on the verandah with

Pandit Ram Sharan and talk. Panditji was delighted to converse with him. Together they would sit and discuss so many things. Sometimes they would become so engrossed in their discussions that he would forget why he had started coming here in the first place. He loved watching Aishani when she helped her father's patients with her soothing and caring advice and suggestions. He was amazed by her knowledge of the *totkas* and ayurvedic cures for the myriad problems that people had. He was also amazed at the faith these people had in her.

He would watch her mesmerised as she went about her work so seriously and kindly. He could not believe that this was the same girl who would so ruthlessly beat her opponents in the martial arts college. But then he had been told about her and how she was the one who would rid the Earth of more than half of the demon scum left over from the time of the *Ramayana* from the demon king Ravan's army.

Sitting here in her father's library he could gauge her personality, so soft, so caring yet so strong and focused, ready to fight for the right and good of mankind. Guruji had specifically told him that Aishani was the real Shakti, the original and real power who would heal the world by annihilating the demons. Everyone else was secondary, even he, Adheesh. Guruji had told him how both their destinies were entwined together and how they would together rid the world of these demons. Guruji had explained to him how he always had to be around Aishani to protect and guide her so that she could focus on her central vocation. She had to trust someone unequivocally to allow that person to come near her. One such person was of course her father but then Guruji had told him that her father would be with her and not be with her, and that he Adheesh was chosen by the Gods to be her guide and protector. But what shocked him was his irresistible attraction to her. And it was not only his heart and mind it was physical as well, as the sparks had proved beyond doubt.

Whenever he crossed her father's shop-cum-library it was as if there was a strong magnet inside the shop pulling him in. Then he knew that Aishani was in the shop. Try as he might he could not cross the shop without going inside. It became so embarrassing that he would retrace his steps rather than go inside. But he could not stop himself. There were many times when he just had to go there if only to get a glimpse of this impressive girl. It was the huge library which saved him from embarrassment every time. He knew that Aishani's father did not allow everybody to use his library. It was only when he felt that a person fully deserved to be in this library that that person would be given permission to sit there. In this context, there was no problem for Adheesh. Pandit Ram Sharan knew exactly who Adheesh was, much more than Adheesh himself. In fact, it was such a great relief for him to finally meet Adheesh that he personally took him to his library every time he went there.

If Adheesh was surprised by his behaviour he did not show it. Apart from the great assemblage of knowledge that this library had, it also served as a face-saver for him. He watched enthralled as Aishani went about her duties cleaning and dusting the shop and helping the people. He knew that there was a special connection as whenever their paths crossed either here or in the college there would be sparks. Thrice their arms had touched. All the three times, small multicoloured sparks had flown. Aishani had blushed crazily and rushed inside the house.

On all these occasions she had turned red and refused to look at him. But every time as she hurried past him he could make out the confusion on her face. Even he could not fathom the origin of these sparks; they seemed to be so pleasant and invigorating. But slowly he was getting the knack of it. He was beginning to understand Guruji's remarks that they were made for each other, that their souls had been together for millennia and in this birth also they would be together—he as her partner and protector and she as his partner and protector of the world.

Seeing her in this role of helping the people, his heart would burst with pride and love. He would himself get surprised by his own reaction—he hardly knew the girl! Well in this birth at least! By what Guruji had told him he could deduce that his and Aishani's relationship was quite old spanning generations, probably centuries! Guruji had told him that she had been his partner from time immemorial and in every birth; one or the other had to awaken the other person to remind him or her about their duties to the world. But he mused how was he going to remind her of her past when he himself did not know about his past, forget about her past and their past together. He had raised this question to Guruji. But Guruji had just looked at him and given him an enigmatic smile.

"All in good time, such memories are not to be rushed. It becomes difficult to absorb them especially if someone else tells you. These memories have to come to both of you on their own. Sometimes, you will have to nudge each other to remind yourselves of some particular incidents; sometimes they will come to you on your own." Adheesh sighed. What was he supposed to do now? He was now fully convinced about his role in this relationship even though millennia of memories were repressed. But what of her? It did not seem that she remembered anything at all. Apart from blushing furiously when their arms had touched and sparks had literally flown she had shown shock at the happening. There were no signs of any flashback or recollection.

Adheesh sighed again. He would have to do it himself. Make her remember what he himself could not remember. Well as Guruji would not tell him anything more, he would have to begin from this birth only. They did have a few points in common in this birth too, he surmised wryly. They went to the same martial arts college; they were star students of the academy which is why they were allowed in the senior library. Even though they recognised and acknc wledged each other in the academy they were never friends or on friendly terms. It was only when he started visiting her father's library that they became aware of each other.

But Pandit Ram Sharan's library had such rare books on *Ramayana* and Vedas and Puranas, that Adheesh would become so engrossed in them he would forget everything. Sometimes it seemed to Adheesh that he had lived some of these stories which were so old that their time could not be fixed. And then it slowly started coming to him! He began recollecting! He was a warrior! He had always been a warrior of very high rank. He remembered that he had always fought beside a woman. He and this woman were one. They had special powers which multiplied hundredfold when they were together and diminished when they were not with each other. They had loved each other from the very core of their hearts; their union had been blessed by the Gods themselves.

To counter the demons there had to be huge amounts of strength and power which could not be bestowed on any single human being, as human beings were frail as compared to the violent and ferocious nature and the powerful strength of the demons. The Rakshasas or the demons and their ilk symbolise all kinds of evil in our myths. They do not have any love or compassion. They do not raise their children with love; their children learn only to survive by any means, the most obvious being to follow in the footsteps of their creators by continuing to live in their hellish dystopia. Their parents killed and tortured for pleasure, so they also did the same.

Only Bhagwan or the Devtas had equal or more power than the demons. But by the time Kalyug came, the celestial beings had left for their heavenly abodes and it was left to the human beings to fend for themselves against the demons. No single human could garner enough vigour, vitality, fortitude or mental and physical strength, not to say of their cunningness, to thwart the demons. Hence superpowers were bestowed on two individuals—a male and a female, with the female being the protagonist in any annihilation and the male equally powerful would fight alongside her and provide her protection. It was the concept of *Ardhnarishwar* or one entity with half the attributes of a female and the other half of a male. These couples were specially and carefully chosen by Hanuman ji and Guruji. There were a few other such couples also in the world. Nobody knew who they were or where they were.

By the time the final piece fell into place, Adheesh's head was spinning. He held his head in his hands and closed his eyes trying to control his overspilling thoughts.

"Will you have a cup of tea or a cold drink or… or anything? I have to go for my evening classes," Aishani said shyly flustered at her own discomfiture. It seemed as if there was nobody in the house, then why did he feel as if the whole house was listening to their conversation with bated breath. In the same breath, the house seemed to be softly coaxing them to talk some more. Adheesh was puzzled. Growing up in a robust, sporty household there was no time to pay attention to these mystical phenomena. But here where there was so much of peace and calmness, he could sense other enigmatical things also albeit of a good kind. But Aishani knew.

The house always spoke to her when she was alone and quite frequently interfered with her affairs also. She sighed. She knew that the house did not want them to leave it. Somehow the house had taken a fancy to Adheesh, why? She did not understand. She made a warning gesture to the house by flicking her hair. The house retreated.

"What? No thank you," his trance was broken, "I'll also leave now." He got up.

"No, no, you stay here and do your research. Just close the door when you leave or ring the bell. Someone will come and close the door."

"It's okay, I was about to leave anyway. I am also going your way. Come, I'll walk you to your institute."

Aishani blushed again. She didn't know what to say. She felt so shy. She was tickled pink at the idea of Adheesh walking along with her to her institute. Ruby would be sure to see them together and tease her afterward but she quickly brushed these thoughts aside. That was not important. What was important was all the feelings welling up inside her; her heart was beating like a small caged bird; she couldn't hold herself straight and was horrified by the thought of Adheesh noticing all these things. But all Adheesh saw was this beautiful, calm and composed girl agreeing to go with him in the most natural manner. His thoughts were in turmoil. This beautiful girl was his partner and had been so for the last so many births! And here he was thinking of wooing her. Well, he would have to woo her to remind her of their togetherness in their past births. He was totally clueless as to how he would do that when he himself remembered only in patches.

They went outside her house very careful not to touch each other or the crackling thing would start again. Both of them had books in their hands, Aishani her college books and Adheesh two books which he had finally borrowed from her father's library. It was a twenty-minute walk to her institute. They did not talk much; when they did it was only about inane things which they both found very interesting.

Slowly, it became a habit for both of them to walk to her institute together. To Aishani it seemed that these walks were the only reason for her living. Her father had returned and this was the first surprise. He was so encouraging of her friendship with Adheesh, so much so that he almost waited for them to walk together. Aishani was totally puzzled by her father's behaviour. Pandit Ram Sharan was a fairly strict father and did not much like Aishani or her brother Jayant mixing with the opposite sex. And here he was literally pushing her to go out with Adheesh. During this time, Pandit Ram Sharan and Adheesh had become very friendly with each other with Panditji sharing his rare manuscripts with him and explaining them also. She gave credit to Adheesh who immediately grasped the texts which were mostly written in Sanskrit and in a language older than that too.

They had become quite friendly in these few days. They talked about their families, their classes and of the two libraries—one which was her father's and the other which was in their college of martial arts.

"I must say Aishani some of the books in your father's library are such gems of knowledge and spirituality that they outshine the books in our library also." By library, he meant the library of their college.

"Yes, I am aware of it. Baba has often shown me these books, but I am afraid I have not shown much interest," she laughed embarrassed at the thought. Here was a complete stranger appreciating these books while she who was so fond of such books did not pay much attention to them. As if sensing her discomfiture he came near her to reassure her. Accidentally his hand touched her elbow. Sparks flew and how! Thousands of multi-coloured stars came out with that small touch—mostly gold, silver, pink and blue. Current passed through her whole body. This was something she could not hide. Mutely she looked at him. He was also looking at her. Maybe the same current had passed through him.

Fortunately, they were in a secluded corner. They looked at each other for a long time then Adheesh said slowly, "Aishani both of us know that this is not a coincidence and this is not magic. This is just our chemistry through the ages. I won't be really able to explain it fully as I don't fully understand it myself. Needless to say, it'll save us the trouble of saying I know you and I love you." Adheesh smiled at his own feeble attempt at humour.

Aishani was stunned, "What do you mean Adheesh?" she said softly her heart hammering again. She did not find his words very shocking.

"Ash, we have been partners from the time we came into this world. You are the protector of the world and I am your partner and your protector," he said simply. He could not think of any other way to explain.

"The sparks?"Aishani looked at him mutely.

"I guess we have met after a couple of generations. The touch must be triggering back old memories embedded in our subconscious. Guruji did say that we are an old soul couple…" his words drifted away. Both of them were quiet for a very long time. Both of them were acutely aware that something great and significant was blossoming before their eyes, exactly what they did not know. Their emotions were so overwhelming that it was becoming almost impossible to control them. Aishani had this great urge to put her arms around him and hold him tightly while Adheesh just wanted to hold her and protect her from the whole world. Slowly she came towards him and he opened his arms and they melted into each other. Stardust covered them from top to toe. Closing their eyes, they travelled together across continents, across oceans, across rivers—they flew in space, they went inside the Earth and travelled to the past and the future too. All the time holding hands and clutching each other. When sanity returned after eons they were still there holding on to each other. The crackling of stars had petered down though they were still touching and staring at each other. Aishani was the first to move. "Adheesh," she said softly, "Adheesh I don't know what happened just now, but all of it doesn't seem strange now."

"I know Ash," he whispered back, "Time had stopped when we were going to so many places in the past and the future also. We were together in all those places. We have always been together and we will always be together." He took her in his arms again. They stayed like that for a long time. Finally, Adheesh drew away from her. Aishani had almost gone to sleep.

"Aishani, we can never be separated, that much is confirmed. Don't you think that this…" he faltered, "This revelation of ours is not as important as the work for which we are destined."

Aishani looked up languidly, "What Adheesh, what is our work?" She didn't want to talk about anything other than them.

"Ash, there are other things."

Ash woke up now. She looked around and came to her senses. She was in Adheesh's arms! What was this! She hardly knew him. How could she do this! Why, she was with Adheesh—her partner, her lover, her protector, and her husband too. Oh God, what was happening? What was true, this or the dream which she had with Adheesh? She looked at him. He looked back, "Yes Ash," he had read her thoughts, "All of it is true. This is true and the dream is also true, the dream more so because we have lived all those lives whereas we still have to live this life. We still have to be told about our goals and how to achieve them.

But, later. Now I have to take you home. Promise me Ash, you'll go to sleep and not think much about all this. We'll try to sort it out tomorrow when we meet in the evening."

"Ok Adheesh, but it won't be easy."

"I know, it's difficult for me to grasp as well. I will go to Guruji and tell him that we have remembered some of our past. I think you can ask your father also. I am now sure that he knows about us."

Ash was also now convinced that her father knew more than she thought he knew. Adheesh dropped her home, then went back to his own home. He didn't look back though she kept looking after him till he disappeared around the corner. Everybody had returned by now. She mumbled an excuse about not wanting dinner then quickly went to her room. She sat cross-legged on her bed and covered her face with her hair and palms. Oh! What revelations! Adheesh, her dearest Adheesh was with her now after so many years, maybe ages. His name must have been different in the previous births.

But that didn't matter. What mattered was now they were together in this birth. And they were going to be together after such a long time. It seemed as if she had two personalities, the past one where she and Adheesh had been partners and the present one where she hardly knew him. She couldn't be seen to be very friendly with him. People around them wouldn't understand. It would be sweet torment for her, knowing what she knew and unable to do anything about it. Well, she was going to face each day as it came, she thought happily. Her father was only too happy to see her with Adheesh and hence her mother also. In the next few days, she did not know what transpired between her parents, but her mother had almost started fawning over Adheesh. It was embarrassing, so much so that even Jayant began noticing their parents' behaviour. But the happy go lucky Jayant didn't pay much heed. If they liked Adheesh then so be it. In any case, he made Aishani smile, which was good for everybody around.

Jayant's Birthday

They were all looking forward to the feast tonight. It was Jayant's birthday. They knew that their mother would outshine herself. She was an excellent cook and many of her recipes were in their family for generations and closely guarded. Aishani was not very fond of cooking; she could barely cook to save her own life. Not that anybody minded, least of all her mother. Aishani was being trained for a much greater destiny and would have to fight tooth and nail to bring normalcy and happiness so that people like her could happily and contentedly cook and feed their families. Both mother and daughter had decided the menu a couple of days earlier and had made a few preparations a day before. It was an eclectic mixture of different Indian cuisines, a sort of fusion to suit their family's taste. Of course, the ubiquitous Ruby had to be there to share everything.

Without her, things wouldn't be so colourful.

On every birthday of his children, Pandit Ram Sharan made it a point to give each child a unique gift. It could be a material gift or it could be a *Diksha*. For Jayant's birthday today he was gifting him the diksha of seeing through solid things with his naked eyes. The process for this had been going on for almost a year now. It had probably begun from his last birthday and today was the culmination of the year-long practice. Jayant could now see through most solids and dense things. This was not a small diksha. It was like opening a small door to a vast universe of seeing things which are beyond normal human comprehension.

It all depended on how much practice and attention one gave to this *vidya (study)*. With it, one could see the past and the future also. As for Jayant, he obediently and sincerely learned what his father taught him, but Pandit Ram Sharan had yet to see the fever in him. After the final initiation was over, father and son went on the terrace of the house and stood at the balustrade encircling the roof. Panditji placed his hands on Jayant's head.

"Son, close your eyes, chant your mantras, then open your eyes slowly. Differentiate between what is there and the extra things that you are seeing."

"Yes Baba," Jayant closed his eyes, then opened them slowly after some time.

"I don't see any changes baba," he said, a bit disappointed then perked up a bit. "Wait, baba, I can see through the trees and now I can see through that wall also," Jayant was getting very excited now. If there wasn't a distance between father and son he would have hugged his father, but they did not have that kind of bonhomie between them.

"Son," Pandit Ram Sharan warned him, "This is the beginning of your initiation of this vidya. This power will be in direct proportion to the practice that you put in it otherwise it will just wither away. Today is your birthday, today is the day that you become an adult with full responsibilities and maturity."

He continued, "Beta, we all have to play a role in the bigger picture of the Universe. It is through our small roles in life, whether positive or negative, that the Universe becomes a whole. Some of us are leaders and play a pivotal role in the scheme of things while some of us play supporting roles which are equally important. It is when all of us play our roles to the best of our abilities that we go forward. I don't want to give a long discourse now, but I cannot reiterate enough that in this part of the world Aishani is our leader; yes, she is your mother's and my leader too. We are here to support her in whatever way we can, sometimes with our lives too."

"Baba, I understand," said Jayant who had been quietly taking care of Aishani right from the time he was a toddler. This came naturally to him and his parents had a very fair idea about it. They knew that with Jayant around Aishani was safe.

Jayant touched his father's feet with reverence. Panditji blessed him. "Let's go down beta, the others are waiting for us."

They were a few of Jayant's friends, a couple of her father's patients who had become friends and Ruby's family with her parents and her brothers. It was almost the same list every year only this time one more person was added which made Ruby smile wickedly and Aishani very nervous and excited too.

Her father had become so enamoured with Adheesh and his vast knowledge that he had invited him also.

"This *ras malai* is pure ambrosia," Adheesh exclaimed with satisfaction. Aishani blushed happily and prettily. Ruby made round eyes while Pandit Ram Sharan beamed. Her mother had made Jayant's favourite mango cake. Ruby had put some candles on it also. With great gusto Jayant cut the cake, everybody clapped and the cake was distributed. Ruby and Aishani distributed the cake slices; some of the old timers took more than two pieces; it was so tasty, soft and gooey with all the goodness of mangoes and butter.

Ruby and her younger brother Tejas were all over the place with Ruby helping in the kitchen, and Tejas generally making a nuisance of himself but in such an endearing way that everybody liked and laughed at his antics. Only Uday was quiet, but nobody paid any attention to him as he was always quiet. Nobody noticed that his shoulders hunched a little. He behaved impeccably, as usual, ate and enjoyed his meal. If there was anything the matter with Uday they didn't know, least of all Uday. After his talk with Guruji, Uday had not even thought about Aishani. She was going to be his leader and he was going to accept her as such.

The party was over sooner than Aishani would have liked, but it was Jayant's day. He and his friends had planned to go hiking in the nearby jungle and couldn't wait to leave. Her heart beating with happiness and anticipation Aishani looked for a chance to be alone with Adheesh. From his surreptitious glances, she knew that he also wanted to talk to her. But it was just not possible. When the party was over and the elders sat in the library to have a cup of coffee, or just relax, Aishani thought of sitting with Adheesh in the back veranda, but as usual her mother asked her to help in the winding up. Ruby was already winding up. If she did not do this work now, Ruby would make her miserable by teasing her mercilessly and even her mother would find it odd. The last thing Aishani wanted was anybody knowing about her feelings. Slowly everybody left and she was left alone with her thoughts in turmoil. Adheesh gave her a fleeting glance before leaving. That simple eye contact had so much of meaning that it sent shivers down her spine and her bones melted. She finished the kitchen work with Ruby and her mother and then sat down with Ruby in her bedroom to discuss the evening.

"That's another birthday gone Ash, I must say Jayant is growing up really fast. Only yesterday he was chasing butterflies. Look at him now, chasing butterflies of the other kind."

Aishani laughed. She was used to Ruby's droll remarks. Yes, Jayant was growing up, yet he would always remain her baby brother and best friend. If anyone understood Jayant it was her. She knew that beneath the fun-loving and the frolicsome person was a very sharp and focused warrior. She knew that with Jayant around nothing could ever happen to her. She sighed. There were so many people to protect her. She could not fathom what they were trying to protect her from. There was another addition to this list now. Her cheeks reddened at the thought. She tried to hide her blushes with her hair but not before Ruby had seen them.

"Oh ho, madam, we are here to dissect the party, not daydream about any person who may have just drifted in," Ruby said wickedly.

The rosiness deepened some more. She decided she was not going to hide it from Ruby anymore. She turned towards Ruby who was looking at her as if she knew what she was going to say.

"Ruby, I have to tell you something."

Ruby waited. She knew as Guruji had already told her. Ruby probably knew more than Ash herself. But she wanted to hear it from Ash. She didn't want Ash to keep any secrets from her, nor did she want to keep any of her own secrets from Ash. Except that she was descendent of apsaras and that her method of protecting Ash was totally different. Ruby knew that Ash would take some time to assimilate this information. Why, she herself had taken time to adjust to this fact. Initially, she had felt chagrined by the role assigned to her, but she adjusted to it fast enough when Manohar reminded her of a few of her past births.

Aishani cleared her throat and flicked the hair off from her face. Ruby knew that she was ready to speak now. "Ruby, I have to tell you something about Adheesh," she paused searching for words. "It's not only that I am attracted to him, but it's also something much more than that. Adheesh and I have been partners from a very long time," she stopped, searching Ruby's face to see if she had understood. Of course Ruby understood, but she wanted the revelation to come from Aishani. She kept quiet.

"Adheesh and I have been partners in our past births also. That is why whenever our arms touch there are sparks, which remind us of our feelings for each other and that we are soulmates from a very long time." Aishani paused. She had expected Ruby to look shocked or at least laugh unbelievably at the thought. Ruby did not do any of these things which was a pleasant surprise for Aishani.

"Oh Ash, I could make out that your attraction for each other is more than skin deep, so to say. Now that you have told me, I can understand. But tell me one thing Ash, what about the sparks, will they continue or will they end after you get married to each other?" Ruby asked impishly.

Ash threw a cushion at Ruby. Ruby ducked laughingly. They sat and talked some more about the party and Adheesh, then Ruby left leaving Ash to her own secret and dreamy thoughts.

Adheesh and Devnath

Adheesh had an extended and happy family though everyone had their own quirks and idiosyncrasies. There was his father Vidyadhar Mishra, a jovial man who always saw the positive side of everything or so it seemed and he always claimed that his large business empire was mainly the result of his positive attitude. Vidyadharji was a stocky man of middling height. He was neither fat nor thin but his physical strength and confidence shone through his clothes. He was fond of wearing western clothes, that is pants, shirts or suits as the occasion demanded, though many times he wore Indian clothes also like kurta and Aligarhi pajama. Aligarh *pajamas* are the more formal kind of pajamas which are broader at the waist and tapered at the bottom. He had a slightly balding head with a thick fringe of hair around his baldness. He had sharp piercing brown eyes which did not miss anything. This was because of centuries of looking after and protecting Adheesh in one avatar or another. He knew his role in the divine scheme of things that even if Adheesh was his biological son in this birth, he was his lord and he had to protect Adheesh at all costs.

Vidyadhar knew all this because it was imperative for him to remember all this in order to protect him. Nobody apart from his wife, Anuja, knew about this, even Adheesh. Vidyadhar never spoke rudely to anyone or even in a harsh voice. Everyone also knew that he was unforgiving only with people who did not to perform their duties as expected. He gave second chances to everybody but not more.

Everybody loved him and he loved everybody. He owned a number of hospitals and hotels. He had only one weakness which he hid quite successfully from others. This was his extreme love for his son Adheesh. Adheesh was the kind of son that any father would yearn for; he was the reason for his living. Vidyadhar was Adheesh's father and patron in more ways than one. He had been with Adheesh through the ages in one form or other. In this birth and in some other past births also he had been his father. He did not remember all of them; he just had a vague knowledge of these births, but what he knew with utmost surety was that Adheesh had to be trained and protected at all costs. Right from the time when he was born Vidyadhar knew that Adheesh was not an average or normal human being. He knew that Adheesh been blessed by God himself and that there was a touch of divinity in him. Vidyadhar also knew that Adheesh was born for a specific purpose, and also that most of the people surrounding him had also been born for the specific purpose of making a strong protective shield around him so that he could execute his work undisturbed and unhindered.

Vidyadhar did not have full knowledge of what Adheesh's mission in this birth was but he did know that Adheesh had been carrying on this work in his past births also and that it was his, Vidyadhar's responsibility to provide him with all cooperation and assistance. He was also sure that Adheesh was aware of his feelings and that he knew that he was meant for greater things which were not really about the material world. As such the best education was provided to him. Adheesh was a naturally gifted scholar plus a natural athlete also.

Then there was Adheesh's other training, the paranormal training, a procedure which had to be undertaken secretly, as the other 'normal' people would not understand and thus misconstrue the whole thing. Adheesh was wired to understand these things as was his wife Anuja, Adheesh's mother. Both the parents made sure that he undertook his training at the fastest pace and in the best possible manner. Adheesh had understood his responsibilities right from the time he was born. This knowledge was stamped in him from his birth itself. He spent all his holidays in his paranormal training school. Nobody questioned him.

What everybody didn't know was that his parents knew exactly where Adheesh was at any given time and that they only sent him to these sojourns many times. The others had in a hazy way however noticed that their servant Devnath would also be missing at these times. But because his parents were not worried so they were also not worried or very curious. They were also aware that Devnath was there in the household especially for Adheesh and thus was given a wide berth as far as other household duties were concerned.

Devnath had been hired by Vidyadhar for Adheesh's security. In the initial part of his life, Devnath had become an ascetic, a follower of Aghori Dharm in the city of Varanasi. The people of this sect were Shaivites or followers of Shiva. These people would stay in cremation grounds to meditate and pray to get rid of vices, their own and of others. Their methods were so different from the normal form of Hindu pujas that generally people did not mix with them and vice versa. The Aghoris practiced Tantra too, the violent supernatural form of Hindu puja. After his understanding of some of the Aghori trends, Vidyadhar had a meeting with the head of the Aghori Panth at Varanasi. Their association with each other went a long back. Though not friends it could be said that they knew each other very well. Aghori baba knew why Vidyadhar had come to him. His ashram was a spartan and simple one, devoid of any luxurious things.

Baba slept on the ground on a thin blanket which was smeared with ashes. He himself was covered with ashes from the crematorium ghats of Varanasi; his hair tied up into a knot on top of his head was also smeared with ash. Vidyadhar knew that these were ashes from the cremation ground. He was familiar with all this. In one corner there were a few bones kept in a small heap. There were three inverted skulls in front of Aghori baba placed on a bed of ashes. Vidyadhar sat down cross-legged on the ground in front of Baba. They looked at each other seriously, no smile on their faces, but each of them acknowledged the other through their eyes. Baba knew why

Vidyadhar had come to him. In fact, Baba was waiting for him. They sat in companionable silence for a few minutes.

Then Baba spoke, "I have trained a person for your son. He will be your son's guard and he will protect him with his life. He is blessed by Mata Hinglaj herself and is a devotee of Swami Dattatreya and of course the omniscient and omnipotent Mahadev Bhagwan Shiv. He will be a great boon to your son and will protect him, so that your son can perform his calling without any hindrances. He is adept in warding off and destroying the evil spirits. In fact, he can smell the evil spirits and demons from a mile ahead. God knows your son needs this kind of protection the most. You should have come to me earlier Vidya, but Shiva desires that I give you Devnath only. Yes, the boy's name is Devnath and he has been brought up with just one goal in mind that is protecting your son Adheesh. Devnath has been blessed specifically by Mahadev and Kamakhya Devi."

Vidyadhar nodded, he did not doubt Baba at all. It was Baba only who had apprised him of the greatness of his son and reminded him of some of their past births together. Though Vidyadhar knew about the great capabilities of Adheesh and his destiny, one corner of his mind wanted to reject all his knowledge so that Adheesh could lead a normal life.

"Vidyadhar," said Baba as if reading his thoughts, "You have become complacent through the centuries. It has always been your job to provide the best and the absolutely true knowledge to this warrior Adheesh whether he is your son in this birth or any other relation in any other birth. I am afraid doubts have started creeping in some other protectors also."

Baba sighed, "This is Kalyug, such things are bound to happen, and we are moving towards destruction both in our thoughts and deeds. Vidya, before I hand over the boy Devnath to you let me explain a few things. You know that your son has been born to you and your wife to fulfill a greater purpose in this life, a purpose which reaches far beyond the boundaries of this Earth. There will be great clashes and destructions on Earth in space, under and inside the Earth, and in water too. He will encounter not only human beings but all sorts of ferocious creatures and super intelligent and aware people who do not have a spark of mercy or emotional understanding in their DNA. In this Kalyug many of these creatures have been modified into hybrid monsters thus making them even more rapacious and unrecognisable. All this is God's maya.

"If God has made evil then God has made good and virtuous people too and myriad ways to counter these vile creatures. God has given us the knowledge to counter each and every maleficent monster. Our ancestors were given different disciplines of knowledge and abilities to counter these demons, for example, Hanuman, Laxman, Bharat, Shatrughan, Bali, Sugreev and even the greatest villain Ravan himself. Each sect of our ancestors was imparted with a certain kind of knowledge to dispose of certain kinds of demons."

Baba continued, "Again, for example, *Betaals* generally stay in the graveyards or in the cremation grounds. They control corpses and sometimes inhabit corpses also. Because of this, the corpses do not decompose till the time they are controlled by the *Betaals*. These souls of the dead bodies cannot attain *Moksha* as they are controlled by the *Betaals*. Anybody who tries to perform the last rites for the dead has to go through a labyrinth of difficult tasks to free these souls from the clutches of the *Betaals*. In the earlier passages of time, many renowned and revered sages had tried very hard to fulfill the atrocious demands of the *Betaals* to free these souls. The most notable amongst them was Raja Vikramaditya whose perseverance in fulfilling their demands had freed many souls from their dead bodies. Later, there were a few other sages also who tackled this problem successfully. Gradually, as in other places in society, greed and corruption crept in. The rich were ready to pay anything for the liberation of the soul of their loved ones. "Inevitably, it became a business for bounty hunters who amassed great powers and fortune by freeing the souls of these dead humans. When this became the main reason for freeing the souls, these people who amassed so much power and money became greedier and more power hungry. They started performing horrible acts to fulfill the demands of the *Betaals*. In other words, they themselves became worse than the creatures they were trying to appease. So we had to eliminate the evil from the source itself that is to demolish and eliminate the *Betaal* also. Devnath with his training in and of the crematoriums has succeeded in eliminating many of them as he is very well versed in the happenings in the graveyards and crematoriums. As you yourself know, much of the knowledge in removing these demons has been written by our ancestors and has been passed from one generation to another by word of mouth—from father to the eldest child, preferably a male one, because women were thought to become impure for four days in a month and then one day more for purification. Childhood and motherhood made it all the more difficult."

Vidyadhar kept his head down and nodded. He knew what Baba was talking about. Everybody was becoming self-centered and losing focus and getting more attached to material things. But Adheesh was his life, his blood. He knew that Adheesh had to overcome insurmountable obstacles mentally, physically and emotionally too, to get rid of the bloodthirsty creatures and that he would be scarred for the rest of his life. Vidyadhar also knew Adheesh's life would continue like that only. These were the thoughts that made Vidyadhar weak sometimes. In spite of being born in an affluent home Adheesh still would have to fight diabolical forces for which he was not fully prepared at the moment, though all efforts were being made to make him stronger than these enemies. That was the reason Baba had called him in his Aghor Ashram.

"Vidyadhar, though Devnath looks like a mere boy, don't take him as such. He has undergone rigorous training as an Aghori. He has more physical strength than three elephants, he is faster than your cars, he can go from one place to another in an instant, and above all, he can tackle any kind of dead and undead entities—above all, he has intuition. He will be absolutely loyal to your son Adheesh. In fact, after Mahadev Shiv Shambhu, Adheesh is his God. Even though Devnath has not met Adheesh he knows all about him and his loyalty to him is unquestionable. It is his life's ambition to look after Adheesh and take care of all his needs so that Adheesh can discharge his duties effectively and freely without any hindrances."

Vidyadhar bowed his head in acknowledgment and gratefulness. There was no need to say anything. Baba had said it all. Satisfied by his response Baba made a gesture to one of the disciples standing outside who bowed and respectfully went away.

While they were waiting, Baba continued, "One more very important matter Vidya." Vidyadharji looked up slightly surprised. Baba had waited for the cabin to be completely emply before he said something else. Must be something important he thought.

"Vidya, though your son has been given the arduous responsibility of destroying the demons it will be a woman who will actually perform the conclusive act of destroying the demons. This woman or rather a girl at the moment is blessed by Goddess Durga herself and has been physically getting rid of the demons through the ages. She is Adheesh's partner and together they will be successful in their annihilations of the demons."

"Oh!" Vidyadharji was at a loss for words. This was indeed shocking news for him but a bit reassuring also. At least Adheesh won't be alone. Silently he thanked God.

"Who is this girl, Guruji? Has Adheesh met her? How will we know that she is the girl?"

"Patience, Vidya, patience, no need to hurry things. You will know and Adheesh will know. No need to involve too many people. When the time comes, tell only those people who are vital to the blueprint of annihilating the demons."

Vidyadhar bowed his head. He had heard enough. At least Adheesh would have a partner to share his work. For the time being he was reassured.

He looked at the boy who he presumed was Devnath. He was of medium height. He was wearing a big turban around his head. He was about twenty years of age with big bulging eyes and a shadow of a beard. He bowed to Vidyadhar and then reverentially touched Baba's feet. Baba blessed him then gestured with his eyes. Devnath respectfully touched Vidyadhar's feet, then stood quietly between them.

"You can take him now Vidya," said Baba. There was nothing more to be said. Vidyadhar folded his hands in namaste. Baba acknowledged.

"How do I return this huge favour?" Vidyadhar asked softly.

Equally softly Baba said, "It's not I who is doing you a favour. It's the other way round. We also want to get rid of the demons as much as all of you. You know we have our own methods of which the general society does not approve, in fact, abhors it. Nevertheless, our aim is the same, destroy these demons and conjoin with Shiva. If you have to return the favour then promise to encourage your son to stay focused on his destiny and not to leave any stone unturned in his quest. You have to help him, Vidya. You have to let go of your emotional attachment."

Vidyadhar bowed again indicating that he understood exactly what Baba meant. He turned around without looking at the boy, knowing that he would follow him.

In his large household, Devnath was just a new servant and they accepted him as such. Only his wife Anuja knew Devnath's true designation. She, too, like her husband feared for her first born and his life and the irreparable scars which he would have. She was at first wary of Devnath but when she saw his behaviour towards Adheesh she was somewhat relieved.

Vidyadhar's house was a huge three-storey one with state of

the art infrastructure. His was a joint family with his younger brothers Kedar and Kalpesh and their families also staying there. Kedar and Kalpesh assisted in the family businesses. Vidyadhar and his wife Anuja stayed on the ground floor. Anuja managed the whole household and supervised everything. There were intercoms on all the floors which helped her in organising things. There was a beautifully decorated hall on the ground floor, two guest rooms and a large office for all the three brothers. Kedar and Kalpesh lived with their families on the first floor and Adheesh lived on the second floor. There were other fully furnished rooms on the second floor also to be used as guest rooms but they were mostly vacant as most of the guests liked to stay downstairs. So Adheesh most of the time had the entire second floor to himself.

A little away from the main house was a cluster of small houses which were the servants' quarters. Devnath was given a room there but he hardly ever stayed there. He had made himself Adheesh's shadow, so much so that he even slept in the balcony outside his room. Slowly this news percolated to Vidyadhar and Anuja. They were again so relieved that Anuja gave a room to Devnath on the second floor itself. Devnath's room was two doors away from Adheesh's room which suited both of them fine. Though Adheesh did not mind Devnath hovering around him, still there were times when he wanted absolute privacy especially when he was meditating and communicating with a higher presence. Being highly intuitive, Devnath quickly understood his need for privacy and left him well alone. He stood far away from Adheesh's room on the balcony. In fact, he did not allow anyone else also to come up to the second floor when Adheesh needed space.

Adheesh and Devnath hit it off right from the beginning. Devnath was in any case wholly committed to Adheesh even before he had met him. Very soon people in the huge household realised that though Devnath did any work which he was told to, the only time he was happy was when he was with Adheesh. Since it was a large household with a large number of servants no one was discomfited by this attitude as long as their requirements were met.

Such was the trust and loyalty of Devnath to Adheesh that very soon Adheesh allowed Devnath to accompany him to his martial arts college. Initially, Devnath was awed by what he saw. He was no stranger to magic or rather practices which seemed like magic. This was just a different kind of magic for him. He quickly adjusted to this new life. Very soon he became Adheesh's shadow there too. No one was bothered and no one knew that Devnath was Adheesh's bodyguard except Vidyadhar and his wife and of course Guruji.

Adheesh got an inkling of Devnath's true purpose in his life very soon in the Gurukul. Once during his training, while he was fencing with another student he noticed Devnath sitting there watching them idly. Adheesh's adversary was a huge boy fully adept in the art of fencing. He had a sneer on his face as he was convinced that Adheesh was no match for him. In a matter of minutes, Adheesh was on the ground and the tip of his sword was on Adheesh's throat. It was a mock match but Devnath was not to know this. In a flash, the other boy was picked up and thrown ten meters away and in a flash again Devnath was at Adheesh's side to pick him up. All the onlookers were stunned. Adheesh was a star scholar. Nobody had beaten Adheesh in anything as yet. Everyone had been casually watching the sparring. They knew that Adheesh was going to be the ultimate winner, thus there was not too much of speculation and excitement. But Devnath did not know that. For him, his God was going down and nobody could be allowed to do that. Adheesh got up slowly with the help of Devnath, more surprised than hurt.

"It's alright Devnath, this was just practice, we are not allowed any bloody fights here," he said soothingly. One thing was slowly becoming clearer to Adheesh. It was that Devnath was always going to go the extra mile for him and much more even. He also suspected that Devnath had extra powers acquired while he was training as an Aghori in Varanasi.

Slowly Devnath began understanding the Gurukul and started recognising the fact that almost nobody could touch Adheesh in any of the subjects and fields which were taught there. One day, while they were sitting near the river bank Adheesh said, "Come and sit beside me Devnath." This river ran on the periphery of the Gurukul, rather the location of the Gurukul was selected keeping the river in mind. It was a tributary of one of their holy rivers and many prayers and rituals were performed on its banks. The Gurukul was not surrounded by any boundary walls and the river also did not pose any threat from the outside world, mainly lurking spies and demons. The river flowed in the "normal" world and then just disappeared. People marvelled at this miracle and just left it at that. It was simply not visible to the outside world. Just like the Gurukul, special mantras and chants were required to view or be near the river. Its banks were the most peaceful and serene that Adheesh had ever seen. He could sit here for hours thinking and meditating. There was lush foliage around the river. It wound through the rich foliage collecting the stray flora and distributing it to the other parts of the Gurukul. It was integral to the Gurukul and was a very strong entity in itself. The sound of its gurgling water had a hypnotic effect on anybody who stopped to listen to it making that person confide his or her closest secrets to it.

Devnath hesitated. The master-servant hierarchy was too strongly embedded in him to sit as an equal with Adheesh. But Adheesh was not going to brook any nonsense. Everyone made sure that the servants were treated with respect. And here was Devnath, a total antithesis of the other servants. He would fawn all over Adheesh all the time so much so that it was beginning to irritate Adheesh. He meant to put a stop to this kind of behaviour. Reluctantly Devnath went and sat beside him.

"Devnath, see I know what you want to do. You want to protect me at all costs and I know that you will always care for me. The thing is, you see, is that I don't need protecting. There is nothing to protect. I am in no danger. I am just an ordinary person lucky enough to be born in a great and loving household. That's it. Look, I appreciate that you care for me so much. If that's so important to you then do it but tone it down just a bit, okay?"

Devnath turned and looked at him enigmatically. There was no confusion on his face. He just stared at Adheesh and did not say anything. Now it was Adheesh's turn to be confused. It seemed to him that Devnath knew something about him of which he was not aware. It was also obvious that Devnath was not going to share this knowledge with him. Adheesh sighed. So be it! But he was curious also. What was it about him that Devnath knew that he, Adheesh himself, did not know? He decided to leave it at that but only for the time being.

Once they were returning from the city. It was late, so they decided to take a short cut which was beside the crematorium. Devnath was not keen on it. He knew what could happen on those grounds at night. He was not very sure of himself too. The cremation grounds always beckoned him like a magnet. His long-forgotten cravings may come to the fore. Along with his other colleagues, when he was undergoing the Aghori panth course, they would regularly eat the roasted flesh of corpses which was part of their learning process. It is said that of all flesh human meat is the tastiest. Somehow the taste had lingered on Devnath's palette and once in a while, he would have a strong urge to bite into a roasted human leg or hand. Devnath had left all of that a long time back as now his life's mission was Adheesh's security and nothing else.

Baba had made him undergo the training in the cremation grounds so that he could protect Adheesh from the evil supernatural forces. These were the only places where he felt one with God—the detached feeling, no revulsion, no sadness, only *anand*, a place where he was truly himself. This was the place where he had power over himself, over others; this was the place where he was invincible where nobody could touch him. But he was not so sure about Adheesh. His Guru Baba had entrusted him with Adheesh's safety at all costs, so much so that in the event of his own death too he had to protect

Adheesh. In fact, it was in Devnath's genetic code to look after Adheesh. It was as simple as that. He had looked after Adheesh through the ages, maybe in different forms and he knew that he would always be there as long as Adheesh was there. It was an almost symbiotic relationship of which Adheesh was not fully aware as of now, although he was beginning to feel it.

There was a parallel mud track running beside the crematorium grounds. There was no boundary wall around the crematorium not that it would have mattered to the *chudails*, *dayans* or *bhoots, praits,* residing there, looking for any human body to inhabit or simply kill to eat and drink flesh and blood to make themselves powerful. There were no lights there. The only illumination which was there was coming from the few burning funeral pyres and the only sound was from the chattering and crackling of the burning wood. The trees were casting long and short shadows depending on their proximity to the burning pyres. Devnath could see and hear some *dayans* eying them expectantly and malevolently, their red and yellow eyes squinting and flickering on and off. He surreptitiously looked at Adheesh who was walking nonchalantly and trying not to inhale too deeply.

Devnath was alert. He knew that they could not do anything to him. They would find out immediately who he was. Their main target would be Adheesh, so muscular and so full of blood! How much power they would have! Suddenly two black shadows slid towards Adheesh. Adheesh stopped and turned though he did not see anything. Suddenly more shadows materialised and now they seemed to be all over Adheesh. Adheesh stiffened. He turned around, "Devnath," he called out. But Devnath was not there. Surprised Adheesh called him again. Suddenly as if in slow motion, he saw Devnath rushing towards him with two long burning bones in his hands chanting what seemed some nonsensical words. He came near Adheesh and started dancing around him all the time continuing with his chanting. He seemed to be thrusting the long burning bones like a sword all around Adheesh.

It was a macabre dance. Long and short shadows were formed by the light of the burning bones. In some places, charred flesh still clung to the bones making the whole process gorier. For a minute Adheesh assessed the situation then swiftly took one bone from Devnath's hand and flourished it all around them. Both he and Devnath continued their sparring with the invisible beings thrusting and pushing the creatures. Even Adheesh could now hear the howling and shrieking of these creatures. Slowly the shadows started falling down and fading away. Some of them had been cut into pieces. These pieces vanished before they touched the ground. Gradually the sounds died down, some shadows vanished, and the rest receded into the crematorium. Devnath took the bones from Adheesh and gently placed them near the burning pyres inside the crematorium. Quietly and quickly they walked away and slowed only when they reached the main road. Both of them did not look back as both knew that looking back would cause the *chudails* to follow them.

On returning they went inside via the back stairs straight to Adheesh's room. It was already quite late and everybody had gone to sleep. There was the night guard at the front gate and another at the back gate. They were used to Adheesh coming home late at night so no reporting would be done in the morning. There was a light burning in one of his uncle's rooms. Probably doing his accounting he thought. What both of them failed to notice was Vidyadhar sitting in the dark unlit verandah waiting for Adheesh and giving a sigh of relief as soon as he saw him.

"Bhaiya, give me all your clothes. I'm going to burn all our clothes immediately. You have your bath with Gangajal. After burning these clothes I'll also have my bath."

From then on whatever little doubts Adheesh may have had about Devnath also disappeared. He started taking along Devnath on almost all of his sojourns.

The Library and Somesh

This was a huge library with separate annexures. Each annexure housed a different subject, their books ranging from single numbers to thousands with varied subjects from astronomy, history, mythology, astrology etc. As well as various versions and interpretations of the *Ramayana*, the *Gita,* and *Mahabharata.* There were other secret subjects also which only a chosen few were allowed to browse and study. These were in an old forgotten language much older than Sanskrit and Pali too. Only a handful of people could read and speak this language. Hence this part of the library was generally under lock and key and was opened only after special permission was granted to the seeker by Guruji. These chosen few were those students who were specially chosen by Guruji. It was rumoured that Guruji was hundreds of years old, that he was sent on Earth by Gods to set things right on Earth and was not born of human parents.

Guruji was also rumoured to be the direct representative of Lord Hanuman or Bajrangbali, the devotee of Bhagwan Ram. Guruji knew everything; he knew which demons were active at present, which demons were hibernating and when they would come out of their hibernation; which demons had become almost human and hence were not so harmful. The secret library housed all the information about these demons. Every year, Guruji would choose a few special students to use this library. These students had special abilities and reflexes. They had an inborn capability to understand and withstand great stress and a burning desire to remove the demonic obstacles of the Earth.

Aishani and Adheesh were among the very few who were specially chosen by Guruji to use this secret library. They knew instinctively how to read and understand these books. This was not an ordinary library. It housed hundreds and thousands of books on the legions of demons from the time of the creation of the world till the present, and how the beasts and demons came to be in existence and how they could be destroyed. Before admitting Aishani and Adheesh to this library Guruji had called both of them to his hut.

"You will know when and how to use these words," said Guruji in a satisfied tone. "Let me take you to the library now. Each of you now has the blueprint for opening the door of the library. You can go to the library any time you feel the need to do so. However, opening some of the books may be another matter altogether."

Adheesh and Aishani looked at each other perplexed. They had been to the library so many times so why was Guruji taking them there? Walking and crossing the main library Guruji went into a small bare hall, and stood in front of a blank wall without a door or window. Beckoning both of them to follow he walked into the wall. They looked at each other in surprise. Guruji was nowhere to be seen. They had no choice but to follow him into the wall. As soon as they touched the wall it started shimmering and then disappeared. They followed Guruji inside.

Why, it was their library! The same old library where they would sit for hours studying! But they had just cut across it. They turned to look at Guruji who just smiled at them and left. The wall closed behind them and they were in this strange library. A smile from Guruji! That was a very big reward. They smiled back at the wall and turned towards the room.

There were a total of ten students there. Aishani and Adheesh knew a couple of them who nodded at them. They tentatively nodded back. The others had their faces buried in their books. They were all senior students. They knew each other but that was about all. Bonhomie was not very common here as there was just not enough time to mix with other fellow students. Too much of friendship was not frowned upon but not encouraged either.

They looked at the librarian who seemed to be waiting for them. His name was Janardan Vashisht. They knew his name because he used to come to the other library too. Aishani had met him earlier but didn't know that he was in charge of this library. As of now both Aishani and Adheesh were clueless about this library. That this was a special one they had immediately understood. They looked around with curiosity. There were rows and rows of neatly lined thick books with their spines facing outwards, everything in alphabetical order and written in a familiar but strange script. They were colour coded also. There were comfortable chairs and tables and low asanas or mats thrown around in case anybody wanted to sit on the ground and read. A cool breeze was flowing from the windows providing succor from the heat. There was stillness in the atmosphere, with sometimes just a muffled hushed whisper as if a few students were discussing points.

Vashisht Ji beckoned them and told them to sit in front of him.

"I can understand your curiosity," he said "This is a different library, not for the average student; in fact, God forbid if any such student enters this library without Guruji's sanction. What havoc can be created if such books fall in the hands of a novice!"

"What kind of books are these, sir?" asked Adheesh. Aishani kept quiet. She had almost understood what these books were for. But still, she wanted Vashisht ji to tell them about them.

"Well to begin with, these books describe the different types of demons or creatures that were left over after Prabhu Ram defeated and killed the asur king Ravan and his army of demons. Many demons and creatures ran away and hid in various places deep inside the Earth or space or deep inside the oceans. Many went into hibernation, many mingled with humans and animals through the ages. This altered their persona so much that it is now almost impossible to differentiate them from the humans, but the demon psyche more or less remains the same even after the millennia. These books contain all information about the demons and *rakshasas*, and hordes of other such beings,—how to recognise them and how to annihilate them. Many of them are very intelligent and aware beings and hence all the more cunning and dangerous. Many of them can take the shape of human beings also."

"How do these books work? Is there any special way to open and read them?" Adheesh casually asked. He had some knowledge of these books. Aishani stared at Adheesh. He never failed to amaze her.

"I am glad you asked this question. There are various ways to open and interpret these books. They tell you how to get rid of the smaller beasts or freaks. These books are not for both of you. They are for the juniors. The kinds of books which Guruji has assigned me to show both of you are very different. There are special methods for opening them. Most of them are in Sanskrit, not difficult for you, others are in code and in an older language. Both of you are familiar with this older language."

"You will first have to crack the codes then translate them into Sanskrit. These books are very very ancient, both of you know this. They have not been written on paper, maybe cloth or hemp or any other such material. They could not have survived the millennia without God's magic or blessings; still, you have to handle them very delicately. It's because of this that so many important things were orally taught to students by their gurus or from father to son."

"It's such a relief sir," Aishani said warmly, "It's so nice that you are here to guide us, otherwise it may take us ages to open these books."

"Well, I must warn you that I won't be of much use for you in this matter. There are so many books here which even I don't know how to open."

Both Aishani and Adheesh looked at Vashisht ji in astonishment. He was the librarian. He had to know how to open these books, otherwise, how would he give these books to the students!

"Yes, I know the same questions had entered my mind. I am a librarian, therefore, I have to know about all the books that are under my jurisdiction. But that is not the case here and rightly so. The contents of this library are very dangerous not to say highly ambiguous. In fact, a misspelled incantation may help a demon rather than destroying it. There have been thefts of some of these books. The librarian at that time knew how to open some of the books. Every week he would lovingly open the books and wipe them clean. Then one day to his chagrin when he opened the books he found that they were just empty shells.

"All the pages had mysteriously disappeared. Nobody had come inside this room. The room and the bookshelves had not been opened. A thin layer of dust was there and nobody had touched anything. Still, the matter of the books had been stolen. It was later revealed by Guruji that whenever the previous librarian opened the books somebody would listen to those incantations sitting hundreds of miles away. After that, becoming invisible, coming to this library and stealing the pages was just child's play for that being."

Aishani sighed, "So all that invaluable material is gone

now. Even if it is found it may be of no use as those devils must have nullified it."

Vashisht smiled, "That's the beauty of the whole thing. They were not able to read the stolen pages. The pages were written in a script older than Sanskrit too and they would become decipherable only after the chanting of certain keywords which would change daily. In other words, they were password protected. Before the new password could be set, the old passwords would be chanted most respectfully and were informed that they were now being set free from their sentinel duties and could now be free to be used as normal words. After that, a new password would be set. Well, the thieves did not know all this. They simply chanted the incantations and the words on the pages just disappeared."

"Ohh, what a relief," Aishani murmured.

"Sir, what happened to the words on the pages?" This was Adheesh, "Did they find out?"

"Yes Adheesh, they all came back. With the right incantations, they all came back slowly one by one. Mind you it took Guruji sometime before everything was set back in place. From that time onwards things became very strict, only on a need to know basis. Even I don't know how many passwords are there and for what."

"Sir this is such a beautiful and huge library with an equal number of secret codes and blueprints. It is impossible for one person to take care of such a large number of books. How do you maintain all this?" Adheesh asked curiously.

"Oh, I do have some help only for the basic cleaning and dusting etc. Somesh is there to help me in these jobs. I want to do these basic jobs also but that would curtail my time in looking after the books," Janardan said wistfully.

"Who is Somesh sir?" Adheesh asked.

"Oh you can call Somesh the assistant librarian," Janardan smiled, "He is basically the handyman of the whole Ashram doing this work and that, always smiling and always ready to do any work. You must have seen him running about here and there."

Recognition dawned. "Oh, that Somesh, yes I've seen him many times. Isn't he the security head's son?"

"Yes, that he is; he has been here in the ashram ever since he was a toddler and knows the ashram like the back of his hand. He comes in the morning with me and leaves after an hour or so."

"There is so much of security around here sir, how does Somesh come here so easily?"

Janardan smiled, "I know you are thinking about the security of these books Adheesh. Since Somesh has been here almost from the time he was born he does have a permission of sorts to go anywhere in the ashram nor has he ever given us any reason to doubt him. As far as this part of the library is concerned he always comes with me and I see him off after one hour when the cleaning is done."

"Yes sir," Adheesh replied.

Aishani had not spoken as yet. She was intently watching the interaction between Janardan Vashisht and Adheesh. She knew that Adheesh was wary about Somesh's role in the scheme of things.

"Both of you go around and have a feel of the library.

Once you master opening and reading some of the books you will find them the most interesting books in the world. But there is a rider here."

They waited for him to speak again. Janardan cleared his throat and went on, "Some of these books will open only when their time comes. Some of them will open only to the persons designated to read them."

"How will we know which books will open for us?" Aishani asked her curiosity aroused now.

"Chosen students like you don't have to worry too much. In presence like yours, they open of their own accord. However, some are bound by time. They will open only when the time comes or unless Guruji feels the necessity of opening a particular book."

They acknowledged their understanding. Janardan nodded and left them. Alone now they looked around. The bookcases were beautifully carved. They were probably made of sheesham or rosewood. Some of the books were covered in gold cloth, some in silver and some in red silk. In fact, there seemed to be a myriad of colours of the book covers and they seemed to be put together in a disciplined manner. Gingerly Aishani put out her hand to pick up a book. It readily came in her hands. Nervously she tried to open it, but it would not open. She did not want to use even the slightest pressure as the books were so ancient and fragile. Somehow she had a feeling that the book wanted to be opened. But how? A number flashed in her brain. What was it? And then it dawned on her. Guruji had whispered the passwords and their time in their ears. Excited now, she looked at her watch and whispered the word preceding the time given by Guruji. The cover opened readily. The words almost jumped at her in their eagerness to be read by her. They appeared and disappeared in one language then another and then another as if cajoling her to read and understand some of them at least. Aishani sighed. She looked at Adheesh. He was reading quietly without any of the interruptions which she was having. She looked at the book in her hands again. She knew that their past was written in the books and to a certain extent their future too. She knew that the moment she would begin reading she would get so engrossed in the books in this library that she would go into a trance and get transported to another reality.

THE ASSISTANT LIBRARIAN

His name was Somesh. Officially he was the assistant librarian. Unofficially, he was a lovable Jack of all. Always smiling, always trying to please everybody, he was an affable easygoing young man. It was difficult not to like him. The college was his home. His mother had died when he was very young. His father was already working in the college in the security department. Since there was nobody to look after the young Somesh, Guruji had very kindly allowed his father to keep him in the college provided he did not get in the way. Somesh never lacked love and caring in the ashram. Right from the time he was a toddler he would follow one uncle or aunty the whole day and return to his father's room at night only. He knew every inch of the Gurukul apart from the very sacred and secret areas which in any case were forbidden to many students and teachers too. But there were many secret places where only he had access not because he was allowed but because he just naturally drifted into these places which nobody really minded. The Gurukul was like his mother loving him every moment, but chastising him whenever he crossed the lines. He studied here and since he was a good student, he ultimately became the assistant librarian, a job which he did effortlessly even though his heart was not in it. The assistant librarian's job in both the libraries of the Gurukul was not much since Vashisht ji liked to look after the books himself. So the work which was left for Somesh was pretty much cleaning only. Every minute that he spent in the library was spent in wanting to be outdoors playing one sport or the other.

It was on one of his sojourns outside the college that he met the man who did not have a face or a name or if he did have either of them, Somesh did not know. It was when he was window shopping in front of a sports shop that this person ran into him. The sunshine was reflecting on the cricket bats that were displayed in the window along with helmets and gloves. It was his favourite hobby to browse in these shops. Sometimes he bought a couple of things too. Till now everything was fun and innocent in his life.

It was more of a gentle nudge than a shove but it completely upturned Somesh's life. Suddenly he was not Somesh anymore. That gentle nudge was a thief's nudge but unlike a traditional thief, this one did not take his money or any other valuable that Somesh might have on his body. It was while the stranger slowly walked past him that Somesh felt a tug in his heart and throat. It was as if his very soul was being dragged out of his body. Holding his throat by one hand he tried to stop the stranger. He tried to say something but gagged on his words. Slowly his will power left him and he was left standing there paralysed not knowing what to do and what to say. A voice seemed to be whispering in his head, "You will do as I say; you will do as I say." Slowly the thought connected in his head that somebody was talking to him. He tried to shake his head. To his horror, he realised that he could not shake his head. There was a sarcastic laugh in his head.

"I told you, you will do as I say and nothing more." Somesh tried to move. Nothing happened. Am I sick? Why can't I move? he thought desperately. It was as if there was another person inside him and he was unable to resist that person. He tried to move once again with all his strength but was unable to do so.

"Ok, now move your left foot forward," the voice ordered. Somesh found that he could move his left foot forward now. "Who are you, what have you done to me and why are you doing this?"

There was chilling laughter.

"No questions are to be asked simply because no questions will be answered. I will get very irritated with questions. If you ask questions the answers will be this." There was a swift pain in his heart as if a huge fist was squeezing it very hard trying to wring out the last drop of blood from his heart. It was so painful that he could not breathe. Tears came out of his eyes. It went on and on and wouldn't stop. It flashed in his mind for a second that this was his death and a very painful one. The pain was so intense that he welcomed the death which would eventually come now. Gagging sounds came from his mouth and his eyes started closing. Suddenly it was all over. He was standing in exactly the same place where he was before the happening. He was taking shallow breaths but that was all. There was no sign of the trauma which he had just undergone. Only a vivid memory of the nightmare remained. He sat down on a bench nearby too scared to even think. His hair rose in fear. "Who are you?" Somesh managed to croak, "What do you want?"

"All in good time," the voice whispered, "You will do exactly as I say or else…"

"Or else what?" Courage was slowly returning to Somesh.

"Forgotten so soon?" the voice whispered mockingly, "Do we need a recap?" Somesh shuddered with fear as the huge icy fist began closing around his heart again. The forgotten pain reared its head.

"Stop," he begged before the pain increased but the pain did not stop. It kept on increasing till the time he fell down in agony, writhing in pain. "Stop, stop, please I'll do anything, I'll do anything you say. Just stop the pain please," he implored.

"Anything?" said the mocking voice, now filling his whole body with more excruciating pain.

Somesh was in a delirious haze of pain. He could not open his mouth. His eyes glazed over. Just when he was losing all his senses and probably his life, the pressure loosened up a bit. He gasped and took a shuddering breath.

"Yes I'll do anything," he stuttered, "Just stop the pain. What do I have to do?" He gasped.

"All in good time, go to the Ashram first. Tomorrow morning, call me when you are cleaning the library."

Somesh was too far gone to ask any coherent questions. The pain around his heart and body was continuous. That person had loosened his grip just enough so he could just think and talk a bit. Though he did not know the actual importance of the books of the library, he did know that they were very valuable and could not be stolen by anybody. Nobody other than the special people designated by Guruji could enter the library. This being, if allowed to enter the library, could create enough havoc and destruction that it would be almost impossible to get it back into shape. Somesh had still some thinking power left. The library! He could not help anyone gain access to the library! He hesitated and tried to stall the conversation.

"I am not allowed into the library on my own. The librarian himself takes me inside the library and after my work is over, he sees me off."The shadow hissed in anger and pressed Somesh some more. Somesh passed out. When he came to his senses he was lying on the side of the road, the shadow was gone and only a semblance of the pain remained. Groggily he got up holding his head in his hands. Was it just a nightmare? A nightmare in broad daylight? He could imagine the other things but not the pain.

He also knew that it was going to happen again if he did not follow the being's instructions. But the library! Instinctively he knew that this library was the sanctum of the sanctums. If this was defiled then there would be hell to pay. Each and every nook of the Ashram was his playground, his mother, his home, his everything. There was nothing to lose except perhaps his life. He took his decision and started walking firmly towards the Gurukul.

Somesh was not scheduled to go to the inner library the next day. He was required to go there every other day. The memory of the pain was so strong and lasting that he decided to take the day off. Nobody really missed him because he was always everywhere. He had his bath with very cold water and decided to go for a walk in the jungle. He knew that he would not meet anybody as everybody would be busy with their classes and the mundane routines of the morning. As he walked amongst the woods he thought and relived every moment of the earlier day's gruelling torture. Living in the Gurukul almost from the time of his birth he knew that there were demons all around even though he had never encountered any. Yesterday was the first time and how! He could not do what the shadow demon was telling him to do. He had to do something fast. He also knew that he was not a selected warrior. Seeing all the students in the Ashram from a very young age he badly wanted to become a warrior. He wanted to prove himself. Here was a chance to prove himself! But how? No matter how much he thought he could not arrive at an answer. Was proving himself more important than saving the library? Both the answers were interconnected. Mulling over all these points he arrived at a conclusion.

The next day he went to the library as usual. He was a mental and physical wreck but determined to save the millennia-old library. The previous night the shadow had come to him and entered his body. Now the shadow was dominating his mind and body. He had no control over his mind and body. His own being would surface from time to time but it was for so short a period that he was unable to do anything. He had spent the whole of the previous night in torture both physical and mental. But he was also confident that the shadow (for want of a better word) would not be able to harm the library or steal anything from it.

After his walk in the forest the day before, he had gone straight to Guruji. Guruji was engaged in his *sadhna (meditation)*. Somesh waited. He knew that this was a huge crisis which only Guruji could deal with. Guruji did not seem to be very surprised to see Somesh. It seemed as if he was expecting him. Without wasting any time Somesh blurted out everything. His words were too hurried and were sometimes slurred too. He felt as if he was not making any sense. He tried to make his words clearer, but he began sounding more and more confused and lost. At last, he stopped, lost in his own confusion and incoherency.

Not so with Guruji who understood exactly what Somesh was saying.

"We were expecting these attacks Somesh. We just didn't know that it would be you. We are prepared and were waiting for this kind of attack."

Guruji then told him very clearly that his life was going to be at stake.

"Somesh, this is a huge sacrifice that you will be making. I shall, of course, leave no stone unturned to make sure that you are unharmed, but the chances may be slim."

Somesh touched Guruji's feet in obeisance. "Guruji it will be my honour to give my life for such a worthy cause. I know that you will do whatever is best."

Guruji blessed Somesh and he left. What Guruji left

unsaid and what Somesh understood perfectly was that he might not survive the onslaught which would be made on the shadow. It was his body, his heart on which the onslaught would be made. For Somesh giving up his life for the ultimate good of mankind was the supreme sacrifice and *moksha*. He was assured that Guruji was going to get rid of the shadow demon and that was that. Guruji was going to do what was the best for everybody.

Somesh had transferred his dilemma and torture to Guruji. Late in the night when almost the whole of the ashram had gone to sleep Guruji summoned somebody. The whole ashram never went to sleep at the same time. There were people on shift duties, guards, teachers, some animals, birds and insects also and some interns too. There wasn't much time to prepare this intern to face the Shadow. But Guruji had faith in this student. He knew that with his experiences of fighting the demons in the past, this student would be able to successfully destroy the shadow.

The student was explained everything about the shadow demon and instructed about his role in its destruction. There was no time to take the intern to the inner library and give him the book on shadow demons. Guruji took a dagger out from his cupboard, took it out of its sheath and gave it to the intern to feel it. Then Guruji and the intern placed the dagger on a small stool which was covered by a yellow cloth. Guruji made some drawings on the cloth then placed an idol of Maa Bagalmukhi, a Yantra of Maa Bagalmukhi and the dagger over it. Maa Bagalmukhi is the eighth doctrine of the ten great components of knowledge of the world. She is prayed to, in order to destroy one's enemies and demons and for attaining expertise in the spoken word.

Both Guruji and the intern offered yellow flowers and a coconut to the deity. A copper vessel with Gangajal was placed beside the stool where the puja was going to be performed. The Gangajal had always been an integral part of reducing the power of the demons. It did not much affect the stronger demons but it did distract them for a while like scalding their bodies wherever the holy water was sprinkled on them. The yantra and the dagger were placed on a small mound of turmeric. The yantra was known as the Bagalmukhi yantra. One side of the dagger was serrated and the dagger itself was in the shape of a half moon. Both he and the intern sat in front of the dagger and began chanting a mantra which was known as the Bagalamukhi mantra. Both Guruji and the intern offered yellow flowers and coconut to the deity. This mantra was supposed to destroy one's enemies. As far as Guruji was concerned he had been chanting this mantra for a very long time for different kinds of enemies and demons which the ashram had been surrounded with.

Apart from the hordes of guards and supernatural spirits and beings that guarded the Gurukul day in and day out, it was strong mantras such as this one which actually destroyed the demons. Maa Bagalmukhi could single-handedly destroy all their enemies and demons of the universe but she could not be requested to prevail on the mundane happenings in the Gurukul every time something like this catastrophe happened. The intern too knew everything about Maa Bagalmukhi and her prowess, and that she alone had the power to destroy every creature of the universe and that nobody in the entire universe could defeat her.

After vigorous chanting of the mantra from night till dawn, Guruji finally concluded their prayers. Then very respectfully he picked up the serrated dagger and placed it in the intern's hands.

"Leave the turmeric on. Don't wipe it," Guruji instructed him and tied a piece of yellow thread on his wrist.

"Remember you have to strike it in its heart and take out the heart itself. For this, the Shadow has to come out of Somesh's body. At least the upper part has to fully come out. Striking it on any other part of the body may harm it grievously but won't be enough to kill it. It may fatally harm Somesh too."

"Yes, Guruji, I'm aware of it. If there's one person I want to save, it is Somesh. I pray to Maa Bagalamukhi that she gives me enough dexterity to kill the demon and save Somesh also."

Guruji raised his hands to the sky which was taking on the hues of red, pink and yellow, "Whatever he desires will happen. We are but carriers of his wishes and desires."

The intern touched Guruji's feet then turned towards the library.

The next morning Somesh reached the library. Dawn was just breaking. The library was still dark. The sunlight had yet to travel and reach the windows of the library. It seemed that they were waiting for Somesh to open the windows and welcome them. That was their daily routine. Somesh would open the windows and laughingly welcome the rays of the sun. The sunrays did not mind if Somesh was late by a minute or so. They remained red for a minute then petulantly turned into orange and then yellow if he was later than that. Pandit Janardan Vashisht made him enter the inner library. Somesh touched his feet. Janardan blessed him then asked curiously, "Are you sick Somesh? Your hands are very cold. Did you stay out late in the jungle?"

Somesh did not turn around, "Just a bit sir, nothing to worry about." Quietly he went and opened the windows without smiling. He picked up the cleaning items from the corner room and began his work from the far end of the room. Janardan was just a bit curious. Normally Somesh was such a chatterbox but today he was very quiet. Today there was no good-natured ribaldry. Everything was quiet. Janardan shook his head and went back to his work. One fact that he did notice was that the speaking books were unusually quiet while Somesh was dusting them. There was none of the friendliness which happened in Somesh's presence. His antennae did give him a warning signal. He shifted his position so that now instead of facing the entrance of the library he was facing the inside of the library. But there was nothing untoward. Somesh was doing his work very quietly but naturally. Had Janardan known what was happening to Somesh's mind, body and heart he would have raised the emergency alarm and got everyone out.

Somesh, possessed by the shadow demon had no will of his own. Since the demon did not know where the most important books of the inner library were, it had to ask Somesh, but Somesh had no will of his own; he could not articulate anything unless the shadow left him for a minute. Not left with any choice, the shadow partially left Somesh's body but clutched his heart tightly. Somesh gasped with the pain but the pain cleared his mind too for an instant. He remembered everything. He knew that Guruji must have arrived there or sent somebody strong enough to kill the shadow demon. The thought gave him enough strength and succor.

"Take me to the innermost part of the library," it hissed in his ears and gave his heart another jolt. Somesh writhed in pain. He hobbled towards the big books but in the opposite direction. Somesh was taking the shadow where Guruji had told him to go. The shadow was not to know this. It relieved his hold over Somesh's heart in order to touch the books and bind them in its own spell. Now a part of the shadow could be seen by the naked eye also. But it was still not enough for anybody to strike it. Its heart had to be clearly seen to be struck upon. It would cause mayhem and chaos in the library killing whoever was there and destroying the library too in the process. Obviously, the ancient texts were protected so well that they could not be destroyed, but the less important books would be totally destroyed. This, too, would take a long time to rebuild and some important literature may be unable to be reproduced. The intern knew all this for he was the smartest in the Gurukul. That was not all. He also remembered the date of his past births regarding the library. He knew how important it was to annihilate the shadow. But the shadow was also cunning enough to keep his own heart inside Somesh's body.

Guruji had instructed Somesh that the shadow had to leave his body even if it was for only an instant. But Somesh was again paralysed with pain. He could not move and he could not think. Slowly, as and when the shadow put out his hand to pull out a book Somesh tried to inch away from him. In its own excitement and preoccupation, the shadow did not notice this. Ultimately in what seemed like ages to Somesh the shadow was almost half out of his body. It reached out to a huge book which was a little distance away. This was the instant the intern struck. Quick as lightening, the intern who was hiding behind the books there, buried the knife in the shadow's heart and pulled it out, gouging it out from its body. For a moment the shadow was paralysed with shock, then with a high pitched howl it let go of Somesh's body and turned towards the intern in a paroxysm of fury. But the harm was done. It was dead the moment it started turning towards the intern.

There was no blood only black acrid smoke which also vanished through the open window. Its heart was still in the intern's hands twisting and writhing as if it had a body and mind of its own. The intern put the demon's heart on a yellow tray which had already been kept there and slashed it into small pieces. As the heart was shredded into small pieces it melted into a black boiling mass, turned into black steam, vaporised and whooshed out of the window.

Everything was very quiet again. Janardan who had heard the furious howling came running to this part of the library. He saw Adheesh calmly putting something back in the folds of his robe and Somesh sitting and groaning with his head in his hands. Janardan understood almost everything and sprang into action. He ran and got a broom and Gangajal. He swept the floor and sprinkled Gangajal everywhere and quite a lot on Somesh and Adheesh.

For Guruji and Janardan, Adheesh would still be an intern till the time he passed out of the Gurukul. The interns were not addressed by their names except in private. Both Adheesh and Janardan were now more concerned with Somesh who had fallen on the ground and passed out. Adheesh seemed to be much more worried about Somesh. Janardan was a little puzzled by this though he did not give it much thought as Somesh required immediate medical care.

"I'll take him to the infirmary. The Vaidya will look after him," Adheesh said to Janardan. He half carried and half dragged Somesh out of the library towards the private lane that led towards the Vaidyashala or infirmary. Janardan looked after them surprise. He knew some untoward happening had taken place in his domain without his knowledge. He also knew that for the sake of propriety Adheesh was an intern. For all he knew Adheesh was already a warrior and he was here just to be reminded of his destiny in his present birth. To be allowed in this part of the library was a special privilege not accorded to average students of the Gurukul.

He did not know whether Somesh would come back to the library or not but he did know that the library was safe now for the time being. Instinctively he knew that a *havan* was going to be performed in the library very soon.

After handing over Somesh in the Vaidyashala, the intern went straight towards Guruji's cottage. Guruji had everything ready. He looked at the intern who nodded his head. Guruji did not need this assurance as he knew what had happened in the library; otherwise, Adheesh wouldn't have been here. He gave gangajal to Adheesh who tenderly washed the dagger with it, wiped it with a clean cloth, and then placed it over the yellow cloth near the Bagulamukhi yantra. Together, master and pupil sat in front of the idol of Maa Bagalmukhi and prayed to her. They prayed and thanked her for a long time. Only when they were absolutely sure that Maa had accepted their gratitude and thankfulness did they get up and place the idol, dagger and the yantras in their respective places.

Kedar and Geetika

Vidyadhar had two younger brothers, Kedar and Kalpesh. He and his wife Anuja had only one child, Adheesh. The age gap between these two brothers and Vidyadhar was considerable. He treated them more like his sons than his younger brothers. In fact Kedar, Kalpesh and Adheesh were more like friends than uncle and nephew. They were not very interested in the family business nor were they pressurised for this. But they had sharp business intellect. They managed their elder brother's business quite well even if they did not take part in the day to day activities of the hospitals and the hotels. As such, all three of them were given the same treatment by Vidyadhar and his family.

Vidyadhar believed in the free will of a person with just the right amount of guidance at the right age. All three of them belonged to this great illustrious family. Though their main business was hotels and hospitals, the family was fully into charities and in helping the downtrodden. They had hospitals with quite a number of free tests and treatments and they had many schools which gave free education.

Kedar opted to study in a traditional medical college; Kalpesh was more into Ayurvedic treatment. Vidyadhar helped his younger brother procure admission in the best Ayurvedic college of the country. He knew that all the ventures which Adheesh would be undertaking or would undertake would always be only for truth and for the benefit of mankind. Sometimes he and his warriors would be so crushed and maimed that immediate medical attention would be required without any questions asked. Vidyadhar also knew that the whole world could not be made privy to the knowledge that demons existed in this day and age in different forms. This is where he knew that Kedar's and Kalpesh's knowledge of both kinds of medicines—Allopathic as well as Ayurvedic, would come in handy. In course of time, even Kedar and Kalpesh had been apprised of their place in the scheme of things. With the grace of God and the blessings of Vidyadhar and his wife, both of them had married girls who were into alternative and holistic medicines, though their wives Geetika and Padma had still to be told of this mind-boggling and stupendous secret.

Of Vidyadhar's two younger brothers, the elder was Kedar and the younger was Kalpesh. Kedar was a tall strappy man. He was the sporty, outdoor type, very fond of various sports like cricket and football and always ready for a prank or two and a laugh. He was a muscular man with dark brown hair and brown eyes. He had an infectious laugh and was always laughing and joking with his patients and his colleagues and the nurses. He was a surgeon. His friends would joke with him that the main reason for his becoming a surgeon was because he liked cutting and sewing up people. Hence he could either become a tailor or a surgeon. Since becoming a tailor was totally going against the family's tradition, therefore he became a surgeon, a joke which he agreed to and accepted with all humility. As he became a senior, Kedar would either be in the operation theatre or hiking in the mountains and jungles with Adheesh and his friends.

Kedar's wife Geetika was a dietician. She and Kedar were in school together and both of them wanted to become doctors. But as they grew up, Geetika started becoming interested in different kinds of foods and herbs, their properties and their uses. She got so engrossed in this that her earlier desire for becoming a doctor was overshadowed. She wanted to become a dietician, to cure people by advising them to eat the right kinds of food at the right time in the right proportions.

The astute and discerning Vidyadhar was quite happy about this and encouraged this friendship with all his blessings as he knew that when Adheesh and his fighters would come back to them, hurt and broken, it was Kedar and Geetika who would tend and care for them with all sincerity and honesty and in secrecy too. At present Geetika was working in a big hospital as the chief dietician and was thoroughly enjoying her job. She was a comely, cute bubbly girl with curly hair, chattering away nineteen to the dozen and laughing at the smallest provocation. She was of medium height with a rounded figure, though she was not fat. She had an elfin smile and was deeply interested in cooking and gardening especially in growing different herbs and flowers, some of which were used as medicines. That was the reason when Geetika finally met Aishani's mother Madhu, they got along like a house on fire, because of their interest in herbs and flowers. Geetika paid very close attention to the needs of her clients making them feel better just by listening patiently to their likes and dislikes; that made them more prone to agree to and like her diets. When Kedar and Geetika got married it was as if lots of happy energies had entered Vidyadharji's household. She was a familiar figure here even before her marriage as she and Kedar were classmates and sometimes exchanged books and notes. She was everywhere at the same time. She was in the kitchen, in the sitting room, in the offices and pretty much everywhere else. Not that anybody minded these intrusions; rather everybody liked her honest and keen interest in their work.

Kedar and Geetika made a beautiful couple. They were madly in love right from their teenage years. They did everything together, but Geetika drew a line where roaming in the jungles with Kedar was concerned. The idea of going to an unfamiliar jungle which could be infested with wild animals and insects was not her kind of place. She reluctantly allowed Kedar to go alone on these sojourns and she felt quite comfortable when Kedar was sometimes accompanied by his nephew Adheesh. Geetika got along quite well with Adheesh too, though sometimes she would be intimidated by his serious aura.

In contrast to Kedar and Geetika was the other couple—Kedar's younger brother Kalpesh and his wife Padma. Both Kalpesh and Padma had studied in the same Ayurvedic college which was the best in the country, though Padma was two years junior to him. Kalpesh was a sober boy mostly concerned with his own studies which fascinated him no end. He was a slim, tall boy just like his elder brother Kedar, but that was where the similarity ended. Kalpesh was the exact opposite of Kedar. He was a loner, a thinker and a philosopher. Kalpesh, right from his childhood, had an idea that he was meant for things other than what he was studying. He did like Ayurveda a lot, he had chosen it himself, but there were other roles he had to play. He had been able to sort out a few questions also but he had never been fully satisfied with the answers. He was lanky and had slightly long hair which had a habit of falling over his right eye. Though an introvert, he did get his share of attention as he looked quite handsome with his seemingly couldn't care less attitude.

Padma had noticed him as a serious senior. She did not pay much attention to him as she herself was a sober girl and totally involved in her studies. Padma was in the second year of her medical college when she started noticing Kalpesh. Her complexion was dusky, her eyes were brown with long black eyelashes. She had long curly hair which she liked to keep in a single braid which was less of a hassle than keeping her hair open. She wore the typical Indian dress of salwar kameez and looked very pretty in it too. She was totally engrossed in her studies and the presentations that she had to give so many times on the theories of *Charak Samhita*. She sometimes spoke about Lord Dhanvantri also as the God who introduced medicine in this world. She would sometimes meet Kalpesh in the library when both of them asked for the same books. Kalpesh did wonder sometims why a junior would want the books which at the moment were way ahead for her junior classes.

It was Vidyadhar who noticed this slim and sober girl twice in two seminars held by the Ayurvedic college of which he was a patron. On both occasions the girl had spoken with utter confidence on topics which seemed to have been very well analysed and explored. She was speaking well beyond her years and she had examples to prove her points too. Vidyadhar made up his mind that this girl was going to be his younger daughter-in-law. A few discreet inquiries about her family and background brought forth good results. It was now a matter of convincing Kalpesh and Padma. Vidyadhar was in no hurry as there was plenty of time. Both of them had to pass out of college first but he, Vidyadhar started making plans.

Adheesh got along famously with both his uncles and their wives though he got along more with his elder uncle Kedar. Kedar was more outgoing with a penchant for adventure. Adheesh and Kedar would go on long treks and hikes together. They enjoyed each others' company, could survive for days without proper food and could beat anybody when it came to mountain climbing. They knew the value of teamwork and were always ready to help anybody in need—whether human, animal or bird. Kalpesh was an equally kind and generous soul, very sensitive to the needs of others, but he was so involved and interested in his studies that he hardly had any time for outdoor activities. He was always thinking so much, that his friends and family had nicknamed him 'Thinker'. He was always reading the ancient texts on medicine, surgery and about the myriad herbs of ancient and contemporary India and the rest of the world also. Though Kalpesh did not much care for the strenuous adventures that his elder brother Kedar and nephew Adheesh undertook, he almost always played a pivotal role whenever he deigned to go out with them. They had had great adventures together and enjoyed every moment of these treks.

In fact, at one time when they were trekking through a dense jungle, there was a hazardous accident which almost took Kedar's life had it not been for Kalpesh. It was getting dark and they were hurrying to reach the nearest village while there was still light, but shadows had begun appearing and sometimes it seemed that a tree was an animal and vice versa. In the dusk the dark shadows of the trees danced along with the wind, jumping here and there. The jungle had become denser. Suddenly, out of nowhere a huge bear lunged at them and swiped at Kedar on his stomach. It was dusk and they had not been able to see it as it crept silently on them. Kalpesh, as usual, was lagging behind not because he did not want to go along with them, but because he found too many interesting herbs, barks of trees, insects, etc. that he had to pause, study and collect them. Adheesh deliberately did not bring Devnath on these sojourns as Devnath with his penchant of protecting him would have totally curtailed his freedom of movement.

It all happened so fast that the other two were caught totally unawares and just could not do anything. Without any warning or sound, the bear just rushed at them, smacked Kedar on the stomach and ran back the same way it had come. It was a huge bear and it had huge paws. One swipe of the paw ripped Kedar's stomach. He just fell to the ground in a faint. Blood flowed out from his stomach like a fountain. All of them did have some weapons with them but they were rudimentary in the sense that they were not enough to overpower the bear. This forest was considered a safe one; this particular bear may have wandered from the nearby jungle. In any case, now was not the time to ponder over these exigencies. There was Kedar to look after who was bleeding profusely. Adheesh felt helpless at that moment. He was ready to fight with the bear and would have won too, but he had only rudimentary knowledge of first aid though they did have a first aid kit with them. And this was an emergency of gigantic proportions. They were miles away from the nearest hospital. In a few minutes, Kedar would go into shock. Helplessly Adheesh looked for his younger uncle Kalpesh but he was nowhere to be seen.

"Kalpesh!" he shouted desperately, "Come fast, Kedar is hurt!"

There was no response from Kalpesh. There was no time to think. Furiously he clawed the leaves and branches and stones and made a sort of a clearing. He spread a towel over the clearing. Gingerly he made Kedar lie down and made a sort of a pillow with the leaves and twigs to elevate his head. There was medicated cotton in their first aid kit box but that would not be enough. Desperately he tore his shirt, folded it into a rough pad and put it gently over Kedar's stomach. He could not see the depth of the wound as Kedar was bleeding so profusely. He took out an antibiotic powder from the kit and sprinkled it over the wound but it was just not enough. It was meagre for the size of Kedar's injury. Somehow Adheesh made Kedar swallow a painkiller. Kedar was slowly sinking. The shirt pad did help the flow of blood to slow down but only a little.

"Hang on Kedar," he ordered. There was not much of age difference between the two young men; moreover, Kedar wanted Adheesh to call him by his name and not by the appellate 'uncle.'

Adheesh looked around for Kalpesh. He knew that Kalpesh was somewhere nearby rummaging through the trees and shrubs. Kedar could go into shock at anytime. There was nothing else to do but wait. He waited impatiently. The seconds were passing like hours. Finally, after ages, he could make out Kalpesh running towards them through the dense jungle.

"Thank God, I was beginning to despair," Adheesh heaved a sigh of relief.

One look at Kedar and Kalpesh burst out, "Oh my God, what happened? How? We'll talk later. But don't worry too much. I believe I have got the ingredients for stopping the flow of blood and even for closing the wound."

He took out a large quantity of herbs and leaves from his bag and washed them. Thankfully, they always carried lots of water with them. Then he gave various kinds of leaves to Adheesh, "Here, crush them with your hands as fast as you can." He then did the same thing himself. Together both of them crushed the herbs into some sort of a paste and then took out their juice. Kalpesh started chanting some mantras and began applying the juice gently all over Kedar's stomach. Even after applying the thick paste and the juice, the wound was like a gaping hole. It had to be closed immediately.

"What do we do now?" Adheesh wiped the sweat off Kedar's forehead.

Kalpesh looked at the gaping wound, nonplussed for a moment. Then as if making a decision, he turned to Adheesh,

"Look after Bhaiya for a few minutes, I'll just come."

Saying this Kalpesh just rushed away hurriedly, leaving Adheesh staring after him. Adheesh had no option but to just hold Kedar as softly and as firmly as possible. Kalpesh did come back after a few minutes.

"You were wondering why I took so long in coming back with the ingredients," said Kalpesh. "Well this is what took me so long. I knew that some stitching had to be required when I saw the deep wound and I had seen these when we were coming here, so I went to collect these," saying this Kalpesh took out a cloth bag from his knapsack and opened it. The box was full of large ants. They were not the normal kinds of ants. They were quite large and they had large pincers too. Kalpesh did not waste any time in explaining anything to Adheesh. He gingerly took one ant and placed it over Kedar's wound in such a way that the ant bit it with its pincers on both the sides of the wounded flesh. Before the ant could open its mouth again Kalpesh broke the rest of its body and discarded it. He then proceeded to do the same with the other ants over the rest of the wound. Very soon the wound was closed with neat sutures made by the ants' pincers which were still attached to the wound.

"There," Kalpesh sat back with a weary but satisfied sigh. "More than the basic first aid has been done. With proper care and rest, Bhaiya is going to be alright now." He sat back exhausted but got up after a few minutes. Adheesh had already cleaned up the clearing. He was not unfamiliar with what Kalpesh had done. The herbs which Kalpesh always carried himself and what he had collected did the work of cleaning and were the Ayurvedic version of antibiotics. The suturing which he did with the help of the giant ants was also prevalent in ancient times. It was naturally not common anymore but Kalpesh had full knowledge of it and Adheesh had also read about it in a few of his classes. It was getting dark now. Both of them looked at Kedar who had his eyes closed and seemed to be sleeping now. They knew that Kedar was awake but was just very very tired after the trauma and the pain.

"Uncle," Adheesh whispered to Kedar, "You have been very brave, but you require immediate hospitalisation. Kalpesh is here with you. I am going to find someone or something to take you to civilization."

Kedar's head moved imperceptibly to show that he had heard and acquiesced. With a look at Kalpesh, Adheesh went off fast. He had to find help quickly. This was not a wild animal infested jungle but still, the bear had come. Granted the bear may have strayed to this part of the jungle and may have struck Kedar out of sheer fear, panic or self-defense or maybe it was a mother with small cubs. Still, they could not rule out its coming back again. In his urgency, he even climbed a tree to see if he could detect any familiar sign. All around him he could see only dense vegetation. He calmed himself. He thought he heard a sound. What was it? It was a mixture of a whisper and a slither but it was definitely not a snake. Oddly, the sound seemed familiar. Where had he heard it? He wracked his brains to pinpoint the sound. Suddenly it came to him. This was how Devnath used to communicate with spirits in the crematorium and other places where he did not want to be heard or exposed. Adheesh exhaled a sigh of relief, Devnath was nearby and he was warning the spirits and hence the animals also not to go near any human beings in this part of the jungle. He knew that Devnath was too far away at the moment. It was an unspoken agreement between him and Devnath that whenever he did not return at the stipulated time, Devnath would come after him without waiting for his permission.

"Devnath," he shouted from the treetop. His voice would not have reached any person other than Devnath. But it was Devnath. He heard Adheesh clearly. Because he was so attuned to his master he also understood that Adheesh was in acute crisis. He also understood that Adheesh himself was in no danger. Devnath had been fretting from the time Adheesh left for the trek with his uncles leaving him behind. Devnath would have ensured that no danger touched them. But Adheesh did not know that he would have to regret his decision so soon.

In about fifteen minutes Devnath was at his side with two other villagers. He had also managed a makeshift stretcher from the villagers. After that, it was just a matter of time before Kedar was whisked away to a hospital and safety and proper emergency care.

The Snake

Aishani was now in the third semester of her training at the Gurukul. So much had happened in this short span of time. Her nightmares had stopped completely; she had slowly begun to know herself and her powers though she still did not understand anything fully. She was getting the hang of the whole thing, slowly but surely. Though she had yet to see a demon at close range or to test its destructive powers, nevertheless she knew now that they were being trained here in the Gurukul for this very purpose. She also knew that her training had been a continuous process from her past rebirths. The first year of her training in the Gurukul was just a revision and reminder of her past training. It was from the second year that her real training had started. Every ten years or so the training methods or the war fighting was enhanced and augmented according to the changing requirements of the times. Though many of the old methods and old weapons were still better than the present ones, still the Gurukul readied them for any contingency as and when it arose.

But the most beautiful part of these years and her training at the Gurukul was her budding friendship with Adheesh. Romance was the correct word but Aishani was not ready to call it that at the moment. She wanted to let things be as they were now and let destiny take its course. Both Aishani and Adheesh had started getting glimmers of their past relationships and knew that they had been partners and soulmates in their previous lives. But Aishani still had to come to terms with her present relationship with him. She was still very shy with him; she was wary of her parents encouraging her so much and of the sparks that invariably brought forth an eruption of emotions and memories. On top of it, her rigorous training left her little or no time to think of these things in the correct perspective. She decided to let things be and let time itself decide on what she had to do.

In the meantime, her father was preparing her for another exercise. Even Guruji was preparing her for this exercise along with her father. There were extra classes for her in the Gurukul, extra time was given to her for meditation and her martial arts training was also intensified. Along with the chanting of other mantras, she was being taught a very powerful and potent mantra known as the Garuda mantra. She was also being trained in the use of Garuda Astra by Guruji himself. Garuda was the bearer of Bhagwan Vishnu and was the king of birds and the killer of snakes. He could fly anywhere faster than the speed of sound and light, and when the need arose, even time. It was said that Garuda devta could move hell and heaven by the mere flapping of his wings. His appearance was that of half bird and half man.

By now Aishani had a rough idea that this special training somehow involved dangerous snakes or Nagas. If any entity in the world could kill these dangerous Nagas it was Garuda, the snake killer. There was no need to tell Aishani to keep it a secret. Periodically, selected students were sent for certain special training. This was a normal recurrent happening in the Gurukul and thus did not incite much curiosity.

After a couple of weeks' training Aishani was introduced to the Garuda Astra. Guruji led her to a special annexure of the Gurukul museum. It had just a table in the centre with a blue and yellow satin and velvet cloth over it. The table cloth had certain designs on it. Aishani did not recognise the designs but she knew that they had a meaning. On a tray was kept a middle sized bow and arrow. It was the Garuda Astra. Initially it looked just like any other copper bow and arrow, but Aishani now had a fair idea about its powers.

"Aishani, you will come here at daybreak every morning and pray and chant to it so that it becomes fully charged and activated. The time to use it has almost arrived." Aishani bowed her head and acquiesced to Guruji's instructions. The Garuda Astra was kept on a platform. A blue velvet cloth was spread over the platform over which a swastika was painted in yellow. The Astra had been kept over it. All the divine weapons were kept in the armoury of the Gurukul's museum. They looked like any other ordinary weapons. It was only when a particular Astra was required to be used against any demon that the weapon was taken by Guruji to the room adjoining his and kept on the platform. It was here that he invoked the particular Astra's deity, took the deity's permission, and then activated it with special kriyas and chanting of specific mantras.

After the initial activation of the Garuda Astra, Guruji beckoned Aishani to introduce her to the celestial weapon. Aishani gasped in awe and wonderment as she espied the shining black bow and its arrows lying on the bed of blue velvet. Guruji smilingly gave her a nod. She lifted it carefully and drew in her breath sharply. Its design was exquisite and elegant and it was perfectly balanced. It had the design of a bird's wings extended in flight. Aishani closed her eyes. For a moment she thought that she heard the sound of a crying eagle. She opened her eyes in alarm and looked at Guruji who was smiling broadly.

"It's not your imagination, the Astra has approved of you. It will help you in getting itself activated."

Guruji had taught Aishani the special mantras which she continued. Every morning she would come and sit in front of the Garuda Astra and pray to it.

One day Pandit Ram Sharan called her to his library. Nobody was there apart from Aishani.

"Beta, the time has come. All your rigorous training will be put to the test now. I cannot be more proud of any child of mine. You have far exceeded my expectations but that was only to be expected." Aishani smiled at her father's compliments and waited. She knew that she was being prepared for a very special and dangerous mission but Baba was going to be there so it was going to be alright and successful too. She wasn't nervous or anxious. Baba would handle if any mishap happened. How naïve she was!

"Beta we will be leaving tonight."

She nodded. Baba knew best.

Pandit Ram Sharan cleared his throat, "Beta this will be the first of your great missions of eliminating the demons. Every mission of yours will make you more powerful and more mature. Normal demons will run away at the very mention of your name and even the more dangerous ones will think twice before crossing your path." He cleared his throat and stopped as if trying to put his words together. Aishani looked at her father and waited.

"But there will be a price to pay also. It's all the will of the Almighty. You along with your partner will gain so much but in the process you will also become tough and hardened too. You might even lose your loved ones. This is a sacrifice that both of you will have to make for the betterment of this world."

What was Baba talking about? How will I lose my loved ones? Over what? And what partner was Baba talking about? A picture of Adheesh flashed before her eyes but she brushed the picture aside.

"Come beta, go to sleep now. Your mother knows about this. No need to go to her now. She'll get emotional."

Again Aishani found this a bit strange coming from her father. Her mother was the strong and stable one in the family. She was the one who kept calm in times of crisis and she was the one who provided practical solutions. Aishani did not say anything and went straight to her room.

It had been a week now, this waiting for the snake creature to come out of the water of the ocean. They were on the farthest southernmost part of the country where the sea met the ocean. A clear beach was in front of them and the dense forest was behind them. The sandy beach glittered under the morning sun, a graceful arc of sand, small soothing waves rolling over it. How could a huge fierce monster hide inside its placid waters? The ocean wouldn't allow it. Its shore is a gateway of the beautiful aquatic world. The salty brine smell was all-pervasive, warm and cool at the same time. Aishani felt intoxicated while her father looked at her just a little sad at the thought of what she was going to face after some time.

On her father's instructions, Aishani sat under a tree which was far away from the sea, meditating and chanting the specific mantras given to her by Guruji and her father. The Garuda Astra or the Garuda bow and arrow were always strung on her shoulders ready to be harnessed at a moment's notice. The demon which they were going to face was going to be a humongous Nag or snake of an unimaginably enormous size related to the giant Nag Kaalia from the ancient times. Kaalia had been killed by Bhagwan Vishnu but a couple of its kin had managed to escape and gone into hibernation inside the ocean bed.

Her father sat at the other end of the lake chanting mantras invoking the snake or snakes to come out. She had been briefed about this snake who had gone into hibernation deep inside the ocean centuries ago. The huge Nag may or may not be in his full senses and they had to take advantage of this fact. If the snake woke up with full control over his senses and memory then they would have to be extra careful and fast.

When Aishani suggested that they sit together and chant their mantras her father explained patiently, "Ash we are chanting different kinds of mantras; my mantras are to agitate and anger the snake so much that it comes out to kill and destroy the person who is disturbing it so much, and yours is to strengthen your focus and your will power plus your weapons too." Aishani glanced at her weapons or rather her weapon, the divine Astra of Garuda devta who was the steed of Bhagwan Vishnu. Both the bow and the arrow were small and archaic looking, the kind one would find in antique shops with its unique design of a flying eagle-like bird. No one looking at them would take them as actual weapons now, and even if someone learned enough to understand this weapon, he would not know how to use it as these particular pieces of bow and arrow could only be used by one initiated into it.

Aishani was one of them. She was trained in these kinds of martial arts. In the right hands, this small bow and arrow could with one shot uncoil hundreds of Garudas capable of killing even the most dangerous of snakes. Its supply was limitless. It was a celestial weapon and could be used only by a celestial being or by a person who was chosen and blessed by celestial beings. Pandit Ram Sharan's heart always swelled up at the thought that such a person had taken birth through him.

The Garuda Astra had become active in Aishani's hands by her chanting the specific mantras and it could now recognise Aishani's feel and aura. What Aishani did not know and what her father knew was that such intense focus and such intense desire to annihilate evil was in her blood, accumulated through the ages. Pandit Ram Sharan was very proud and happy that he was blessed to have her as his daughter. He did not want to lose her. But he also knew that in these dangerous missions he would not always be there to share her glory. It would not necessarily be him losing her, rather it would be her losing him. In any case, they would be losing each other. Pandit ji was under no illusions that he was merely a medium in leading Aishani to the demons after which she would take over. He was a Brahmin but he knew that his daughter was a Kshatriya even though she was born a Brahmin. Maybe she was born to him to facilitate her understanding and chanting of mantras. Terrible loneliness filled his heart and mind.

He knew that they would be separated during this mission; he had known about it from the beginning; his mind, values, and skills were just not geared for destroying such demons. He glanced towards her. So beautiful, so full of dignity and poise, so slim—who would imagine that such a normal looking girl would be capable of such unimaginable huge feats and merciless killings with such strength of character. One thought which gave him some peace and consolation was that her partner and soulmate had arrived and had almost recognised and remembered his role, which was to protect and provide succor to Aishani. Pandit ji knew that Adheesh was going to be Aishani's partner in the truest sense of the word and together they would reach heights of glory in achieving their aims and getting rid of the demons everywhere. One critical factor was that Aishani's training could not be completed in time for the annihilation of the Nag. This was because the Nag was coming out of its dormancy earlier than calculated. One of the factors could be global warming. The point was that Aishani was not fully prepared even though she did not know it herself. Pandit ji and Guruji would have to rely on her emotions to do the needful.

Pandit ji closed his eyes and continued with his chanting. He could sense that the creature which was indirectly related to the Naga king Kaalia was getting disturbed and was very slowly coming out of its hibernation. His instructions were to agitate the nag so much that even before it fully came out of its comatose stage Aishani would kill it. They both knew that Aishani was not yet fully honed to kill the creature with timing and precision. But what Aishani did not know was that the impetus for the supplemental killer instinct would come only when she was in shock or would have to be in such a rage as to be able to use the bow and arrow or the Garuda Astra to its maximum capacity. Pandit Ram Sharan knew that this is where the scarring would begin, the scars so deep that they would take ages to heal, if at all.

He could now feel the water of the ocean warming up. Small ripples of dark green waves billowed but gave up as if too afraid of the creature that was coming out of the ocean's bowels. The whole jungle had become quieter. Birds had stopped singing; trees were standing bolt upright as if they wanted to bolt away. He looked at Aishani. Nothing had changed in the girl's demeanor but he knew that she could also sense the change in the atmosphere. Both father and daughter stared at it fascinated. Aishani was ready, her hands poised with the bow and the arrow when suddenly the scene changed. From the mountainous snake which had just shot up hundreds of ice snakes regurgitated from its body trying to lap up everything around them. They were jet black, squirming and swirling, about four feet in length with poisonous green slush oozing out of their pores. Their red-rimmed eyes and mouths were spewing black ice ready to devour anything and anybody that came in front of them. Black, red, yellow and black! It was a sight to behold! All of them were susurrating and hissing at the same time, some of them spitting out the sea water which they must have ingested during their dormancy.

Aishani closed her eyes in reverence to her bow and arrow and pulled her arrow. A volley of arrows came out of that single arrow and went deep inside the snake's sheath. There was a roar of pain, a mixture of hissing and the howl of hyenas. The creature had not fully come out of its stupor which was a good thing for father and daughter. But it would not take a long time to assess the situation and then all hell would break loose if that was allowed to happen. Taking a fistful of the powder which they had brought in a sack, Pandit Ram Sharan threw it at the creature and then bombarded the snake with the powder. Wherever the powder struck, the ice snakes jutting out of the Naga immediately liquefied and disintegrated followed by deadly painful screeching.

The creature was just coming out of hibernation and was being struck by Aishani's arrows on one side and by the deadly powder from the other. But its pain was now precipitating more by the powder. In massive agony and rage, it turned towards the source of its pain. Pandit Ram Sharan, now almost shouting his mantras, was standing there waiting for him. He threw another fistful of powder at the creature. It howled with pain and fury again searching for its tormentor and then detected him. Before Aishani could do anything it spat a huge ball of fiery venom at Pandit Ram Sharan. Pandit ji was burnt to cinders in that instant. What remained of him was just black ash.

There was complete silence. Pandit Ram Sharan's loud chanting had stopped. Horrified, Aishani stared at her father's ashes. It was incomprehensible. But there was no time, the creature had started searching for other victims; it was now trying to fully come out of its stupor. Aishani was heaving with rage and grief now, a rage so great that it could destroy anything which came in her path. Her bow and arrow understood her rage and grief; they were now fully compliant in her hands almost willing her to shoot at the creature!

She turned to face the serpent, the killer, the murderer of her father. Gone was the shock of seeing her father's ashes, gone was the extreme sense of loss and confusion. There was no confusion in her mind now, only rage and hatred so great that it consumed her whole mind and body and she became that and that only—rage and hatred. She took out a bow from the quiver, chanted her mantra to energise it, and then shot at the creature. The arrow which was fretting impatiently till now whizzed buoyantly. Within seconds that small arrow turned into a hundred razor sharp arrows which in turn turned into eagle-like birds with sharp steely beaks. They effortlessly cut the ice snakes in half and then entered the central body. It roared in pain. Huge flames leaped out of it, angry flames annihilating anything and everything that came in its way.

But Aishani was not there. She was quick if not quicker than the serpent. She knew her homework. It had been dinned into her that the serpent coming out of hibernation was her greatest enemy. It was taking sometimes for the huge Nag to adjust to this new age, to his surroundings and the sharp steely beaks of the divine Garuda arrows which were boring into it. Aishani was now on its left side. Again she aimed an arrow at the creature and released it. Only this time they were not arrows of razor-sharp beaks rather they were beaks of fire. The serpent paused for a moment; these were excruciatingly painful arrows and were piercingly hot. The heat was something he understood, it was his arch enemy. He had faced it earlier and he knew how to effectively overpower it.

He was getting stronger. He had started feeling just a bit comfortable when suddenly the arrows turned into beaks of cold icicles, only this time they were serrated and not melting and they were slowly turning around cutting his gut surely and steadily. The creature screeched loudly, the sound exactly like a creature being gnawed by a thousand knives deliberately and dexterously. No time was given to the gargantuan snake to pinpoint the location of its enemy. It was consumed by the excruciating pain in his body. It screamed and lashed out. Colourful spots flashed in front of its eyes. With each cry its pain worsened, its bloody muscles quivered, its consciousness waned.

The water of the lake had turned blackish red, its surface covered with fire. Aishani was like a whirlwind now shooting at the snake from all sides, totally focused and calm, the bow and arrows singing in her hands as if they had finally accomplished their long-forgotten purpose in life. The Garuda arrows were making mincemeat of the Nag's body. The serpent finally could not take it any longer. Its body had turned into a sieve, flesh, sinews, fat and blood pouring out from everywhere. With a long painful wail which seemed to reach the farthest corners of the Earth and Hell and Heaven, it fell down and succumbed to its injuries, half its body out of the sea on the waterfront.

Aishani saw the huge dead snake falling but still did not relax. She kept on shooting all three kinds of arrows at it, the steely beak arrows, the fire arrows, and the non- melting serrated ice arrows. After some time she paused. There was no thought in her mind except to be absolutely sure that the Nag was dead. Only when she was totally sure that the snake was dead that she loosened her grip on her bow and arrow. Slowly the body of the snake turned into a jelly-like mass and began mixing with the water of the sea. After some time the jelly was totally submerged in the water and swept away by the waves of the sea.

Aishani watched it floating away till it totally disappeared. Then she turned towards her bow and arrow. They had become innocuous and inoffensive again like a child's plaything. Aishani rubbed them clean with the sand then wiped them with a soft cloth. They shone once to show their appreciation, then they became dull and lifeless again. They would be returned to their exalted place in the armoury of the Martial Arts College where they would stay till the next mission. Aishani did all this very deliberately as if that was the most important thing in her life. She sat down cross-legged on the sand of the beach, her shoulders and heart heaving and her body shaking like a broken leaf.

She didn't know how long she sat like that. Her body had stopped shaking and she could now comprehend and look around at her surroundings. After that, there was nothing else to do except to face the horrible fact about Baba. Her baba could not die. He had merely left things to her so that she could have faith and confidence in herself that she could destroy that horrendous snake. He would come out of the woods any time now and applaud her for a job well done. She waited, and then sat down and waited some more. Slowly she traced her steps back to the spot where she had seen her baba being burnt to cinders. She closed her eyes. She had stopped breathing. Slowly she opened her eyes and searched for her father. There was nothing there except for a small pathetic mound of black ash which the waves were trying to lap up. She couldn't let that happen! Quickly she took out a small bag tied to her waist. With trembling hands, she scooped up her father's ashes in the bag and tied it with twine. Her whole body had started shaking again. She knew that her baba was not dead and these ashes were not his and she was not going to cry. There was nothing to cry about. They had come to kill the snake and they had killed it. That was that. She sat down on a nearby rock waiting for her father to come back.

A few hours ago the ocean had been absolutely cool and calm almost like a sanctuary, now it was ugly and the home of her deadliest enemy. Her whole world had been destroyed by this freak storm. Everything had dissolved in the ocean—the Nag, her father, the plant and aquatic life and everything around her. She took a deep shuddering breath. Her father had disappeared like he was never there. She was numb with pain. And yet she would have to live, to fight and kill and lose her loved ones. This was a dystopian nightmare.

After Father's Death

There was nobody in the house except Aishani and her mother. The evening's natural lights had drained away but the twilight was still not enough for shadows. The darkness would come whether she liked it or not. The warmth of the afternoon ebbed away making sure it was going to be a cold and soulless night.

The dusk would become a highly perceptible lightening of the gloom. In happier times the house used to make sure that everybody had had food but now it was itself so distraught that it forgot to nag them to eat.

Her brother Jayant was in the Gurukul. As for her mother, she would finish her daily responsibilities then she would go to her bedroom, sit on an *asan* on the floor and meditate for hours. Aishani instinctively knew that her mother's pain was too much and that meditation was the only panacea for her emotional suffering.

She knew that her father and mother had always shared a special bond with each other, a bond which seemed to be made in heaven. The aura of happiness and contentment which emanated from them when they were in each other's company had to be observed by a keen sensitive observer to understand these feelings. Aishani tried to hide her tears but there was such a flood of them that she could not control them. But now that her beloved Baba was killed by a creature, the awful truth dawned on Aishani about her mother's loss.

Initially, she was distressed by her own grief, feelings of guilt and the conviction that she had somehow killed her father. Try as she might she could not rid herself of this horrible feeling. But she had to go for her training and Adheesh was always there. Slowly and gradually she began coming out of her haze of pain and could now see beyond her own misery. The first person she looked out for, was her mother, her mother Madhu whose world began and ended with her father and now her father was no more.

Aishani was appalled at herself. She was so engrossed in her own grief that she could not pay close attention to her mother who had been shattered by her father's death. Slowly gathering up her courage she went to her mother. Her mother was sitting on the verandah preoccupied with knitting. The light of the day was depleting and the sun was sinking lower in *the sky,* it was time for the mosquitoes and crickets to come out. The air had become cooler, the close silence ushered in the dim evening light. There was gloom everywhere. The house kept on sighing, not allowing even the sunrays to come inside its windows.

Grief surged through her body as she expelled her breath and went and sat on the verandah beside her mother. Tears silently spilled from her helpless eyes. She gazed sightlessly at her mother's herb garden, for a moment surprised. The herbs seemed to be doing quite well. Though her mother did not tend to them these days she did water them, so they were growing and surviving. It seemed to Aishani that time had only stopped for them. Her mother's shoulders were hunched up as if she had the weight of the whole world on her shoulders.

"Ma," she whispered softly. Madhu turned at the sound of her daughter.

"Ash," she said softly, "Come beta."

Her face red with grief, Ash was sniffling by the time she went and put her arms around her mother. They were alone now, the relatives and friends had left; mother and daughter could now share their mourning in peace. Holding each other tightly they wept. Aishani could not hold herself anymore. The heartbreak of losing her father and the guilt that she was somehow responsible for not being able to prevent his death was killing her. She cried and cried, for how long she did not know. Aeons passed, but she kept on shivering and crying. There was no other thought other than sharing the agony of the bereavement with her mother. After a very long time, her mother shook her very softly.

"Ash beta, control yourself."

"Ma, how will we live now," Ash sobbed, "Without Baba, nothing is the same. There will never be anything that will make us happy."

"Shh Ash, what has happened had to happen. It was all predestined. Your father had to die."

"No Ma, he did not have to die, it was too early for his death. How will you live, how will all of us live?" she wailed.

"Beta, we will live the same way the world has lived without its loved ones. Our agonies and our heartaches continue and the world goes on. Now it is up to us to let our wounds fester or treat them and go ahead with life."

"There is no treatment for the absence of Baba's life ma," she sobbed, "Baba was everything, that snake should have killed me instead."

Madhu shook her daughter again and said softly, "Ash I have to tell you something. Things are not always as lost as they seem to us." Madhu took her hands in hers. She felt her daughter's hands. These hands should have been soft and supple for a girl her age; instead, they were hard, fleshy and rough, because of all the hard training that she was undergoing. A wave of pure love and emotion passed over Madhu's face. Aishani was born for a very noble cause, for the purpose of eliminating all the evil energies of this world and she had been doing this for the last so many births with this single focus in mind. She did not deserve to be so emotionally distraught. Madhu made up her mind. There was no good in hiding the truth from Aishani. Jayant could be told some other time but Aishani had to be told now only. Hiding the truth from Aishani would only weaken her emotionally and physically and temporarily deflect her from her cause.

"Ash, your father and I knew that this was going to happen. We deliberately did not tell you because then the impetus and the anger required in you to destroy the Nag would just not have been there. You have all the strength and valour to destroy any demon but some of them are so powerful that just that extra springboard or thrust is required to demolish them. In this case your shock and your anger had to exceed the power of that particular snake and your father's death gave you just the right impetus."

Aishani sat up, "Ma what are you talking about! You mean both of you knew that baba was going to die and both of you let it be so and allowed Baba to die! I don't understand, baba was your life. To hell with the creature, Baba was much more important than that snake! Ma how could you!"

"Ash," her mother said gently, "There is nobody more important or precious for me in this world than your father. I would never have allowed such a thing to happen, but God closes one door and he opens another."

"Ma, what door are you talking about? How can God open another door, even one which can make up for Baba's loss?" Aishani was thoroughly confused now. Her mother never talked stupidly or said things in a lighthearted manner. She was a very dedicated wife, mother, and housewife. So what was she saying now? Had she gone on some defense mechanism to counter her grief? Or had God or maybe Guruji guided Madhu in some way to lighten her sense of bereavement? If so, what was it? Aishani waited mutely for her mother to explain her statement.

"Ash," her mother said gently, "Your father and I were not only partners in our married life but our destinations were also the same, that of getting rid of the demons. But we are human beings blessed with some supernatural powers," she stopped. Ash stared at her mother amazed, "You too ma! But you never showed any inclination towards these things or gave any hint," she exclaimed. Even if she wanted she couldn't visualise her mother harming a fly let alone killing a demon.

"Yes," Madhu said wryly. "Remember, I am a wife, mother, and housewife, each job more demanding than the other. Initially, your father and I were totally into it. But as our family grew, both you and Jayant were born. Your father became increasingly busy in training the students of the college and I was left alone to look after the house, the shop and both of you. Then when you were born you started showing your powers immediately. This had to be hidden from the outer world if both of you had to lead a normal life. I could not accompany your father on our excursions anymore. Gradually it became a routine affair with your father being away most of the time either on his missions or training the students. Even though both of us very much wanted to be together there was this very important job of raising you two as normal children."

It took Aishani some time to figure out and assimilate this information about her mother. Madhu waited. Finally, Aishani sighed and looked up. She was looking at her mother with different eyes now, "But ma, Jayant has never shown any inclination for these things," she said.

"Yes Ash, Jayant is not overly interested in these so-called activities, but he is your brother and our son," her mother said proudly. "As you know, he performs herculean tasks effortlessly. He is also cut from the same cloth. We have deliberately let him be. Sometimes the fire in the heart and mind comes later than usual. The fire is there in Jayant, it just has to be ignited at the proper time with the proper training."

Tears came to Aishani's eyes again, "And now baba is not there, who will look after his training, who will look after us ma!"

"Your baba is still looking after us. He will never leave us," Madhu said softly and deliberately.

Aishani looked up sadly, "What do you mean ma, you mean to say we have his blessings. But that is not the real thing ma. I know that Baba will always be there to bless us. Oh, ma! What are we going to do?"

"Ash, listen to me and this time don't interrupt. When I said your father will be with us I meant physically and metaphorically also. You know the Parijat tree which flows into our backyard."

Aishani stared mutely and expectantly at her mother. She knew all about the Parijat or the wish-fulfilling tree. She also knew that her mother used to pray to it daily. Every morning she would collect the small fragrant flowers and put them in water in a flat bowl. The flowers were so beautiful with their small white petals and bright orange stalks. They filled their whole house with their heady subtle sweetness. She had a dim and hazy idea that praying to the Parijat tree brought marital bliss. But, but Baba had left and gone!

"Yes ma, I've seen you praying to the Parijat tree. What has that to do with Baba?"

Something was happening of which she was not aware. Was it going to be true? Was baba alive and in some other realm? Was the Parijat tree in anyway responsible for baba's coming back?

How could this be possible! She waited impatiently but held her breath. There was something definitely in the air. Her mother was going to tell her something of momentous and far-reaching importance and consequences. Her mother was forming her words and taking her own time to articulate them. Aishani's anticipation was heightening. Her nervous energy was tingling through her like electrical sparks. Her mother continued, "Both of us knew that this was going to happen. Guruji knew right from the beginning. He has given us the diksha of travelling into the past and the future—that is travelling in time. We come from that fraternity of warriors who can travel into the past and the future too sometimes to prevent crime and if we cannot prevent, then to meet it headlong and demolish it. The Parijat tree is instrumental in sending us to different realms especially if a partner is involved."

Aishani was fascinated; momentarily forgetting her grief she blurted out, "Ma you too! Do you meet Baba in the past? Is this what you have been trying to tell me?"

Would the shadows disappear? Would the light be back in their lives? There was absolute silence now. The house had stopped sighing and creaking. Both the house and Aishani were now straining themselves to hear Madhu' snext words.

"I have travelled to the past and yes, I have met your baba there after his……." Madhu faltered, she could not use the word death, "After your father passed away," and before Aishani could say anything she hastily continued, "This diksha given to us by Guruji has not been given to us just for the purpose of travelling back and forth oı to have fun or to meet our friends and loved ones. We have been blessed with this great diksha to fight evil and prevent it from happening. We cannot be immature and use it for our personal desires or any other motive. The dikshas have a mind of their own; if they sense that they are being used for purposes other than those for which they were created, they peter off, and the people using or misusing them are left without any powers and sometimes in a different time and mental frame also."

But Aishani was not paying attention. For her, the keywords were 'they could see baba again.' She was on cloud nine! To see baba, hold him, talk to him as if nothing had happened; it was sheer happiness! The house too did a small jig and some of the things fell down from the table. Nobody noticed. They were quite used to the idiosyncrasies of the house.

Madhu could make out that Aishani had heard her selectively and was more than eager to meet her father again. Her euphoric flight had to be curtailed now itself.

"Ash listen to me," she said urgently and shook her daughter. "There is no way we can meet your father in the past only for the sake of meeting him. If we are sent by Guruji for some mission, then only can we meet our loved ones to be with them for some time. Even then the other person may not know that you have come from his future. That would only confuse them and a new mess could be created."

Aishani was now dimly becoming aware of what her mother was saying. "Ma has it been the same with Baba? When he saw you did he recognise you as his wife from the future or from this time—was Baba confused when he met you after his passing away? And why were you sent back into among past ma?"

"Ash beta your, father and I have been the very few persons to have been selected from our generation for time travel. It's not possible for everyone to learn this powerful skill." Her mother said this as a statement without any consciousness of pride or arrogance. But Aishani knew that Madhu was trying to evade her question so she just looked at her mutely and waited expectantly. Madhu sighed. She knew her daughter. She knew that Ash was not going to leave her until she got to the bottom of the matter.

"Ok beta, yes your father knew from what future time I had come, in the same way both of us knew that he would have to die," she drew in her breath. "That is the reason I have not been able to fully grieve your father's loss knowing that I will be able to meet him a few times during the rest of my life. It's not the same but beggars can't be choosers. We chose this life and we will make do with whatever time we have with each other no matter how fragmented it is. As for why I went there, let that be for some other time. That is another story altogether."

"Ma does this mean that if there is work related to my training or destruction of the demons, I may be allowed to go back in time to complete my training or to kill any demon which has come out of its dormancy in the past?"

Madhu could hear and sense the elation in Aishani's voice. And who was she to blame her daughter when she herself had wished the same thing so many times! She patted Aishani's cheek, "Ash, don't be so hasty with your dreams. We are in *Mrityulok* where each of us has to take birth and die. That is the rule of nature here and we cannot go against it. As far as going back in time is concerned, it all depends on how much of your training was left with your father and if any demon is there in the past who has to be annihilated immediately. Some of the demons are so intelligent and cunning that they can come out of their hibernation at those times when there is the least resistance to their survival."

"Ma I never thought that I'll welcome the appearance of a demon so much as now!" Both mother and daughter smiled and laughed in spite of their pain. There was still so much to ask and so much to learn. Today she would give in to her deliriously happy feelings and revel in them. Baba was there somewhere. And she knew that he was missing her and waiting for her. Oh! What a lovely thought!

Finding Themselves

Aishani left for the Gurukul content with her mother's answers. There was a light breeze and the sun was shining. The clouds lazily drifted here and there. The trees and their leaves were shining after last night's rain. In some places, small new plants had sprouted and there were some new budding flowers too. Was it her imagination or had the world started looking better and more beautiful? But in her heart of hearts, she knew that there was a possibility that she could meet her father. Her burning hope was that Guruji would somehow send her to the past so that she could meet her Baba. She had not been to the Gurukul for quite a long period. Nobody had questioned her also. Everyone at the Gurukul was shocked by Pandit Ram Sharan's death. They knew how important he was in the scheme of things. Ruby had been with her all through, but in spite of being her bosom friend, even she could not penetrate the haze of pain in which Aishani had shrouded herself.

They left for Guruji's ashram. Adheesh had come to pick her up. Ever since her father's unprecedented death, it had become a practice for Adheesh to pick her up and drop her. It was because of him that she could go out of her house. Everybody in their house was grieving; they didn't know how to console each other. It was only after her heart to heart talk with her mother last evening that Aishani pepped up a little. There was hope in her heart. The Gurukul had begun looking beautiful again, well, not fully, nevertheless it was looking better. If Adheesh was pleasantly surprised he did not show it.

They reached Guruji's cottage and went inside. They touched his feet and sat cross-legged in front of him. Everyone around Aishani knew that she was depressed, most of all Adheesh, Guruji and Ruby. Guruji spoke to them for a length of time and gave them a sermon. Aishani heard him absentmindedly. She hoped and prayed that Guruji would say something about a new demon cropping up in the past or that she had to complete her leftover training in the past. At present, it was only because of Adheesh that she could go out anywhere. Even Guruji knew that she was unable to pay attention to his sermons. He could not let Panditji's sacrifice go in vain. Aishani had to be shaken out of her stupor. But there was a subtle difference here today. The palpable dark gloom was not so dark today. Guruji blessed them and began his sermon.

Aishani casually heard him. Guruji continued, "Prabhu acts in mysterious ways, and according to the need of the hour.

He gives everybody whatever he or she requires at different times. He takes with one hand and gives with the other."

What was Guruji saying? God had taken away everything from her and she did not want anything in exchange. She wanted her Baba. Nobody and nothing could replace her baba. There was the familiar catch in her throat again along with the expectation that Guruji would announce about some demon who had appeared from the past and they had to go back to the past to destroy it. But no such luck. She could barely catch one or two sentences of what Guruji was saying. But she also knew now that if there was any person in the world who could send her back to her Baba it was Guruji. She tried to pay attention to what he was saying.

Guruji pursued the topic, "In your case Aishani beta, the demon killed your father or let's say God took away your father. Your father was your friend, guide and philosopher. He provided you and your family with emotional succuor, love, and protection. But God has already chosen a befitting person to be your mentor and protector."

She looked at Guruji then at Adheesh but Adheesh was looking down at the ground paying full attention to what Guruji was saying. Even if he did know anything, he was not going to divulge it at the moment.

"This person will protect you with more than his life. He will support you in all ways—mentally, physically and emotionally. From the beginning of time, Prabhu had created him and chosen him for you."

But he will not bring back baba, Aishani thought tearfully. She was neither interested nor curious to know about this person. Her only objective was her father and how she could meet him.

"True," Guruji concurred as if reading her thoughts, "But strange are the ways of God. Sometimes when you wish too much for something or someone, He may grant you your wish albeit in a miraculous and extraordinary way. Sometimes things are not as they are seen to be; sometimes a great shock has to be given to a person to jolt him or her out of their comfortable cocoon. In your case, it was your father who gave the supreme sacrifice. Though you have always had the power to destroy the demons in any form, you did not have the required impetus to kill it. You were quite comfortable in the fact that since your father was there, everything was going to be alright in the end. At that time your training was incomplete, and you lacked the perfect focus. You still have to train for these two things. To compensate for this, your father had to sacrifice his life. I still shudder to think what would have happened if Pandit Ram Sharan had not given up his life. We would have lost both of you and half of the world's population too."

Aishani did not like to go home and she preferred to stay in the Ashram. She immersed herself in her studies but today she allowed Adheesh to take her home. Dimly she realised that Guruji had been talking about Adheesh. It was Adheesh who chanted the mantra which would take them outside the Ashram and it was Adheesh who made her sit in her father's library. He pulled up a chair and sat in front of her. For some strange reason, Aishani became nervous. She could not sit on the chair nor could she look him in the eye.

The house had somehow sensed Aishani's anticipation and so allowed a few bits of sunlight and air to come inside the library. Reflections and shadows had also begun dancing in the room. The house had permitted this interplay of lights inside the library. Just like Aishani, it seemed as if a heavy weight had been lifted from the house's shoulders.

"Will you have tea?" she asked him shyly. He nodded his assent. In the kitchen, she could not make the tea properly. Did he like brewed tea or boiled tea? With milk or without milk? Oh! What was she thinking? There had been so many revelations in the last few days each more momentous than the other! She took out some chocolate biscuits and *mathris* from their jars and carried them to the library. There were so many questions she had to ask. They had their tea in silence. After some time she could not hold back anymore.

"So," Aishani said in a small voice, "You are the chosen one." Adheesh looked at her in a neutral way.

"Adheesh, what I understand is that the chosen one is ageless; he has to undergo years of *tapa* and meditation and years of harsh and rigorous training in fighting with and understanding the weapons and making them his own. And above all, he has to be purest of heart and mind! That person is you!" Aishani almost accused him but also stared at him in awe.

After what seemed ages, Adheesh broke the silence. "Come now Ash, don't be so perturbed, you did have an inkling right from the beginning."

"Yes I did, but this is so different, Adheesh. It seems I don't know you at all. Who are you, who are your parents, your real parents? Your studies, where did you do your studies and your training, who taught you?" Words tumbled out of her mouth incoherently; she was now looking at him with different eyes, with a mixture of awe, respect, admiration, and reverence. But where was that one emotion that he wanted to see in her eyes? The tenderness for him that he had earlier seen in them.

"Ash, look at me, I am the same person; I am your Adhee."

Aishani looked at him. He can't be my Adheesh, she thought desperately. My Adheesh is a normal person, not this—this God man! Oh!

"Ash, I'll try to explain as much as I can. I, as well as my parents, are descendants of Kshatriya warriors from the time of *Ramayan*a. We have been in the royal army of King Dashratha and his ancestors from time immemorial. Now wait Ash," he admonished, "Don't interrupt, hear me out fully before you start asking questions. When Bhagwan Vishnu in his avatar of Raja Ram, son of King Dashratha, came to this Earth for the sole purpose of killing the Asur king Ravana and his army of *rakshasas,* demons—*bhoot*, *praits, chudails*, even hybrid demons that were more dangerous and cruel than the normal ones, he succeeded in killing them all. But it was Bhagwan's *maya* and the great intellect and cunning of the demons that some of them escaped as they had come to know beforehand that God was coming to destroy them. So they hid, not in normal places but deep inside the Earth and Water and far-flung places in Space.

"Many changed their appearance so much that it was impossible to recognise them and weed them out. Bhagwan Ram along with Sita and his brothers went back to their abode that is Vaikunth, leaving Hanuman in charge of eliminating these creatures and protecting the Earth. We are the special warriors of Shri Hanuman, and hence Shri Ram. Sometimes we are successful in annihilating the demons and sometimes we are ourselves killed. We are born again, we are reminded of our previous births and we continue with our mission from that time onwards. In a nutshell, this is what we have been doing these past ages."

Aishani's head was reeling. She heard everything but could not grasp anything. She just looked mutely at Adheesh. Her mind was getting befuddled with the information. Adheesh looked at her, he knew what she was thinking—either he was mad or she was mad!

"Ash, this will take some time to fully comprehend. There's some more."

She looked at him not knowing what to say, "The question in your eyes—will I always be away fighting these demons, well the answer is yes and the good part is that many of the times you will be alongside me fighting them," he said easily.

Aishani was still without comprehension, "What will I do?" she whispered hoarsely.

"Ash," he took her hand in his, "Ash you are everything. You don't know your powers. You alone can demolish more than half of the demon population. Your ancestors have been personally blessed by Maa Durga."

"Adheesh stop!" she said imperatively. "I know that I have an affinity with Maa Durga, but this. How can I be blessed in such a way to—to fight demons! Where are the demons? I do not see them anywhere!" Her head was reeling.

"No?" he said softly. "Then who killed your father? Why

did he send you to that training school in the forest where in some places even he could not enter without your help? And what were you taught there? Why were you taught the martial arts at all? Why did your father give you that special cloak and other such things?"

"Most of Baba's gifts were related to astrology, mantra, *tantra and totkas*. How do you know about these gifts and you mean to say that Baba knew about all this?"

Adheesh looked at her quietly. She kept her head down, her hair covering her eyes. At one level she was stunned by these revelations, but a niggling doubt was rising in her that all this was not unfamiliar.

Nor did it seem unfair. Did Adheesh know that she had killed the snake? And what had compelled her to kill the snake? She, who could not look at slithery things without a shudder, had gone ahead and killed that humongous snake without a thought except that she had to kill it. Why did she not think about it beforehand?

"Oh, I killed it because it killed Baba." Tears welled up in her eyes at the thought of her father.

Adheesh looked at her, "Ash look inside you. Just because your Baba did not tell you in so many words does not mean that you never thought of it. Your Baba had always wanted to tell you but he did not want to give you a shock nor did he want you to resent the fact that you were the chosen one. You were not only his chosen daughter, you had been chosen by the Gods themselves to rid the world of all the demons or all the cruel and negative beings who have camouflaged themselves so well throughout the ages to continue with their ghastly deeds. Just imagine what the human race has had to endure."

"How do you know all this Adhee? Are you a celestial being or a normal human being?" she asked tremulously.

Adheesh laughed out loud. "Far from it. I am as human as you or the next person." Then in a softer tone he said, "Look both of us are as human as possible, but the sooner we recognise ourselves, the easier it will be for us, our elders and the world around us."

"Who are we Adhee? How do we recognise ourselves? Do we have superpowers?" She asked mystified, "I do know that the demons have superpowers, but then they are a different species altogether. They just have raw supernatural strength, lust for power and raw flesh and blood and extreme cunningness; they are extremely intelligent and have powers in the air, water and on earth too. Are we different too Adhee?" She said all this in one breath.

"Yes Ash, we are different too. But there is a bigger difference here. We are human beings. Human beings are physically weaker than the demons; there is no doubt about that. What is different about us and our teams is that we have been in the armies of Bhagwan Ram and that many, including us, have been blessed by the Gods and Devtas. These are special blessings which give us special powers. Like you have been blessed by Maa Durga to destroy the demons. This means that just like Maa Durga, in the case of the most dangerous demons, the final blow will always be yours. When Uday has to kill somebody there is no mercy in him. This may seem demoniac, but Uday will always kill for a good cause. Such people are required to destroy the lesser demons. Dithering will just not work; it will only harm the core team. Or take Ruby the descendent of apsaras. There are so many demons whose only weakness is beautiful women and lust. The Gods have to maintain the equilibrium between good and evil but it seems that evil is winning. The apsaras reside in the heavens and are the courtesans of the heavenly courts. They are beautiful, sensuous and very aware and intelligent too. They are at the beck and call of the devtas. For a demon to get entangled with an apsara is a sure means of his destruction. Tejas—his small form and swiftness and elasticity will open so many doors and pave your way. Or Jayant. Jayant and you have a symbiotic relationship. He can anticipate your requirements even before you think of them consciously."

"And you Adhee? How will you be there for me?"

"By simply being there with you and looking after you personally," he smiled guilelessly and melted her heart. In her heart of hearts, she knew that Adheesh was the strongest of all with a sharp calculating brain who would always be with her.

"Human beings are being demonised. This is Kalyug. All this has been written and foretold in our Epics. Each and every member of our team has one or other special power. That way we can be termed as having superpowers, but we are definitely not superheroes of the comic book variety. We are very much human, we have all the strengths and weaknesses of human beings, but we are stronger, more focused and totally pledged to look after you and pave the way for you to fulfill your destiny and hence ours too."

"But Adhee, I don't feel so great or so powerful to be able to stop all these demons, forget about totally annihilating them."

"Now this is your human feeling coming to the fore, which is underestimating yourself. But not to worry, I am there to boost your ego and give you confidence whenever you lag behind."

She smiled tremulously and went into his arms.

After some time Adheesh lowered himself on his knees in front of her. A faint balmy breeze was blowing softly so as to hear what Adheesh was going to say next. He came nearer to her and said almost in a whisper, "We are not given direct guidelines as to how to discover ourselves and our destinies. We search and our paths unfold themselves slowly in front of us. We have to go to Guruji and ask him to bless us for deep meditation for it is only through strongly focused meditation that we shall be able to find ourselves."

This was a month ago. It had taken Aishani that much time to adjust to the new revelations of her life with an inkling of what her destiny was going to be. When she came to terms with her new life, Adheesh suggested that they go to Guruji. Manohar, their friendly teacher and guide of earlier times was hovering outside Guruji's cottage sometimes tending to the plants or just tinkering with something else. They wished him. Manohar's presence implied that a very serious and secretive matter was going to be discussed with them and Guruji was not to be disturbed at all. Sensing this, they themselves became very serious and geared up for whatever Guruji was going to tell them. He was waiting for them.

"It's time now for both of you to fully remember and recognise your destinies. It is not humanly possible even for me to apprise both of you of the full history of your past. Even

I may not know of the subtle nuances. You will have to learn it from each other and from nature."

Without wasting time Guruji took them to a clearing in the nearby forest. "This is where both of you will recall and find the essence of your lives. You will live the life of ascetics, survive on the offerings of this jungle, choose a tree each and meditate under it every day. Once you reach your higher state of awareness, the trees will talk to you and affirm your place in the chronicles of mankind. They will not guide you, they will not direct you, but they will just enlighten you of what you are and what you have been in the context of the larger picture of the things and happenings in the universe, and beyond it too. How soon you arrive at these conclusions depends on the purity of your thoughts and the depth of your meditation. The earth, the water and everything here, that is the *panchbhutas* or the five essential elements will teach you and remind you."

They touched Guruji's feet. Guruji blessed them and left. They saw him briefly and then Guruji shimmered and just faded away. They knew that Guruji had crossed the invisible barrier to this part of the jungle. They turned to look at each other. They were now alone in this forest. It was their forest now. Aishani blushed and Adheesh smiled; they held hands and started walking.

They spent the first three to four days roaming about in the forest. It was a huge forest full of greenery and other myriad colours. On the fifth day, it began raining. They took shelter under the lush branches of a huge tree but got wet nevertheless. Not that both of them minded getting wet. They looked around after the rain stopped. Aishani caught her breath. The water had polished everything in the forest and their true colours had come out. The leaves were greener, the small flowers were redder, the trees and the ground were shining—everything was given a freshly bathed look—what a blessed sight!

After a long time, Aishani's heart was singing. Maybe it was Adheesh's company or the veiled promise by Guruji that they might be sent to the past where her father would complete her training.

There were long stretches of plain fields too. There were huge patches of green and golden yellow where the grass had dried up. A few clouds did float lazily, but apart from that, there was nothing to break the tranquility of the place. It was as if God had made these fields so that hermits and ascetics could just enjoy the calmness of the scene and become peaceful themselves to be at harmony with nature. After a mile or so the real forest began with huge trees and small bushes too.

They discovered small streams in the forest. It seemed as if the birds were also welcoming them with their songs and whirring of their wings. It was all so beautiful, quiet and peaceful. Food had never been a problem for them. They knew how to survive in jungles. They knew how to make a fire, which leaves and branches could be eaten raw and which had to be roasted or boiled. Both of them knew how to make basic utensils from mud. They also dug out edible roots and enjoyed them too. It was all such a big adventure for them. Guruji had instructed them to be just be.

They did not need much in the way of coercion. They had quite correctly presumed a lot about themselves. What Guruji told them did not come as too much of a surprise to them. Walking around the jungle they chose two huge trees for themselves. These were huge banyan trees next to each other. They cleared the area below the trees so that they could sit and meditate. The branches of the trees were so ancient and long that they were inadvertently touching each other. They were guiding the new couple to reach heady heights of imagination opening the doors of heaven. The thick lush green leaves of the branches wanted to hug them and remind them of the roles which their past souls had played.

All the better for us, Aishani mused, I can live here with you all my life, my love, she thought and looked at Adheesh. He also turned and looked at her as if he perfectly understood what she was thinking. Brushing aside these thoughts they sat down in their respective places, closed their eyes and began their meditation. Meditation was not new to them. But this was a different kind of meditation. This was not only about their personal lives but about the history of their lives together. Guruji had left them in this place so that the trees, the brooks, and even the breeze would tell them about their past lives and their responsibilities.

There were so many memories, so many roles they had played through the centuries, sometimes as rulers, sometimes as servants, so many faces, so many characters. All their friends and relatives were also around them most of the times though in different roles. There was no end to the different kinds of roles they had played. Slowly and imperceptibly the gentle breeze started making sense of another kind. It carried them to different levels of their subconscious minds. At one time it would carry them to one part of ancient history, another time to another instance in the past. Even the tinkling and gurgling water of the stream had begun making sense.

Enlightenment came to them at almost the same time. It was like they were two separate entities but in the same cocoon. Because of their long past association with each other, when the trees spoke to them it did not take much effort on their part to understand the language of the trees. When the wind passing through the trees spoke it was like a kaleidoscope of pictures moving at the speed of light. Their strong mental strength enabled them to grasp all the pictures in the same order. When they came out of their reverie and faced each other it was as if they had been together all the time.

It had taken them almost two months of living like hermits in that part of the Gurukul's forest when awareness about their past came to them. They had come to know almost everything about themselves apart from a few stray incidents which they knew would come to them as and when the need arose. But they knew that the present was the most important part of their lives now. It seemed to them that they were already quite late, late for what they weren't quite sure as yet. They knew now that their powers proliferated when they worked together as a team though it would be Aishani who would be precipitating the final act of destroying any demon. In the last two weeks she had learned so much about her existence on this Earth, her relationship with Adheesh and with everyone around her and their fight with the demons. Why did she feel as if she was not ready to face her opponents and beat them? Finally, she made up her mind to share her thoughts with Adheesh.

"Adhee I do not feel scared of the demons, I can face them anytime. But many times I've felt that something is lacking in me, that I am not ready to challenge them as of now. Everything around us is telling us to destroy and annihilate these demons from the face of our Earth," she stopped. Adheesh took her hands in his. He knew that she was thinking of her father. He waited for some time for her thoughts to settle down then said, "Ash, I know that you are not the type of girl to have misgivings just for the heck of it. Even I have noticed your hesitation and I believe you may be right too. But I cannot understand your apprehensions nor can I begin to solve them. Even the least harmful demon will be astute enough to recognise our weakness."

"So what do we do Adhee?" she almost grumbled, "If only Baba was here, he would have known what to do." Tears came to her eyes. She wiped them away angrily.

"Ash, I believe we have learned whatever we had to learn here, at least for the time being. It's time for us to leave this lovely place and go back to the Gurukul. We will have to go to our homes too."

"We will go to Guruji tomorrow and tell him everything—about us, about our enlightenment, about our conversations with nature and about our own doubts. Guruji will have a solution," he said simply.

"Yes Adhee, we'll meet in Guruji's cottage tomorrow morning."

Guruji was in a sombre mood when they went to meet him the next morning. They touched his feet. He blessed them and told them to sit in front of him.

"Your self-doubts are totally justified. Both of you recognise your own capabilities and to a large extent, the capabilities and qualities of the demons also. What you find lacking in yourself is the recognition of the fact that you are really lacking in a number of aspects of demon warfare."

Looking at Aishani Guruji continued, "Because that Nag came out of its self-imposed stupor earlier than expected, your father had to give the supreme sacrifice of his life. A part of your training has been left incomplete because of his untimely demise. This particular training could only have been imparted by Pandit Ram Sharan and nobody else."

Aishani's heart started hammering. Did she really understand Guruji or was there any other meaning? Her mother's face and words came to her mind. She became very still. She dare not look at Adheesh lest Guruji said something else and she missed it.

"I have no choice but to send you back in time because only Pandit Ram Sharan can complete your training."

Then turning to Adheesh Guruji said, "Yours too."

Eyes wide, heart pounding, Aishani now turned to look at Adheesh who was listening attentively to Guruji.

"Do you agree?" Guruji asked them. It was a perfunctory question not really requiring an answer as both of them were more than ready to go back to the past, both to meet her father and to complete their training.

Back in Time

Her heart was singing. Guruji was going to send her back to the past. She would meet her beloved Baba! And the icing on the cake was that Adheesh was going to be with her. "And what about you, Adhee? What do you have to learn from Baba? How much do you know Baba?" She asked him all in one breath.

"Ash I also have to learn a lot from your father, but my learning is different from yours. I am a warrior, you are also a warrior, but you have the power bestowed on you by Maa Durga herself. Nobody can compete with that power Ash."

"Then why did Baba die, why could I not save him," she had whispered with tears in her eyes.

"This had to happen Ash. The snake was coming out of its hibernation earlier than the calculations had predicted. We had no choice, rather your father had no choice but to sacrifice himself. Your training still had to be completed. What you lacked in training had to be compensated by your extreme emotion of rage and hurt at the death of your father."

"We had no choice?" Aishani looked at him in confusion; "Adhee were you aware of it, of—of Baba's death?" her voice broke.

Adheesh looked at her sadly, "I had no idea, Ash, at least not in the beginning. Your father Pandit Ram Sharan has been one of the greatest keepers of the ancient texts of the martial arts as well as the keeper of the list of all living beings in these three worlds. He was or is the greatest guru of *mantra* and *tantra vidyas*. A person with such great powers can utilise the *panchbhutas* at his will or at the will of the Almighty. He is the master of illusion or maya; he can change into any form, he can travel in time, he can change history without anybody being the wiser, his powers are so great that he can do almost anything. His sacrifice was a must, he could kill the serpent himself but the serpent was destined to be killed by you."

"And Guruji?" she asked her curiosity getting the better of her.

"Guruji is your father's guru. He cannot be compared to any human no matter how strong or capable that human being is. Guruji is the direct avatar of Lord Hanuman. He supposedly comes from a higher genealogy than ours."

Adheesh paused for a minute then continued, "Since the Nag came out earlier than calculated, your Baba had to die and your training was left incomplete. This leftover training is of the utmost importance; you just cannot learn it on your own nor can anybody else teach you. It was only Pandit Ram Sharan who could teach you and it will be only Panditji who will teach and train you."

"What do you mean Adhee?" She had a fair idea of what he was going to say now—it was something that she so desperately wanted to hear. Her mother had given her very good hints and her hopes had soared from that time only.

Adheesh smiled at her. He understood her anticipation and excitement, "It means Ash that Guruji will send us to the past so that your father can complete your training."

"Guruji? Do you mean that Guruji will teach us how to go back in time? Won't that take a long time Adhee? Time travel is no small feat to learn," she said impatiently.

"Yes, it will certainly take us a long time to learn this *vidya* and we don't have the time. Because of the accelerated environmental changes, many of the demons are coming out of their hibernation earlier than they had planned. Some of our calculations went haywire because of this. Time is of the essence here. Nothing can be left to chance. From our side, we have to be fully prepared and more. Hence it has been decided that Guruji will send us to the past where you will complete your training and Guruji will only bring us back to the present. And Ash you are just plain lucky that this training will be imparted to you by your father. It could have been any other instructor whose syllabi you had to complete."

After dropping the bombshell of sending them into the past Guruji had sent them to their respective homes and instructed them to come to the ashram on Purnima or full moon night, which was three days away. He had already done the calculations of the time of the beginning of the ceremony. This gave them enough time to mentally prepare themselves for their crossing ahead. Aishani's heart was thudding so loudly that she could hear it. Her mouth was dry with fear and anticipation. There was excitement, she was going to meet her baba and there was fear that something may go wrong. She held Adheesh's hand tightly and silently kept on chanting Maa Durga's mantra.

Guruji had told them to hold each other's hand, close their eyes and concentrate on Maa Durga and mentally chant her mantra. Guruji's strict instructions were that no matter how long it took they were not to open their eyes and under no circumstance doze off to sleep. They would know when to open their eyes. It would be when a very bright light would shine on their faces. They had no idea how long they had sat in Guruji's cottage silently chanting Maa Durga's mantra. Somewhere in the distance they could hear Guruji also chanting some special mantras. Intermittently Guruji would also sprinkle some water on them. It seemed as if they were being pulled into an extraordinary current, as if gravity was pulling them like the strongest magnet on Earth. Their limbs were going to be pulled apart now. It had become impossible to bear the pain and the pull and push of the magnet. At the same time, they felt as if they were being enveloped in a cocoon made of the finest and the lightest gossamer kind of microfibers. They were unable to breathe. Life was being slowly sucked out of them. They did not know whether they were dead or alive.

Suddenly it was over. They could now breathe easily. Both of them felt as if they were flying and soaring and floating in the air. Suddenly a blaze of light hit them, a light so strong that they had to unclasp their hands and cover their eyes even though their eyes were closed. This was the sign which they had been waiting for. Slowly they opened their eyes. They were in the same cottage though everything seemed to be a little different. Guruji was nowhere to be seen.

They looked at each other and smiled hesitantly. Adheesh took her hands in his and gestured to her to go out. Slowly they went out. Even if Adheesh was aware of her hesitation he gave no sign of noticing it, a sign that he was so tense that he could not pay attention to these things. Normally when such things happened Adheesh was the first one to notice them. But their greatest emotion at the moment was curiosity. Had they really come back to the past? There was this fear, this trepidation also. Aishani was going to meet her father, her Baba whom she had seen being turned to ashes by the deadly fire of the serpent Kaalia or his hybrid descendants. This was going back in time.

"Adhee, Baba is still alive?" Her voice was quivering.

"Yes Ash, but not as when you had seen him last. We have gone back two years. Your father was alive then. We are going to meet him as he was back then, that is two years earlier." Adheesh stopped. "Don't ask and think too much now Ash, everything will become clearer slowly. As of now concentrate on meeting your father", he gave her hand a reassuring squeeze. She looked around. Everything was the same and very familiar, but there was a subtle difference, exactly what, she couldn't point out. Of course, déjà vu was there but this was more than that.

After a short while, Aishani couldn't stop herself, "Adhee are we going to my house?"

"No Ash, we are going to Ruby's house."

"Ruby's? But why? Why involve them? They are such simple normal people, plus they won't understand! Can't we meet Baba at a more appropriate place?" Aishani tried to reason.

Adheesh sighed and turned to her, "Ash there are many things which have to be disclosed to you, but they will be told to you by your father. Even I do not know about so many things. These great secrets are divulged only on a need to know basis. Only the great Gurus know about the whole strategy. But this I do know—Ruby and her family are *Rakshaks,* they are your defenders and have some idea of what is happening, but their basic job is to protect you and you only. Now, Ash, I suggest that you put all your thoughts on the back burner and concentrate on meeting your father," he said softly.

Aishani's head was spinning. But she stopped herself. Adhee was right. She had to immerse herself in the present moment. Baba! she thought exultantly, Baba I am coming to meet you!

By now they had reached Ruby's house. Aishani was surprised. The usual hustle bustle and the happy ambience was not there; instead, its aura was quiet with a palpable expectancy.

"Where is everybody?" Ash whispered.

"Don't worry; everybody is here except that they have been instructed to be quiet for your meeting with Panditji."

Slowly they went inside the house and into the room which was a sort of a study. Her eyes scanned the room for someone and there he was! Baba! His back was turned and he was looking out of the window.

"*Pranam Guruji*", Adheesh folded his hands in greeting then turning to Aishani he said, "I am leaving now; I'll see you after a couple of days."

But Aishani hardly heard him. Her eyes were locked on her father.

"Baba!" her voice broke. Pandit Ram Sharan turned. Aishani stared at him; he was the same, her Baba, same serious half smile, the same impeccable dhoti and kurta, the only difference was that his hair was less white. Aishani noticed this unconsciously, her full focus on her father.

"Ash," Pandit Ram Sharan spread out his arms and Aishani ran into them, even his smell was the same. The last few weeks had been almost a blur to her, they were so incomprehensible, but now they rushed back at her and overwhelmed her. She was crying now and shaking too.

"Ash beta, it's alright, it's fine, it's me and I am alright, see." He kept her at arm's length and she looked up at him. "Baba I could not kill that serpent in time, if I had been faster you would have been alive today!" She cried.

Pandit Ram Sharan shushed his daughter, "No beta you could not save me, it had to be so. I had to distract that beast so that you could kill it. There was no other way. But let's put that behind us," he smiled, "Or in the future." Then on a serious note he said, "Ash you have been brought here in the past for a specific purpose."

Aishani looked at her father. Taking a deep breath he said, "Your education in these matters is incomplete. That serpent was intelligent and cunning enough to anticipate great danger to it if it had come out of its hibernation in his own time which would have been catastrophic for our world. Who knows he could have destroyed Mother Earth herself. My death was a very small price to pay for such a huge level of destruction."

Aishani mutely looked at her father trying to comprehend what he was saying.

"But Baba, I am two years back in the past—what about the other Ash who is here and what about me in the present... I mean the future," she smiled tremulously.

"Yes beta, there is an exchange of both your selves. Now you have to be very careful. God forbid if anyone starts suspecting they might think that you are not you. Though they all know and understand their duties, it's better that only concerned people know about it. It's not that you don't talk to them just be a little taciturn. Don't mingle too much and don't talk for a long time."

"Okay Baba, I understand," Aishani smiled.

"Your training begins tomorrow. You are already trained for the next two years. Now you will have to be trained for the leftover two years." He looked at his daughter with pride.

"Yes Baba," Aishani said almost happily now.

"Now go and take rest. Do *Shavasan* and sleep. Tomorrow come to me after your *Suryanamaskar*.

"Yes Baba," she said, "Do I sleep here or do I go to my room in our house?"

"Go to your own room, you'll be more comfortable there."

Aishani walked across to her home. She did not meet Ruby or anybody on the way which was slightly unusual; they were probably told to keep out of her way, she mused. A sudden thought came to her mind. This is where the Shakini had entered her body. None of her friends were here now. They had been instructed to give her space. She blushed at the thought of Adheesh. Uday and Tejas were also such good friends. All of them would have been delighted to know about her. She sighed. There was no question of telling anybody. This was no small matter. She was lucky to be one of the chosen few who were allowed time travel because of their destiny.

As soon as she entered her house her mother called out, "Aishani beta dinner is ready, come soon."

"Coming ma, five minutes," she called out, relieved that there was no sadness or suspicion in her mother's voice. But she was thinking of her mother of two years in the future. This ma was in the past, a happy and contented woman who was not fully aware of what the future held. Freshening up she went and had her food. Ma did notice that Aishani was preoccupied but then that was her sweet daughter, always sober and quiet.

Aishani lay down on her bed; everything seemed to be the same. There were differences, but she did not want to think about them now. She was too exhausted by the events of the last couple of days, mostly unbelievable, but then nothing in her life could be termed as normal, yet, she would not exchange this life for another. Taking deep breaths she slowly drifted off to sleep.

Pandit Ram Sharan was waiting for her when she went to their shop after her breakfast.

"We have to go to the Gurukul to meet Guruji." Aishani nodded. She knew where they had to go. Father and daughter left. Today they were not going by their normal route to the Gurukul. Pandit Ram Sharan wanted to avoid meeting anyone on their way to Guruji's cottage. There were many invisible nondescript doorways all across the Gurukul. The Gurukul was so vast that many of its gateways opened in other states too. It was just that they were not visible to the normal eye nor could they be opened just by touching them. Both father and daughter were required to be there.

This was just a room. There was no furniture, no paraphernalia, no doors, no windows, no other person even, just a faint smell of incense, which was just right for them. Pandit Ram Sharan sat down cross-legged in the center of the room facing south and slowly began his incantations. Aishani waited and when her father finished his ninth verse she went to the wall and flatly put both her palms flat in the middle of the wall. Pandit Ram Sharan continued with his incantations. Flickers of blue and pale yellow sparks flew out of Aishani's palms and disappeared into the wall. It was like different keys entering differently coded locks. Both of them did not pay any attention to this as it was a routine affair and not of much importance to them. These things happened to Aishani whenever she was concentrating or feeling emotional, sad, angry or very happy. This was in her blood handed over to her by her ancestors. Much power had been inherited by her and so much more had to be learned. Baba's death in the present had only precipitated the fact.

After ten minutes of chanting, the wall shimmered and began fading. They waited patiently till it became a small opening. They entered into it one by one, her father first as Aishani had to be protected from all sides. The room was safe. There were such strong protective energies in the room that no demon could enter it, in fact, nobody could even suspect that the room was anything other than a normal room. The moment Aishani stepped inside the door it closed softly behind her and the room was as it was—plain and hermetic, just a nondescript room.

They had entered a dense part of the forest, but both of them knew exactly where to go. The major part of Aishani's supernatural and normal training was over, what was left now was honing up of all her skills—more focus, more breathing exercises, holding of breath for very long periods, mentally making up her own Raksha *kavach*, reacting so fast as to become almost invisible, merciless killing of demons; differentiating between shape-changing demons and other living beings, choosing and using her celestial weapons judiciously, swinging from trees, virtually flying, teleportation, using sound to pinpoint her enemy. One would expect to see other people and living beings in a training center of this magnitude but there seemed to be nobody there but Aishani and her father. They were in that secret part of the forest which no one could see.

Finally, they reached Guruji's cottage, the simple two-room hut with a thatched roof. There were flowering plants around the hut and on the sides were patches with vegetables planted in them. This was the place where Aishani felt most powerful and at peace.

Guruji was expecting them. He was sitting erect on a wooden settee. *Asanas* were laid out for them to sit. There were two *asanas* for each of them. One was a thin woollen carpet over which another mat made of Kusha grass was kept. The dimensions of both these asanas were two feet by two feet. Father and daughter first touched Guruji's feet and then sat reverentially on the Asanas. Guruji turned towards Aishani and smiled with a twinkle in his eyes.

"Happy now?"

Aishani smiled back. This time she saw something else in Guruji's eyes. A question? She brushed away the thought. They had come to take Deeksha and inspiration from Guruji. But she too had become a bit intuitive now. Guruji's eyes were going to state or ask another question. She would have to wait. He could not be rushed.

"Yes Guruji," she smiled back, "Very very happy."

"All in His Hands," Guruji looked up. Father and daughter acknowledged with a nod of their heads. Guruji became serious, "We don't have much time. These demons," he paused then continued, "Millennia ago when they went into hiding and hibernation they managed to steal a few *Divya astras* (celestial weapons) and took these along. But they do not know how to use them. Some of them have tinkered with them and they have been a little successful also. In most cases, they have paid a heavy price for trying to use these celestial weapons. They have died, exploded, imploded, been maimed, incinerated and discovered many other ways of annihilating themselves through these divine weapons. The celestial weapons though technically weapons have much higher levels of intelligence and awareness. Each *Divya astra* is represented by a deity and that deity is invoked to bless and bestow powers to the astra. Huge numbers of demons have died or been killed or blown apart by their insufficient knowledge and maleficent intentions. Though these astras are weapons only, they are divine. They react differently in different hands. The

Asurs have disrespected the *divya astras*, hence they will never succeed in fully utilising them. Nevertheless, even if they are able to use a small fraction of them, that will be enough to harm mankind for more than a thousand years."

Guruji continued, "Through the ages, even our power has decreased. Earlier one warrior could annihilate a hundred demons easily. Now, there is mayhem, chaos, crime and corruption everywhere. The line between good and bad has blurred. Our power has weakened. Sometimes more than one warrior is needed to counter these evil creatures," Guruji looked at Aishani again. She was slowly beginning to comprehend Guruji's words but her guess could be still totally wrong. She waited. Without mincing his words Guruji continued, "Adheesh and you have to work together. This is your destiny. You have worked together earlier also in your previous births. Many of these demons are so strong that they cannot be destroyed by a single human being no matter how strong he or she is. It will take more than one human being's superpowers to destroy them."

He looked directly at Aishani, "You will work together as one, then only the real power will come to counter and annihilate these creatures with the *Divya astras*. Since this is Kalyug, you cannot work as one because of the social stigmas attached, you will have to marry."

Seeing Aishani's startled expression Guruji said, "Nothing will happen without your acquiescence. My telling you this, is just reiterating the fact that you are already partners. You must get married now in this birth. It is already too late."

Aishani looked at her father. There was a benign expression on her father's face but he wasn't meeting her eyes. Oh God!

Baba knew! Finally, Pandit Ram Sharan gave her an innocent look. So it was all decided. It was then that the thought struck her. She was getting married to Adheesh! She blushed. The man of her dreams! She was getting married to him. A thought struck her. Was Adheesh aware of all this? She looked questioningly at Guruji. Guruji nodded, "Yes, he knows beta, he knew it much earlier."

She sat back, flummoxed. So she was the last one to know. What else did these people know which she didn't? But this was a very insignificant thought compared to the incidents which were happening in her life now. She looked at Guruji and her father. Guruji replied to her unasked question, "Yes, those things are not possible. Neither your people nor Adheesh's people can come here," he said.

"Yours and Adheesh's marriage will be *Gandharv vivah.* Only your father and I will be there."

Aishani kept her head down. She did not want Guruji to see her confusion. How could they get married without their loved ones? She was bewildered.

Guruji said, "It is God's will. What has to be done has to be done. Even this marriage is not necessary but in this Kalyug's social context, your marriage becomes mandatory if both of you have to work together." That Adheesh was her partner was a foregone conclusion in her heart. There were no doubts on that score or about their love for each other. But she loved her people of this birth too. Her sweet and brave mother who had sacrificed so much for her home and her children, her happy go lucky brother Jayant, with whom she felt the most comfortable, her darling friend Ruby without whom there could be no celebration. Oh! She loved them so much! The euphoric feeling of being married to Adheesh and the heartache that none of her people would be there to share her happiness and excitement, even her mother or Ruby or Jayant had dampened her spirits.

She had read about Gandharv vivah. It was a marriage where a boy and a girl fall in love with each other and decide to get married. They pledge themselves to each other with or without the knowledge and blessings of their people though sometimes it is with the blessings of their elders. Her marriage would also be the same though it would be blessed by Guruji and her father. Not exactly a Gandharv vivah but a very very quiet affair.

"You will be married in Kintoor in Barabanki in the vicinity of the Parijat tree which is also known as the Kalpvraksha or the wish-fulfilling tree. There are many stories regarding Kalpvrakshas, we will go into that some other time. There are about seven other Kalpvrakshas in other parts of the country of which the Kintoor one is supposed to the most benevolent and powerful. These trees are meant to fulfill your greatest desires. The Kalpvraksha had emerged during the time of *Samudra Manthan* when the ocean was churned by the devtas and the asurs, almost at the beginning of time. It has great powers, now forgotten because of the dirt and corruption sweeping in society. Needless to say, it grants boons to selfless and pure souls who totally focus their thoughts on communicating with the tree."

There was a slight sound near them. Aishani turned towards the sound. It was Adheesh sitting a little behind them.

How long had he been sitting there? she wondered, her face reddening. Their eyes met. Adheesh caught his breath. The rosy tinge of her cheeks made her face glow. She was the most beautiful girl he had ever seen in his life. She had always been beautiful, so full of character and strength. And now they were to be married again in this birth. They smiled at each other with their eyes and their hearts welled up.

They were in Kintoor near Barabanki. There was a manmade boundary around this huge tree. There was a small temple also on the boundary of the tree. She had heard many stories about the Kalpvraksha or the auspicious wish-fulfilling tree. She had come here with her father and Adheesh. When they reached the Kalpvraksha, Guruji was already there waiting for them.

Aishani held her father's hand, "Baba," she whispered, "Till now I didn't really know what a Gandharv vivah was. Now I don't want it."

Pandit Ram Sharan put his arms around his daughter's shoulder, "Ash you don't want to marry? You just have to say and no marriage will take place, destiny or no destiny."

"No Baba, I did not mean that," Aishani said hurriedly, "What I meant was that everybody should have been here."

"I also wish so beta, sometimes we just have to go with the flow, your mother will understand. They walked towards the tree where Guruji and Adheesh were waiting for them. Both Aishani and Adheesh were not wearing any special clothes. It had to be kept a secret from everybody especially from the demon clans and the nefarious supernatural forces. Guruji had created a *Suraksha Kavach* around them.

Could one be acutely happy and sad at the same time? Both Aishani and Adheesh had the same feelings on their wedding day. Extremely happy with each other but they were missing their families and friends. Along with these feelings, there was another feeling of excitement. This was following their destinies, of proving their valour, of removing evil from the face of the earth. This was what they were born for; this was what they wanted to do.

Their marriage was simple enough. They had to make their vows themselves. Hand in hand they went around the Parijat tree seven times and then came and sat in front of Guruji and her father. Guruji whispered some mantras and placed some sacred *samagri* on the ground and evoked the sacred fire.

"Make your promises to each other," Guruji prompted them. He did not conduct the ceremony himself as theirs was a Gandharv vivah. Aishani looked at Adheesh and said, "I accept you as you are now and who you will become. I will always support you and I will always accept your support. I will always love you and have faith in you and follow you everywhere. I will look after you to the best of my abilities in this world and beyond too." She stopped her heart too overwhelmed to say anything more, her eyes filled with tears; this was the moment she had been waiting for throughout her life, the culmination of her wishes and desires.

Adheesh took her hands in his and said, "I will always look after you and cherish you in all spheres of our lives. I will always be with you in this world, beyond this world, in this life, and in all other lives too."

They exchanged garlands. Then with folded hands, they

touched Guruji's feet and then her father's. Both of them blessed them profusely.

Pandit Ram Sharan wiped his tears. His daughter was in safe hands now. He knew that now Aishani would always be protected and loved. He looked at Guruji. There was just a shade of smile on Guruji's face; it seemed to Pandit Ram Sharan as if it was a smile of relief. Guruji blessed the newlyweds with more chanting of mantras and then sprinkled *gangajal* on them. Aishani and Adheesh turned towards the Parijat tree or the Kalpvraksh, touched its base, and asked for its blessings.

Honeymoon

Everyone had returned to their places. Aishani and Adheesh had commenced their training in the martial arts college and their academics by studying in the library. Things were back to normal. After the classes in the evening, they always met on the periphery of the ashram. Nobody came to this side. It was their special place and they looked forward to meeting and sitting here for some time every day. Adheesh knew how stressed Aishani was. He took her in his arms and looked at her. There were tears in her eyes.

"Don't cry my love; I know how conflicted you are at the moment. This should be a happy time for us. As for me I am happy wherever you are happy."

"Oh Adhee, without the others I do not feel married. I love you so much, but it seems as if I am being pulled in opposite directions. I cannot abandon the love and sharing of our people for our own sakes."

Aishani closed her eyes. A couple of sparkling tears escaped from her. eyes, "Adheesh, this is not how I had imagined my marriage to be. Of course it had to be you, but not this way."

"I totally understand Ash and I love you and respect you for that. I also wished that my people were there for our marriage, but we have to bow to the directive of our commander and that is Guruji. It is when you walked into my life like a breath of fresh air and sunshine that I have finally understood the meaning of living."

So nothing had changed. And that was what was worrying Guruji. He knew that both Aishani and Adheesh were very much in love with each other and had wanted to get married to each other. But there did not seem to be any excitement around them. Guruji was perplexed. He thought for a long time and then it struck him. Not being a family man Guruji was not really in the know of relationships. Even Pandit Ram Sharan seemed a bit worried about this lack of response between Adheesh and Aishani. And then he realised. Adheesh and Aishani, even though they were very much in love with each other, were feeling guilty about their *Gandharv vivah*, about keeping the whole thing a secret and not involving anybody even their parents and siblings and friends. They had not really planned their wedding but whatever had been there at the back of their minds definitely included their friends and families. But Guruji knew and Pandit Ram Sharan knew that in order to kill the demonic forces it was imperative that Adheesh and Aishani consummate their marriage.

Guruji looked at Panditji, "Don't worry Ram Sharan. The children will come together in all ways. I have sent for Kameshwar and his partner Rati. They will take care of everything."

Pandit Ram Sharan was perplexed as he did not know who Kameshwar and his partner were. He looked at Guruji quizzically. Guruji smiled at him and then it dawned on Panditji. Guruji was summoning the God of love himself albeit in the modern form. Guruji was calling Kamdev and Rati themselves! They would be playing Cupid to Adheesh and Aishani. Well, greater times required greater ingenuity also.

"Ram Sharan let us go outside, we will meet them there."

"Yes Guruji," Pandit Ram Sharan agreed though he was a bit puzzled. Why did Guruji not want to meet Kamdev and Rati in his cottage? He mulled it over for some time. They had walked quite a distance by now. Then it struck him. Guruji was the disciple and follower of Hanuman who was a confirmed bachelor who never went near a woman. Same was the case with Guruji. Kamdev and Rati's mere aura radiated sensuousness. That could not be allowed in Guruji's cottage. Hence they were meeting outside somewhere in the Gurukul.

They waited. Very soon a very handsome man strolled in. With him was a very beautiful woman. Both of them were dressed casually in adherence to the prevalent fashion wearing torn stressed jeans and t-shirts. In spite of their casual attire, his masculinity and her sensuousness shone through. They were smiling and oozing confidence. The only way Kameshwar could be described was by his classic features. His eyes were brown with flecks of green in them. His lips were pale pink, his nose thin and pointed. His strong jaws and neck were gracefully attached to his strong muscular shoulders and biceps. He had a strong chest and strong bold thighs and calves. Other men would naturally pale in comparison with him. One word from him was enough to make a woman swoon. To top it all he had a stylish guitar strung around his neck.

Rati, on the other hand, was so beautiful and sensuous that not only men but even women found her irresistible. There was a hint of her cleavage showing from the top two open buttons of her thin shirt. Her soft and silky golden hair flowed till her waist. Her arched eyebrows and pink pouting lips spoke volumes.

They came and made the gesture of touching Guruji's feet and waited for instructions. Without wasting time Guruji told them about Adheesh and Aishani.

"These children, Adheesh and Aishani, have been each others' partners and soulmates through the ages and are totally in love with each other. They have just been married too," Guruji paused. "Unfortunately, in this birth they had to come two years back into the past for which they were not ready and even though they are married now, it was a Gandharva vivah and none of their family and friends were present there to share their happiness. This thought has troubled them so much that that they are unable to consummate their marriage." Kameshwar and Rati looked at each other knowingly and smiled politely at Guruji. They had made Gods love each other, these were but mere human beings albeit superior ones. This was child's play for them. Meanwhile Guruji had summoned Adheesh and Aishani also.

"This is Kameshwar and his wife, Aishani and Adheesh," Guruji introduced them. All four of them folded their hands in namaste. Then turning to Adheesh, Guruji said, "You know from time to time we get people from other Gurukuls. Kameshwar and Rati are our highly esteemed guests. They would like to do a tour of the Gurukul. Seeing the whole place may take more than a week, but we can show them the primary areas. The college will be closed for a few days. But you all will have to stay here because moving outside at the moment will not be very feasible. Kameshwar and Rati are new to these parts. They will also be staying here. Why don't both of you take them around till the time the college opens up again."

"Yes Guruji," Adheesh said respectfully though he was a bit surprised at this strange request. Even Aishani was surprised. Anyone could have shown the guests around the premises, in fact, there were people designated for this very purpose. But Guruji wanted them to do this work. So be it.

They turned towards the guests and smiled, "Come, we'll show you to your quarters. After you freshen up we'll first start with the outer periphery of the college." Adheesh escorted them outside Guruji's cottage and led them towards the guest quarters. Both Adheesh and Aishani met them after sometime and they started walking towards the outer periphery. "It is mainly a forest but not like any kind of a normal forest; if one knows just a little about forests then one can live here for years amongst the flora and fauna, it is so enchanting," Adheesh paused. Why had he used the word enchanted? He had never even thought of the jungle as enchanted. As they walked around, he had to admit it did look much better and more beautiful than the last time he was here. He was puzzled. What had changed? Not a single thing. He looked at Aishani for confirmation. She also seemed a bit disconcerted. Aishani looked at him. The world had suddenly started to look very beautiful. A silent song had started playing in her heart. She looked around. Had the branches of the trees sprouted soft light green leaves or was it just her imagination? Were there pink flowers also sprouting? Beyond in a clearing was a small deserted hut. Nobody lived there now. It was probably an old guard post from ancient times abandoned because now there was strict hi-tech round the clock surveillance around the Gurukul.

"Oh look, it's so pretty," Rati cooed on noticing the cottage, then turning to Adheesh she asked, "Can I go inside? Does anybody live here?"

Taken by surprise, Adheesh answered, "I suppose so, nobody lives here, I'm sure there's nothing inside, but of course you can go in."

"Oh, thank you so much," Rati clapped her hands in childlike glee and went inside the hut. Kameshwar smiled sheepishly at them, shrugged his shoulders, and then followed Rati inside. Adheesh and Aishani waited outside. From inside came the sound of the strumming of the guitar. It had a hypnotic soothing effect on them, as if somebody was singing to their souls. Its sweet sound was a balm for their bruised souls in the most divine way.

Adheesh and Aishani sat down on the stump of a tree and waited for them to come back. Aishani had this strong urge to go near Adheesh. She went up to him and took his hand. Sparks flew. The sparks had sort of faded away in the past couple of months. But now they flew and how! Electricity crackled between them and it seemed to go on for a long time. They were getting attracted to each other again and they just wanted desperately to be with each other alone. There was so much to talk about, so much to share. From the corner of her eye she saw Kameshwar and his wife stare in shock when their sparks flew. To Adheesh and Aishani there was spring all around. A soft wind was blowing, a cuckoo was singing, fluffy clouds were chasing each other and the world was again becoming such a wonderful place. All her dark thoughts and problems receded. There was only Adheesh in front of her; Adheesh her lover, her partner, her everything. She forgot that she had to show Kameshwar and his wife the college and its myriad offerings. She had even forgotten about them. When she looked at Adheesh she was surprised that he was also looking at her in the same way. Everything faded into oblivion. There were only the two of them. They embraced each other. How good that felt. They were now on fire for each other.

Very soon Kameshwar and Rati came out of the hut holding hands and smiling at each other conspiratorially. Kameshwar and Rati looked at them. It was not a normal gaze. It was the enchanted and amorous love arrow of Kamdev and Rati, an arrow which had pierced the hearts of even celestial beings. These two were mere humans who were in love with each other. They were not even required here, but Guruji's orders had to be followed. Little did they know about the unleashing of Adheesh's and Aishani's superpowers and the importance and essence of time!

Kameshwar watched them and then smiled at his wife. As soon as they saw the sparks flowing between the two of them Kameshwar knew that they did not have much of a job here. He casually gestured to the hut. Immediately that place was turned into a most beautiful arbour with a bed made of flowers. The air was redolent with the heady scent of jasmine and roses. Both Adheesh and Aishani were shocked when they saw such obvious magic. But they were so far gone in their love for each other that they could not pay much attention to these mundane things. They just wanted to melt into each other.

"You two seem to be a bit off colour," said Kameshwar meaning just the opposite, "Why don't go and relax in the hut for a while. Rati and I will continue on the tour by ourselves." He winked, "It will be more adventurous too."

Adheesh and Aishani did not require any more suggestions or persuasion. They meekly acquiesced and went inside the hut. They did not know how they sat on the bed and how the bed was covered with the most beautiful canopy giving them complete privacy. They just held each other tightly and drifted into love.

Space

The stage was being set very swiftly. It was another matter that the preparations may have taken years, decades or in some cases even ages, all depending on the incubation and cunningness of the beasts and the groundwork and preparedness of the fighters. They had been expecting these female demons for some time now. They could spawn hundreds of their own kind in a matter of minutes and scatter them into space. These offsprings became adults almost immediately and in turn, could produce their own spawns. This way they were used to terrifying the other beings in space. All this had stopped when Maa Durga and then Bhagwan Ram had annihilated them. These were space creatures and brilliantly cunning. When their ilk was being demolished by Bhagwan Ram and his formidable army, they flew high into space much above the Earth's solar system, changed their forms and hid and became dormant.

They fixed their internal clocks for waking up at different times according to their age and powers. On one hand, Aishani was raring to go with her newly released powers; on the other hand, there was Adheesh with his sober analytic brain, assessing the situation from all angles. And then there was Guruji in deep meditation almost in a trance in front of them. By now Aishani and Adheesh knew that this meeting was about a legion of evil creatures that had come out of their hibernation and were now roaming in space creating chaos and havoc. Both of them had ideas of their own.

Aishani was thinking that if only they had a cloaking device with which they could become invisible and destroy these demons. But sadly the invisible cloak that she had was not very strong, to begin with, and she could not fly with it. It was just something which her father had given her to play around with. Adheesh also knew that even if the cloaking device was strong enough to fool the demons, they would still have to have divine weapons to demolish the demons, all of which seemed impossible as of now. They kept on mulling over these problems and waited for Guruji to give them instructions. Eventually, Guruji opened his eyes and smiled at them. They touched his feet respectfully. Guruji smiled and blessed them.

"It warms my heart to see such a beautiful, warm-hearted couple. Both of you are a balm for my sore eyes and broken heart," Guruji declared.

"Broken heart?" Aishani looked at Guruji questioningly.

"Beta, when you have lived as long as I have and seen such

great upheavals and chaos, good and great people killed and dying in front you, your heart is bound to break into irreparable pieces. The heart mends a little when it sees and meets warm and loving people like both of you." Both of them smiled and waited for Guruji to tell them why he had called them.

"Well children, now the time for actual warfare has come. We are the guardians of the galaxy and even the great universe beyond. Some of the demons have come out of their hibernation but are still in hiding. Initially, they were just a couple of hundreds. In the vast sea of space, they were lost. Now that they have gained consciousness they found that they were too lonely and too far apart. There was almost nobody to fight and kill and torture. So they did what naturally came to them. They started multiplying which was less of multiplication and more like proliferation. So now our space is full of these demons. They will anytime now dive down on the Earth in hordes and cause destruction and mayhem everywhere. It will be akin to the tsunami waves except that these waves will not erupt from the seas but swoop down from space. This will result in the destruction of the Earth itself. It is already quite late."

Adheesh and Aishani waited patiently. Both of them now knew why they had been summoned here. Guruji had been waiting for their marriage to be consummated. Aishani blushed at the thought. Guruji knew that both of them together now had more power than all the demons put together. Saying this, Guruji took them to another part of the Gurukul. Though both had thought that they knew every part of their college and the forest, this was one place they were not even remotely aware of. When Aishani dared to ask Guruji about this he said, "Yes beta, there are many things and many places in this forest of which both of you are not aware. In fact, this also is like passing your exams. One has to graduate to these things gradually. There are faster ways also, for that you have to have Bhagwat Kripa of which both of you have in plenty," Guruji said seriously. Aishani and Adheesh looked at each other with a hint of a smile. There was no arrogance or pride in their smiles just a graceful acceptance of the fact.

"These divine weapons are handed over to selected people for one-time use only, after which they automatically return to their original owners, the devtas and the Gods. But since these weapons become friendly in human hands there is always the fear that humans can recall them. Human beings may use the celestial weapons indiscriminately and in their foolishness bring pandemonium and heartbreak to everybody on Earth. Hence, after their one-time use, their memory is obliterated from those human minds. Remember, human beings are not very far removed from *rakshasas* or demons as far as greed and violence are concerned."

Guruji continued, "You will be given a team to work with and provide the necessary back up. These are the Divya astras which will help you in destroying these demons in space. I don't have to tell you much about it. I have called you to discuss the strategy of these attacks and to bless you." They both touched his feet. Guruji blessed them and then drew them together to discuss their strategy.

"Remember, surprise and total secrecy are of the utmost importance and don't underestimate your enemy. Can you imagine any human being going into hibernation for centuries and then coming out of this dormancy with all their faculties intact? There is only one factor where human beings score over demons. This X factor is their kindness, mercy, empathy and compassion. These demons will attack your psyche and emotions. I have no doubt that both of you will be successful in demolishing them. But you have to be more careful. The date and time have already been fixed according to the position of the stars. But there is a time when their energy lags a bit. That is the time when we have to hit them. We also have to make sure that there is no hint of any eclipse as that makes them stronger. We also have to ensure that we hit them when we are the strongest. All these calculations have been painstakingly done. We cannot afford to leave anything to chance."

Both Adheesh and Aishani were listening to Guruji with rapt attention.

"Now we come to your divine weapons," Guruji smiled. "You probably know much more about your weapons and how to use them than I."

"Adheesh, you will be using the Vayu Astra and Aishani, you will be using the Narayan Astra."

Both Aishani and Adheesh nodded their heads. It had taken them more than a month to master these divine weapons. Apart from knowing the mechanical aspect of the weapons, they also had to attune their minds, body, and emotions to that of the accoutrements of these weapons. If any of these did not perfectly match they knew that the weapon would refuse to function. Adheesh chanted the Vayu mantra while Aishani chanted the Narayan mantra at dawn and at dusk, sitting in front of their respective weapons. In the beginning, nothing happened but after a couple of weeks, they sensed an imperceptible change in the demeanor of the weapons. This was something which only they could make out. Gradually after that, these weapons began responding to them. After four weeks they knew that the weapons were ready to be used.

The Vayu Astra was the weapon of Vayu devta. It had the power of raising anything from a light breeze to the most violent storms and tornadoes in this world and above it too, that is, it could create huge tempests in space and absolutely no one and nothing would be able to counter it. It could rage for hours, days or weeks and suddenly disappear as if nothing had happened.

The other astra was the great Narayan Astra which even the devtas yearned to possess. It was the astra of Bhagwan Vishnu, one part of the holy trinity of Brahma, Vishnu, and Mahesh. The Narayan Astra was a destroyer in all its totality. It would latch on to its target, chase it to any lengths and destroy it. There was another option, however. The astra gave its victim the choice to either get destroyed or surrender to it unequivocally. Either way, the enemy was destroyed or had changed by surrendering to it unconditionally.

No human being could ever hope to see these weapons let alone use them. It was their accumulated karmas through the ages that Gods bless and bestow on them the one time use of these weapons. Adheesh and Aishani were the most qualified to use these celestial weapons. One life's prayers and yogas were not enough for them to be allowed to use them. Through the ages, Aishani and Adheesh had proved themselves, again and again, to be fit to qualify to use these weapons.

They sat with Guruji for some more time discussing and listening to his guidelines. Finally, when he had painstakingly given them each and every instruction, he led them to a part of the forest which they had never seen or even been apprised of.

They had been coming to this part of the forest for almost a month now. It seemed nobody was aware of this kind of forest in the ashram. Even Adheesh and Aishani were not conscious it. They had got to know about it only when Guruji took them there with their divya astras. For them entering this part of the forest was easy enough. One could not see the celestial weapons or touch them till the time one qualified for them. It was a sort of an exercise for them to enter this part of the forest which after a week became second home to them. After leaving the main jungle they would start walking towards its northern side. They were given the Invisible mantra by Guruji so even if there was any negative energy or demon lurking nearby, it would not be able to follow them to their destination. This was a very strong and effective mantra, for example, if they crossed a tree or any other solid object, it would not be obscured by their silhouettes.

They were praying to the deity or the possessor of the particular celestial weapon. Depending on the proficiency of the person praying to it, the weapon's deity would respond or not. In this part of the world, only Adheesh and Aishani were accomplished and blessed enough to attain this high level of communion with these weapons and their respective deities. Guruji knew that for Aishani and Adheesh to use the weapons successfully, the essence of the deities would have to enter inside them. Only then the weapons would begin to recognise them and respond to them.

In the beginning at Guruji's behest when they touched these weapons nothing happened. The weapons were just like any piece of antique metal or artifact. There was no question of any response; after all, they were just carved out of iron and wood and a few other metals. But both Aishani and Adheesh knew better. Not to be deterred, both made a clearing for themselves to sit in front of the weapons. Everyday they would sit in front of the weapons with folded hands and meditate. They waited patiently and continued praying. These were the weapons of Devtas and Gods. They would open up to them only if approved by the Gods and Devtas.

Gradually, they started noticing an imperceptible luminosity in the weapons which seemed to be increasing. Then they thought they heard a low pitched humming from the weapons. They held their breaths and touched hands. As soon as their hands touched the humming increased so much that it was almost like a loud melody now. The astras had recognised their deities in them and understood that they had personally blessed this couple. They knew now that they would be soon guided by the weapons on how to use them. Very soon they were allowed to touch the weapons and feel them. They made two platforms, one for each weapon, spread clean, red and yellow cloth over the platforms and lovingly and respectfully placed their weapons over them. It was as if they were becoming one with their weapons who sensed that Adheesh and Aishani had been blessed by their masters—Vayu Dev and Narayan or Bhagwan Vishnu. In a sense, it was the weapons themselves which were teaching both Aishani and Adheesh on how to use them. Not that they actually used them, because they would be using them only once. That would be enough. The weapons were so powerful that they would annihilate all the demons and malignant spirits who had multiplied and were now roaming freely in space. All this was done in total secrecy. The demons were smart and intelligent enough to sniff out any planned warfare and strike against them. And like so many innumerable times they would thwart this plan too if they got only a whiff of it.

At last, the day for which they had been preparing arrived. Guruji came to meet them which in itself was an unprecedented thing.

"Well children, tomorrow morning is the time. It will be Pushya Nakshatra and Amrit Siddhi Yog too, the perfect time for us and a bad time for them. I don't have to tell you anything, both of you know the drill very well. The weapons are prepared. Pay your obeisance to them again, this time to actually fire them. The Vayu Astra once pulled will enter space at supersonic speed and blow all the demons to the Eastern side of our solar system where Surya Dev would be just coming out. The weaker of the demons will be burnt to cinders by the fire of the Sun, but these will be few in numbers. There will be hundreds of stronger ones to whom apparently nothing will happen, but they will be most uncomfortable confronting the rays of the Sun and hence become somewhat weakened. They are not used to being in light and heat. Only after Vayu Dev blows and throws all the demons in one place that the Narayan Astra will be released."

Turning to Aishani Guruji continued, "Just before you release the Narayan Astra you may see lots of hallucinations and hear many voices from your friends and loved ones imploring you to postpone or cancel this endeavour and go and immediately help them. They will beg you not to use the Narayan Astra now. You may also see me telling you about some change of plans. Do not pay attention to these entreaties as they will be there only to distract you. There will be many other distractions and beguilements, your own self-doubts will be foremost. The demons are masters in creating illusions and hallucinations. But you, both of you are bigger and greater than the demons. Be firm on your focus. Don't let anything or anyone distract you. You just have to keep your mind and body steady to give the order with full courage and determination. The weapons will take over after that. With my blessings and by God's grace, you will succeed."

Before leaving, Guruji handed over a small satchel like bag to them. "There are some Ayurvedic medicines here. I know you have some with you. I am just adding some more to them. Your short supply may get depleted. There may or may not be any requirement to use them, but it's better to keep them just in case you need some more time to recoup," Guruji was deliberately vague.

Guruji sprinkled mantra infused gangajal on them and left. His body shimmered on the boundary and then slowly faded away.

The next day both of them got up before dawn. The sky was still a dark blanket. After completing their ablutions they went and sat in front of their respective weapons. The weapons were shining luminously and there was a low hum emanating from them. By now both Adheesh and Aishani were so attuned to the weapons that could make out that the weapons were bursting with energy and were raring to go. They folded their hands and prayed. The sky had turned a lighter shade of grey and pink and very soon there would be sunrise. Adheesh got up first. They had held hands earlier and derived strength and sustenance from each other.

Now they were not even looking at each other. They were totally focused on their own jobs. As soon as the first rays of the sun rose in the sky Adheesh picked up the Vayu Astra, touched it to his forehead, and whispered some mantras into it. The astra responded to him immediately. Slowly and deliberately, Adheesh pulled the string and it went off in the North West direction. It was in the shape of a huge half disc. Adheesh knew that from the north west it would fly towards the East where the sun was now coming up. Very soon with their new found powers and far-sighted vision, they would be able to see these happenings in space.

It started off as a small gust of wind and then quickly began building up. They could now see the phenomena in space. It was exciting to see and hear the power of the rising wind proving that its creator was definitely more powerful. It was on a gargantuan scale, a scale which their finite minds would fail to understand. This was a savage and unyielding wind showing its angry raw power and this was just a sample. The demons tired after their nighttime orgies were caught unawares. The sheer magnitude of the cosmic tsunami sent shock waves throughout the solar system and even time was shocked to a standstill.

The wind was so powerful and tenacious that the demons could not combat against it even if they had wanted to. The strong gales herded them from all directions and pushed them towards the north-east direction. There all of them floated in space against the tornado, screeching, howling and protesting. The weaker ones would die the moment the Sun's rays struck them, but it would have no effect on the stronger ones though they would feel a bit uncomfortable. Very soon the strong wind turned into a huge tornado. The huge tornado multiplied into many tornadoes and began sucking the demons in its tail. No matter how hard the demons tried to break free from the clutches of the tornadoes they could not break off. Their bodies and limbs strained against the onslaught. And there they kept on hovering and writhing till the time all the demons were together in the same space.

Dawn approached and the eastern sky was lit up. The sun was going to ride on his golden chariot beginning from the horizon. It was a sad beginning though for the demons. There was no rest for them now and no sleep too, only unexpected torture, misery and agony.

By this time both Adheesh and Aishani could see what was happening in space, how the Vayu Astra had created not one but several tornadoes which were engulfing all the demons in a vice-like grip. So intense was their power of sight and sound that they could actually see each and every demon being swept up in the funnel of the tornado and then being swallowed up in its upper part. They could also hear their hideous, blood curling and eerie screeching as they were being swept away in the vortex of the tornados. The numbers were so huge that it seemed that the entire solar system was covered by these locusts like demons.

The sky was lightning up but the sunrise seemed to turn into night again as a result of the great multitude of demons. Jagged streaks of lightning would periodically light up the whole sky reassuring them that all the demons were in one place. This kept on happening for the next sixty minutes or so. Finally, all the demons were entrapped in the tornadoes, which were dancing a macabre spin in the growing sunlight.

It was Aishani's turn now. Folding her hands in obeisance she reached out towards the Narayan Astra. Bolts of electricity were coming out from the astra.

"Aishani beta, wait!"

Aishani whirled around. It was her father Pandit Ram Sharan. But how could this be possible? Baba was dead. But they were in the past and Baba had undertaken her training also. Baba was alive in the past.

"Baba?'

"Yes beta, it's me. I had to come to you because this is not the right time. You cannot use your astra at this time. It will go waste and its power will dissipate."

Aishani paused, "But Baba, Guruji specifically told us about this time."

She saw someone behind Baba, but she could not see the person clearly. She tried to go closer to see who that familiar-looking person was. For a moment she forgot that they were not to cross the periphery of this part of their base.

Before she could do that or say anything she felt a strong arm around her shoulders. Baba had slightly faded, but there were tears in his eyes. Shocked Aishani looked at him. Why was baba crying? Her father was the strongest man in her life, both mentally and physically. He faced every adversity squarely. Then why were there tears of despair and helplessness in his eyes? There had to be a very strong reason for this. She put out her arms to embrace her father. For that, she would have to cross to the other side of the jungle which was just a few feet away. She again felt the tug of the strong arm around her shoulders. She turned around. It was Adheesh. He was looking at her very intensely and urgently. Baba moved a bit and now she could see the other person who had earlier been hidden from her view. It was Guruji!

"Aishani beta wait," Guruji said urgently, "There has been a miscalculation! The exact time for destroying these demons is not now; it is at a later stage. The scientists are working overtime to pinpoint the correct time."

"Ash we're losing precious time. You have to begin your operation now," Adheesh said impatiently.

"But Adheesh, look, Baba is here, he is saying that the timing is not right and the work has to be postponed. And look, Guruji is also here, he is also saying the same thing!"

"What! Where is Babuji? And where is Guruji?"

Aishani turned towards her father and Guruji. They seemed to be fading away. Aishani knew this was because they were on the other side of the impassable territory. Neither they nor the others could pass this line as the consequences would be grave if they did so.

"Ash I don't see them anywhere. Focus Ash, use your astra now. There is no time to be wasted," he said sharply. "Your baba and Guruji are not here, this is the sorcery of the demons, just to shift your attention. Look at the Narayan Astra. Had it not been the precise time it would not be crackling and humming. The astra's timing is more perfect than ours."

Aishani stood there undecided.

"Don't waste time Ash," Adheesh almost implored.

"Beta," it was Pandit Ram Sharan again, "Trust me, the time is not right, it has to be postponed. Don't use the Vayu Astra now beta. You won't be able to use it again," he said urgently.

"But baba, the Vayu astra has already…" Aishani stopped short. Baba did not know which astra she was going to use. He thought that she was going to use the Vayu Astra. She looked at Guruji. He was looking unconcerned. Her father's apparition faded. Guruji was also looking hazy. In her father's place was a huge black mass which rapidly disappeared. Guruji was still there but growing dimmer by the moment.

She looked at the Narayan Astra. It was shining brightly and humming almost impatiently. Had there been any error, the astra would have just become silent. She shook her head. Adheesh knew that there would be such a contingency and he was prepared for it also. They had been made partners not only because they were in love with each other but to give power and sustenance to each other, too. He took both her hands in his and held them strongly. Aishani shook her head and looked at Adheesh only for a second. She was ready to execute her work. Pandit Ram Sharan and Guruji were not there anymore. Guruji had warned them earlier about such happenings which would distract her. They would bother her more because she at one level was more emotional than Adheesh. Secondly, the demons would always select and pinpoint her, as the last nail in their coffin would always be hers.

She picked up the Narayan Astra, touched her forehead with it and whispered the Narayan mantra into it. Her concentration was at its peak now. Initially, the astra was like a small round disc which increased gigantically in size as it went up in the air. It was like two huge discs joined together. Between the discs were millions of multiple guided missiles and interceptors. The discs rotated clockwise and anti-clockwise. The lower disc generated enough magnetic field to provide the necessary lift to the Narayan Astra. The upper disc provided the speed and maneuverability to the astra. The main feature of the Narayan Astra was the launch of two astras at the same time, one acting as an interceptor and destroying the incoming missiles or enemies or demons; and the other destroying the base of the enemy which would attack the Narayan Astra. This was the only astra which once released could not be reversed. Once the missile locked on to a target or victim it had to destroy it. There was no escape for the victim.

The intensity of the Narayan Astra would increase proportionately with the resistance shown by the enemy or the demons. But like its possessor, Vishnu Bhagwan, there was always one door left open for the victim for his or her redemption. In this case it was total and unconditional submission in utter humility to the astra.

Aishani activated the astra exactly as she had been trained. There were a couple of clicks, and then with a whoosh the astra started rotating its top disc in a clockwise direction and the bottom disc in anti clockwise direction. It started climbing up, its momentum increasing as it went up and very soon it was out of the Earth's atmosphere and out of human sight. Adheesh and Aishani could see and follow its trajectory as they had been given special powers for this very important and dangerous mission.

Soon the discs were inside the swarm of the screeching demons. It was as if a big top was spinning on a dark bed of swarming insects. They also knew that the whole operation was in the radius of hundreds of miles. Fascinated and repelled, they watched and heard the painful, ear-splitting screeching of the demons. The Narayan Astra was demolishing and killing the demons without any discrimination. The demons were not even aware of the loophole which could save their lives. But some of the very cunning demons did remember something about the Narayan Astra, reassured in the knowledge that the astra was with Bhagwan Vishnu and nobody else could use it.

Never in their wildest imagination had they dreamt that the Narayan astra would come back to maul and haunt them. Even after knowing about the catch, many of them were too egotistical to bow down to the might of the Astra as that went against the very grain of their existence. However, some did take the decision and humbly surrendered to the might of the astra and its lord Bhagwan Vishnu. They folded their hands and bowed their heads humbly in total obeisance. This surrender was in totality and not for the moment only. The demons knew it and the Astra knew it. Without pausing even for a moment, the astra skimmed over this rare handful of demons and continued its annihilation of the others. Adheesh and Aishani watched this breathtaking sight in awe and bewilderment. They were hundreds of miles away yet they could see and hear each and every sound and sight of the destruction. This carnage which was taking place in space was far away from the Earth's gravitational pull. Since there was no gravity in this part of the space, many demons were either thrown away or just floated in space, their dead bodies mutilated and crushed. Suddenly it was all over.

Gently they placed the celestial weapons in their cases and then prostrated themselves in front of the astras with their hands folded. They prayed and thanked them for saving humanity and the Earth from the demons. They prayed and chanted their gratitude and thankfulness repeatedly till they got a response from the astras. This was in the form of a mental message from the astras acknowledging their gratitude. They opened their eyes and looked at the weapons which were humming and shining more than ever now. Slowly, in front of their eyes, the lustre and radiance of the astras began dissipating till the time they totally disappeared. They knew that the weapons had returned to their original slot in the antique room of the museum of the Gurukul.

Adheesh and Aishani found themselves looking at a clearing in the jungle. Exhilarated they looked at each other. What an experience! Their bodies and minds felt lighter. They hugged each other giddily. They had done it! Wait! Wait! What had they done? And who and what had they destroyed? Puzzled they looked at each other. Their memory of the whole operation was fading fast, though they tried very hard to remember all the incidents. But these were the weapons of the Gods. That they were given the honour to use them was in itself the greatest approval. Did they really use these weapons? If so then where were they? It did not matter whether they remembered or not, what mattered was that they had done something great.

Adrenaline was still flowing through their veins; their hearts were hammering against their chests as they walked. Guruji would be waiting for them. Yes, Guruji would tell them everything about this great adventure of theirs. They were positive that they had done something great out there and that they had won the battle too; this feeling just would not leave them. They did not know what their euphoria was for, but they intended to find out.

They had now walked for two miles at least but they were nowhere near the Gurukul. It was getting dark. Soon it would become very difficult to go back.

"Ash I think we were probably not meant to go back today. We don't get lost anywhere," Adheesh stated this simple verifiable truth without any pride or any kind of self-consciousness. It was a fact and he said so.

"Ok, Adhee. I'm very tired; we must have done a sizeable amount of work for us to feel so tired. I don't think that I'll be able to go to sleep even if I lie down. My heart has never beaten so fast. I want to run but here I can't take even a small step."

Adheesh tenderly took her in his arms, "I think I have understood a bit of the mystery. We have undergone an exercise in demolishing the demons by using celestial weapons. As per the celestial rules, in the first place, humans are not allowed to use these weapons, and then even if they are allowed to use them, after their use they will have to forget about the whole incident. Our minds forget, but our body remembers the stress, the heightened focus, the dangers involved, the rushing blood, the flowing adrenaline. It'll take some time for our bodies to come to normal. Probably this is why in our heightened sensitivity, we are unable to reach home. We will probably not be able to behave normally in the Gurukul and people will notice. Let us relax here for a few days, take the extra Ashwagandha and Brahmi capsules, which Guruji had so thoughtfully handed us, do simple yogic exercises and lead an uncomplicated idyllic life. Guruji knew that we would be in this kind of predicament. That is why he had given us these nerve-calming medicines. We will just wait. Guruji will himself call us after some time."

Back in the Present and Marriage

The feeling of achieving and succeeding in a great feat was refusing to leave them. The euphoric sensation diminished. But for the life of them, they could not remember what it was that was making them so happy and elated. It was almost a week now and they were still in this jungle. They could have gone back to the main Gurukul but something would stop them every time they tried to leave this part of the forest. They understood that Guruji wanted them to stay here for some more time. They decided that they would try to leave this paradise only when Guruji beckoned them. Even the trees and the birds and the small animals danced with them. Birds of all hues twittered on the treetops, the wind sang softly between the trees and their leaves. It sang love songs making them all the more intoxicated and they fell in love with each other all over again.

"Ash, what are we doing here?" She was lying in his arms under the huge mango tree, redolent and sleepy with their love. She didn't answer; she did not know the answer. Even she knew that they would leave the place only when Guruji called. But in this paradise, there were a couple of disturbances also though not very frequent. Mostly they sat beside the gurgling creek with its silvery tinkling water. Food was never a problem for them. They had been trained to survive in the jungle without so-called normal food. Both of them cooked the produce of the jungle. They would sit under the mango tree eating either fruits or the food they had cooked and they talked. There were a couple of beehives on some of the trees. They also knew how to extract honey without harming the bees.

Sometimes they talked about their immediate past, sometimes about whatever they remembered; they talked about their past births and sometimes about their future but not their present. This was one hurdle which they did not know how to overcome. They had no doubt that they had to go to their present.

"Adhee I think that these mood swings of ours have something to do with some great mission which we have accomplished successfully. It must have been on such a gargantuan scale that we cannot get over it, hence our mood swings. Our minds have been made to forget but our bodies have not forgotten as yet. All our anxieties and uncertainties have to be because of this."

"Yes, I think you're right Ash. Guruji did tell us that whenever we deal with celestial weapons after we use or operate them we will have to forget about them and the mission for which we had used them. We are humans. We cannot be allowed to use the celestial weapons except under extreme circumstances; also because we are humans we cannot be allowed to remember them because our vices may affect the utility and strength of the weapons."

Aishani shot up from his arms. "Does that mean Adhee that we have just used some sort of celestial weapons and though we have forgotten about them our bodies and brains have retained some of these experiences and hence our mood swings?"

"Yes, I think so. That is why we are in this new part of the Gurukul's forest. This is why Guruji has told us to wait here till the time our bodies return to normal and we fully forget about our mission."

"Oh, Adhee are you sure?" Aishani was all agog with wonderment and awe, "Have we really used the celestial weapons?"

"No Ash, I am not completely sure but all the clues point in that direction. Nor will we get to know about it. Who will tell us? Only Guruji is qualified to tell us and he will not tell us, you know that. Even your Baba will not know how and what we have actually done."

Aishani sighed, then brightened up, "Adhee these are stolen moments. Who knows when we'll have this kind of carefree life again? We must enjoy every moment of our life here together alone."

Adheesh gathered her tightly in his arms again. "Yes Ash," he whispered, "We won't get this time again. Let's make the most of it." She sighed and he kissed her softly.

Holding hands they walked towards where they thought

the ashram would be. They did not face any disorientation this time. They knew that now they had been totally purged of their temporary afflictions. Very soon they reached the Gurukul. They went straight to Guruji's cottage. As usual, Guruji was waiting for them. He seemed to be more relaxed and happier too.

"Come, children, I have been waiting for you; come and sit here in front of me. Guruji patted the *asan* which was lying in front of him. They sat down. Guruji sprinkled gangajal on them, placed his palms over their heads and whispered some mantras. Then he spoke;

"Both of you must be very curious to know why and what you both were doing in that part of the Gurukul. Both of you have accomplished your particular missions with more than flying colours. At least one species of demons are no more there to terrorise the people of this world. The credit for this goes entirely to both of you and God," Guruji folded his hands in supplication to God. Both Adheesh and Aishani did the same. They knew that Guruji had told them more than enough and they had to be content with that. Guruji became serious.

"Aishani you have completed your training which was left over after your father's untimely demise. Both of you have excelled in your training and proved it too beyond doubt. There is now no need for you to stay in the past. You have to go back to your present."

Aishani's heart started thudding. She was going to meet her mother. But, what about Baba? She would now have to leave her Baba! She almost wrung her hands in despair. She would never see her baba again. A plethora of emotions passed over her face noticed by both Guruji and Adheesh.

"Go and say goodbye to your father Aishani, he is waiting for you in the library," Guruji said softly. "Come back here in an hour's time. You will be meeting your mother this evening."

Aishani gave a tremulous smile, touched Guruji's feet and they left his cottage.

Adheesh took her hands in his. There was no response from her. He looked at her. She was miles away. He knew the turmoil she was undergoing. It was best to keep quiet and leave her alone with her thoughts. This was not a problem which could be solved. It just had to be borne. Adheesh walked with her to the library.

"I'll wait for you outside in the garden." She nodded and squeezed his hand and went inside. Janardan was sitting in his usual place. Somesh was nowhere to be seen. Aishani went towards one of the inner rooms where she knew Baba was waiting for her and where they would not be disturbed.

Pandit Ram Sharan's eyes lit up when he saw Aishani.

"Ash! I have been waiting for you for the last so many days!"

With tears in her eyes Ash went into her father's arms. "Baba," she sobbed, "Baba, how can we live without you. What will Amma, Jayant and I do without you!"

Pandit Ram Sharan patted her shoulders. His eyes also turned moist.

"I will always be with all three of you. Don't even presume for a moment that I have left you. Remember your destiny and why you are here on this Earth. God has gifted us such a beautiful place to live in, there is such a huge plethora of various living beings on this Earth, the earth itself, its exquisite colours, the trees, the flowers, the animals, the birds and above all the human beings. We cannot allow anybody to destroy our mother earth. We must not allow our emotions to come in between our missions and goals."

Sobered by her father's far-reaching and meaningful speech, Aishani smiled tremulously.

"Yes, Baba, I know. You know Adheesh and I will do everything to destroy the demons."

"That's the spirit, now go; it's time for both of you to go back to the present. Another thing which I have been waiting to tell you," Pandit Ram Sharan paused.

"Yes, baba?"

"Just this beta, I am very proud of you. And now with Adheesh at your side, I am totally reassured that you will always be secure and protected. Together both of you will destroy all the demons and soar victoriously in the skies."

"Yes baba," she said, tears in her eyes.

"What should I tell Ma? Should I tell her everything?"

"No need beta, Madhu knows everything; she is also a warrior albeit of a different kind."

Aishani went into her father's arms, "Oh Baba, Amma misses you so much she seems to have lost all interest in life. She works almost as if she is waiting for her death so that she can come to you," Aishani was sobbing. "I want to go to her but I want to stay with you also; Baba what do I do?"

"Beta, you have no choice. You cannot stay back. Your place is not here in the past. God knows how much you have suffered in the past. You have to live in the present and prepare for the future. Your Ma is a very strong woman. Remember she is also a warrior and she can never give away that admirable trait of hers. Who knows now that she has time on her hands she might take to helping both of you. God willing your Ma and I will meet in our next births," his eyes became moist.

That was that. They had gone back to Guruji. His mantras took half an hour to teleport them back to the present. This time when they opened their eyes they were still in Guruji's cottage and he was sitting in front of them. He blessed them again and they left for their homes.

They were still holding hands when they reached Aishani's house. Adheesh turned towards her, "This is where we part my love. We'll be together again very soon, as soon as we work out how to go about our marriage again."

"Bye Adhee, take care, we'll meet at the Gurukul after two days. So much has happened in these two years. Let's see how much and how soon I adjust to my new surroundings and people," they smiled knowingly at each other. Neither the surroundings nor the people were new to them. The only variable was time.

Adheesh kissed her lightly and turned towards the main road. She too turned towards her home. Everything was so strange but so familiar. Oh! But nothing was the same. She had got much more than what she had bargained for—happiness, unhappiness, and nail-biting excitement, much of which she did not remember, but both of them knew that they had achieved impossible targets. They could relive the excitement though not the exact happenings. Mulling over all this she went inside. It was quiet inside as usual, quieter because Baba was not there. Jayant was also not to be seen anywhere, but that was to be expected. It was dusk and getting darker. There were no patients. The number of patients had thinned ever since Baba's demise and her own intermittent absences.

Amma was sitting in the courtyard under the darkening sky. She always said that she liked this part of the evening the best where a tired day met an eager evening eagerly waiting to wear the mantle of the queen of the night. Softly Aishani switched on a light and quietly sat down beside Amma. Amma did not change her stance but she knew that Madhu knew that she had returned. After a very long time, Amma turned to her and looked at her mutely. Tears came to Aishani's eyes. She put her arms around her mother. Mother and daughter held each tightly and cried.

"Oh Amma, Baba's alright. He misses you and sends his love. He said that you are a warrior first and a wife second and he feels privileged to have you as his wife!"

"I know beta, your father was always full of love and appreciation for me. He loves us even from the other world." Then holding her at arm's length she looked closely at her daughter.

"And how have you been sweetheart? Why are you blushing? Where is that boy? You did go along with him, didn't you? So where is he now?" Amma asked everything in one breath.

"Amma stop," Aishani couldn't help herself from laughing, "One question at a time, but I have a question to ask."

Amma looked at her expectantly.

"How did you know that it was I and not my shadow who was sitting beside you?"

Amma smiled, "You are my daughter beta, and I will know you wherever you are, in whatever state you are in. In this case, it was your vibrant happy energy that I recognised. Speaking of energy I love it when you are happy. Nothing could make me happier, but this new vibrancy of yours is making me wonder. What has happened in the past to make you so vivacious and joyful?"

Aishani blushed, "Oh Ma, I don't know from where to start."

Madhu's eyes narrowed. "So something big has happened. What is it beta? What has made you so sad and so happy at the same time? I know you are sad because of baba. Now you tell me the rest of it," she said.

"Ma, I'm hungry," then seeing her mother's expression she laughed. "No, no, I am not deflecting the topic. Let us go to the kitchen. I'll sit on my high stool and tell you everything while you cook. Is that fine amma?"

The last six months had been a buzz of activities in their household. After the shock that her baby was married off by Guruji and her husband in the past, Madhu now had to make everything official. She could understand and empathise with Aishani's agony and bewilderment and of course her happiness too at her marriage. This was their destiny and that was that. She was happy that both she and her husband had witnessed her marriage, albeit separately and in different time periods. Madhu and Jayant had gone to Adheesh's home with their marriage proposal, which was just a formality as Adheesh had also apprised his father about their marriage. It did not come as a surprise to anybody in Adheesh's family as they already had an inkling about his relationship with Aishani. Adheesh's father Vidyadhar felt quite peaceful now. He and his wife Anuja had always worried about Adheesh and his dangerous activities. Vidyadhar had been told about Aishani by Aghori Baba at Varanasi.

The star of the show was, of course, Ruby, who naturally took on the responsibilities of everything concerning the marriage, right from the shopping to the catering, to the reception and everything in between. Even Aishani got caught up in the whole razzmatazz. Which girl wouldn't get excited by all the attention, all the preparations and all the shopping? Though Aishani preferred pastel colours and sober styles, Ruby would have none of it. However, she did allow a few clothes of Aishani's taste; most of them were chosen by Ruby herself, without any arguments from anybody. There was no question about her impeccable taste in clothes and style. She was an apsara who really knew how to make herself attractive and beautiful. All the three boys had never seen Ruby as a harried vixen earlier and didn't want to face her now. They knew when to leave well alone.

They quietly and efficiently did whatever they were asked to do. In fact, they did each and every job eagerly and enthusiastically. They worked nonstop to make things smooth. Madhu was not too much of a help as she still missed her husband so much. Not to miss anything, their house butted its head into almost everything. If it didn't like something in the preparations it would just bang all its windows or close the door on somebody's face and not open it. After Pandit Ram Sharan's death, it had taken over the extra mantle of looking after everything especially Aishani's mother. Due respect was given to it as an elder, anticipating its likes and dislikes. Sometimes they spoke in whispers lest the house heard something which it didn't like and create a shindig.

Ruby outshone herself on the day of Aishani's marriage. She had chosen an absolutely beautiful sari and exquisite Kundan jewelry for her. Her sari was a dark maroon Benarasi silk with a broad golden border. Her kundan necklace and danglers complemented her face and sari. She hired a hairdresser for Aishani and gave her precise instructions. The end result was a very attractive bun with wisps of her silky hair covering the sides of her face. Aishani had never done anything to enhance her looks. But now she had undergone a total metamorphosis under Ruby's tutelage. Notwithstanding the fact that she was already married to Adheesh, she had not dressed up for the earlier marriage at all, because it was performed under extraordinary circumstances and the ceremony was held under total secrecy. But today she was enjoying herself so much. This is what a real marriage should be, she thought happily. Everybody was so happy. How she wished that her Baba was here. But baba had already given his blessings and they had to accept it as such. Everybody was so happy. It was as if a heavy burden had been lifted from their heads.

Aishani looked perfect. Adheesh and the others caught their breath on seeing her. She looked so shy and hesitant; her heavy maroon sari looked perfect against her fair skin. She was glowing with a hint of a shy smile on her face.

Aishani's transition to her in-law's place was as smooth as it could be. Adheesh was the only son, though his two uncles and aunts were nearer to his age. The big difference here was the number of family members, the huge household and the large number of servants and then, of course, Adheesh's shadow Devnath. There was a flurry of activities in the mornings and quite a lot of comings and goings as there were two working offices also on the ground floor where Adheesh's two uncles Kedar and Kalpesh worked in the morning and the evening, before leaving for their offices and when they returned. Their wives would also leave for their jobs in the morning. Besides, Aishani was bewildered by the array of servants in this house. In her house, there were two servants, one part-time and one who stayed with them. Here there was so much buzzing and hurried chatter in the morning that she didn't know what to do and how to behave.

She used to cherish her early morning meditations and readings but now found that she could not do either anymore. Everyone wanted to get to know Aishani and make her comfortable in this household. There was too much eagerness to please on both sides and that was taking a toll on Aishani. She loved her yoga, her walk in the fields with the breeze flowing through her long hair and kissing her cheeks, she loved to sit in a corner and read for hours; she loved her enchanted life and the life that had been chosen for her by her destiny. She liked the rush of adrenaline in her veins whenever they were given a new assignment. She was not getting any of this here though everybody wanted her to be happy and comfortable.

It was Vidyadhar who was the first one to notice Aishani's discomfiture. He persuaded both Adheesh and Aishani to expedite their honeymoon dates. Both of them hadn't much thought about this for the obvious reason that they had already been for their honeymoon, but a second one certainly wouldn't hurt and would be most welcome.

Aishani was pleasantly surprised when everybody jumped in to discuss the matter of their honeymoon. And this is when she discovered what a warm-hearted family this was. They genuinely gave their suggestions sometimes without even being bothered whether their opinions were wanted or not. Everybody had a favourite place where they wanted the newlyweds to go. A European tour was suggested by Geetika; somebody suggested Kashmir. Goa and Andamans were also in the pipeline. Aishani wanted to be in India and to go to a scenic place which had mountains as well as lakes and gardens. A fevered search began and ultimately they zeroed in on Ooty.

They took a small villa in Coonoor on the outskirts of Ooty. It was peaceful and scenic and private, exactly as Aishani wanted. Ooty was just a few miles away. One day they went to the Botanical gardens as Aishani had heard quite a lot about it.The huge garden was laid in tiers, each tier having a different kind of design and vegetation. Some of the trees were hundreds of years old reminding them of their own trees in the Gurukul.

Aishani touched the bark of one tree; it sighed happily. She knew that the tree was ready to talk to them. She reassured it that they would come and sit with it for a very long time on their next visit. They did some river rafting in Lake Pykara. But what she mostly liked was sitting all cozily bundled up in their lovely balcony holding hands with their cups of freshly made coffee and staring at the Nilgiris, the blue mountains.

Sometimes they would see rows of women plucking leaves from the tea shrubs with huge cane baskets on their backs. Every morning, a woman, presumably a gardener's wife, would bring them a small basket with the most exquisite flowers. Not that she was unfamiliar with the flowers but their sheer bewitching colours took her breath away. Apart from the tulips which were rare in North India, there were dahlias, carnations, gerberas, liliums and so many others.

"Oh Adhee, I wish we could stay here forever," she mused dreamingly, closing her eyes at the heady fragrance of the roses.

Adheesh became a bit restless at times. This place was quite far from their homes and he had to be careful of any kind of demon following them here and creating havoc in their idyllic love life. As for Aishani she was in a totally blissful state now and would not let any negative thought enter her mind. After a very long time, she was relaxed and Adheesh wanted it to be so. He just wanted her to be at peace and in love, at least for the time being.

Very soon it was time to go back. They bought lots of gifts for everybody. They were mainly Toda tribal jewellery pieces, lots of different kinds of cheeses, medicinal oils like eucalyptus oil and the famous Nilgiri tea. Aishani saw some beautiful needlecrafts in Ooty. She took many of these for both the families. They even bought a painting of the Nilgiri Mountains for the house. She knew that it would like it.

Dr Shambhu

"Adhee will you do this?" She held out her hand to him; he held it as soft blue, pink and white electricity crackled around their hands. Their thoughts were on something much more important.

"I know Ash, it has to be done the proper way," he said simply.

"I don't want to kill Adhee, I want to live peacefully," she said.

"I understand Ash, but nonetheless we are the precursors for peace. It is our job to make the world peaceful again. God knows how many kinds of demons are there. There are so many crossbreeds that it has almost become hopeless to differentiate the good from the evil. Some of these demons are so advanced intellectually and culturally that it is almost impossible to identify them; also they are so intelligent and cunning and they have mixed and interbred with the humans on such a large scale that it has become an insurmountable task to track them down."

"But Adheesh our people are also intelligent; our people also have trackers to find these demons; our people are also so well placed in the right places and have tracked down so many of these demons. Why, we can and we will disseminate these people from the society!" she stopped, Adheesh was staring at her with a bemused smile, "What! Why are you looking at me like that?"

Adheesh smiled again, "Nothing, just now you said that you did not want to fight and you wanted peace and in the same breath you say that you want to annihilate these demons."

"Oh, Adhee, you know what I mean. I definitely want peace but I still don't want to fight and I don't want to kill," she sighed, "Yes, I know it is not possible but we have to fight and destroy."

"If it's any help to you the circumstances will be such that you will kill of your own volition and you will have no choice. Who are we to decide who to kill and who not to kill? We have not made them nor do we have the right to destroy them. God will decide who will have to be destroyed and He will destroy them, albeit through us. We live in this illusory world; this is all Maya or illusion that gives us the perception that it is we human beings who know who is a villain and who is not and also who has to be destroyed and who has to be saved. True, we have a fair idea of right and wrong, but we take decisions in our haste and tend to judge things at their face value without knowing their past histories and circumstances. You don't have to feel responsible or guilty for these killings; for one, these are our direct directives from Lord Hanuman via our Guruji. As such you will search and hunt and ferret out these monsters and criminals of the human society—no wait, the criminals and villains of this world and beyond too.

"Yes Adhee," she murmured sadly, "We don't have a choice, and I wouldn't want a choice also."

"Ash, don't ever fall prey to the feelings of regret. For all you know, this may well become the beginning of our downfall. The enemy is very intelligent and very cunning. It will sense your indecision even if it is for a fraction of a second and then all mayhem will ensue."

"Okay, okay, no more sentimentalism—let's continue with our research," she smiled.

"Yeah, that's the spirit." Adheesh hugged her.

"So, what's next? I saw you walking with Guruji."

"So, nothing, it was just a walk. Sometimes Guruji also wants to talk of lighter and insignificant things."

Aishani smiled and just looked at him and waited. She knew that he was teasing her.

Adheesh kept quiet for some time as if mulling over what to say. Then with a sigh, he said, "Ok, I didn't want to trouble you so soon after our honeymoon. God knows you don't get much time for peace of mind and tranquility."

Aishani waited. She knew that Guruji had directed Adheesh for another mission and that it was a big one. That is why he was told first so that he could make the preparations for yet another assault on the demons. Guruji would call her later on to apprise her of the facts.

"This one is probably one of the most dangerous demons that we have faced till now. He is a wolf in sheep's clothing."

"What do you mean, Adhee? Has he mixed with human beings or has he mixed with some other species?"

"You are right there Ash. This demon's ancestors have been mixing with the humans from centuries but have very religiously kept their demoniac traits intact, that is they have kept all their beastly nature alive in themselves. Only their outer shells are that of human beings. They have very successfully mingled with the humans and some of them hold very high and respectable positions in society. It's a herculean task to weed them out and destroy them."

"Who are we talking about Adhee?"

"One of them is Dr Shambhu Nath, the scientist, and the other one is his assistant Veeju. He was conferred with the India Science Award a few years back."

"Adhee, I can't believe it! Dr Shambhu Nath is one of the most respected and celebrated scientists in our country. For interested people, there is nothing secret about his professional or personal life. How can we suspect him?"

"It's not a question of us suspecting him. We got this information from the Intelligence wing of the War training school. We'll be just following orders and these orders are to dispose of the valiant doctor. Along with our orders, there is a long list of dos and don'ts."

Adheesh continued, "Dr Shambhu Nath's life, both professional and personal has been under intense scrutiny since a very long time. It seems that he is completely without any blemish at present and in the past also."

"What do you mean by past Adhee? Is it his near past or his ancestral past?"

"Both Ash, everything about his life is perfect. He belongs to an upper middle class family, not that it matters to him; he is at such a level that money is immaterial to him. He has a son who stays abroad, and his wife died a decade back due to some illness. After her death, he spends most of his time in his state of the art laboratory. He has no friends, his only companion is his faithful attendant, his man Friday who looks after all his needs and accompanies him everywhere."

"Oh, okay, so what is this man Friday's actual name? Does he have a family? That might give us a clue."

"His name is Veeju and he doesn't have a family. He follows only one person whom he serves religiously with complete faith and loyalty."

"Adhee, if there is nothing suspicious about these two then why are we chasing them?" Aishani asked a bit exasperated.

Adheesh looked at her seriously, "There is always something Ash, otherwise we wouldn't have been summoned to look into this." He was referring to their high status in the hierarchy of warriors. He stated this as a matter of fact, without any airs.

"It seems," he continued, "There have been gruesome murders and killings in Dr Shambhu Nath's vicinity. There has been no need of any alibi because in such circumstances, the good doctor was always surrounded by people. That itself puts him in the light of suspicion. He is often referred to as a loner not wanting any company. Moreover, many a times when these incidents have taken place his trusted aide Veeju has not been around. But during these grisly murders near them, there has been constant whispering and chit-chats between the doctor and Veeju."

"But that doesn't prove anything Adhee!"

"There have been rumours Ash. Rumours that Veeju has been killed many times," he looked at her.

Aishani looked at him uncomprehendingly for some time. He could see her brain assimilating the information and then she gasped, "Adhee does it mean what I think?" she whispered, scared and excited at the same time.

"Yes Ash, it actually means what you are thinking."

"Oh! Fill me in on the details Adhee."

"Ok Ash. I don't have to tell you about Durga Saptashati or how Maa Durga killed the demons Shumbha, Nishumbh and Rakta Beej. Our elders suspect that Dr Shambhu Nath is the descendant of the demon Shumbh and his trusted aide Veeju is descendant of Raktabeej. You know whenever Maa Durga struck, his blood spilled on the Earth and each drop of his blood produced hundreds of demons just like him and as strong. Maa Durga was in a dilemma as to how to destroy him. No doubt she could kill all of them but they would nevertheless multiply. It was then that Maa Durga directed Maa Kali to drink their blood before it dropped on the ground. That was the end of Raktabeej."

"But Adhee, if Maa had totally destroyed them, then how come they are still here?"

"That's the thing, Ash, a few drops of the demon blood must have gone inside the Earth and may have thus escaped Maa Kali's wrath and immediately gone into dormancy. That is how they have survived all these centuries, by hibernation, by camouflaging and by mingling with the human beings. So Raktabeej dies and another takes his place with the help of Dr Shambhu. Both seem to be in a symbiotic relationship, each doing what the other wills it to do. So while Veeju kills whoever the doctor wants him to kill, Dr Shambhu Nath brings Veeju back to life whenever he is killed."

"But how? Raktabeej came to life whenever his blood spilled on the ground. Out of one drop of his blood, hundreds of the same demon would spring forth of their own accord. Shumbh and Nishumbh never created Raktabeej. He had the power to create himself manifold through his blood."

"The number of destructions and killings which have followed Dr Shambhu and his cohort Veeju, especially Veeju, are too many to be passed off as stray incidents or as the responsibility of other gruesome killers. The elders have got their proofs and now it is up to us destroy these two."

"I get it Adhee, but how do we do this? Have the elders sent any guidelines? I have heard that Dr Shambhu's laboratory is like a fortress what with the govt on his side giving him a free hand. How do we break the multi-layered security? And when we do manage to do that, how do we kill them?"

"The security should not prove to be too much of a problem. Ruby and her family have already been briefed on how to go about it."

"Oh, said Ash, relieved but feeling a left out also.

"Ash, first of all, don't doubt Ruby and her family. Ruby would never voluntarily hide anything from you; secondly, these were the orders given to her and her family when you had gone to your Baba in the past to complete your training. Everybody thought that you were missing your father so much that you had given up on everything. Ruby didn't know what to do, she tried to confide in you many times but you just gave her a blank look mainly because you were not there."

"Oh," Ash said in a small voice, "I was actually devoid of any feelings during those days. I still shudder when I think of those days without Baba. I don't know what I would have become had I not met Baba in the past."

"It is presumed by the elders that the powers of Veeju or the descendant of Raktabeej have watered down so much that he cannot replicate himself on his own and that too in large numbers. Therefore, Dr Shambhu helps in replicating him or rather helps himself. Raktabeej was Shumbh's commander and this is the same now also. Veeju is Dr. Shambhu's commander or henchman or anything else, totally subservient to him. Both of them are demons and though very intelligent ones, their basic nature remains the same—killing, murder, cannibalism, playing on other people's minds and emotions, revelling in playing with flesh, blood, and bones. Their other traits are pride, greed, lust, envy, sloth, wrath and gluttony. Even when they were in their original forms, our Goddess Maa Durga or Shakti had faced problems in annihilating the demon Raktabeej. It is only now when his descendants have become weak by hiding, cross-breeding, lack of proper nutrition through the ages, that weakness has entered their genes, and our elders have been able to track them down and now it is our dharma to destroy them. I can show you their real forms though in imagery only."

Aishani was listening to Adheesh very carefully. Completely thrown off guard by his last sentence she blurted out, "What do you mean Adhee? You mean you can show me Shumbh and Nishumbh and Raktabeej? Do you mean how they are in the present or at the time they fought with Maa Durga? What kind of pictures are you going to show me?"

"Whoa, stop, stop with all the questioning, I was merely telling you that I will show you their images, how they look today in our society and how they should look in reality as per their temperament."

"Do you have their photos Adhee? How did you get them?" she demanded then stopped when she saw Adheesh smiling.

"I did not tell you this because I did not know it myself till now. I did not know that I had the power to conjure up images of people in their present forms and in their real forms."

"Show me Adhee; show me what they look like now."

"Ok," Adheesh put his hands in his shoulder bag and took out a sort of ash or *bhasm*, brought it in front of his face, chanted a mantra a few times and then blew on it. There was dark smoke all around which very soon conjured up into two huge shadowy images. She opened her mouth to say something but Adheesh stopped her with a gesture. The dark smoke seemed to be settling down and a proper image was getting formed. Aishani stared at the evolving image. It seemed to be of a huge giant. Gradually features began developing on the image's face. It was a huge, hairy giant, with protuberant red eyes and bulging biceps. Cruelty and hate emanated from it even though it was an image only. In his hands he was holding huge sharp and heavy weapons. Its head swung around everywhere as if looking for any victim to kill, maim, torture and eat. Two huge teeth thrust out from the corners of its mouth. She half expected it to roar anytime and she could almost smell the fetid blood and flesh of its victims on its person. Such a creature could just not be allowed to live. It was as if its super scientific brain had preserved a pinhead drop of its blood for centuries and it came alive now and was raring to go on its rampage of mutilations and bloodshed.

The bizarre silhouettes extinguished many souls at the same time. The message was clear "Join me in this world of greed and hoarding or suffer and die. Be complicit or be under our feet. Where do you want to be?"

Adheesh continued, "I can show you the images of the other demons of this era too, but that will be just wastage of our time and the *bhasm* also. Needless to say, the other demons are also a prototype of this image only. I will now show you what the present Shumbh and Raktabeej look now. We'll just wait for this image to dissipate."

After some time Adheesh again took out a fistful of *bhasm*, chanted a few mantras and blew on it. This time the image that emerged was of a slim and very distinguished looking man with a cigar in his hand. He was very well dressed and was wearing glasses. He had an aura of seriousness and dignity around him.

Nobody even in his or her wildest imagination could think of Dr Shambhu to be any different than what he looked, that is, a scientist. Beside him was his assistant Veeju or Raktabeej. He did look like he came from a class of people who were into physical labour. Veeju also did not give the impression of being a mass murderer that he was. Instead, he just looked like a typical assistant.

Totally disgusted by the sight in front of her Aishani was becoming more confident and stronger by the minute. "Adhee I'm so proud of you and your knowledge of these things. Like you say we have been chosen by the elders to complete this job. I am more than sure that with proper and systematic planning we will be able to kill these demons. I am just curious that we did not kill them in our earlier births."

Adhee looked at her for some time then he seemed to make up his mind, "There are other things also Ash," he said quietly.

She looked at him expectantly. Instinctively she knew that he was going to tell her something big, something which he did not want to tell and something which she did not want to hear. She waited.

"It's just that we have done this together and have not been successful."

"What? What do you mean Adhee?" she was perplexed, but a familiar unpleasant knot had already begun tightening in her stomach.

"In a couple of our births we were given the herculean task of killing Shambhu and Veeju but we were not successful. These two are very formidable enemies. In the millennia of time, in some births, even our powers decrease a little. When the two us are together, our powers get multiplied. The demons know this. They do everything to ensure that we do not come together. It is the death knell for them when we merge as one. Once in a while, they have succeeded also."

"What do you mean they have succeeded? Have they

defeated us? Where? When?" She looked at him questioningly.

Adheesh looked at her seriously and sighed, "In one of our previous births we were about to get married. Our elders had to wait for an auspicious time for the marriage. Though all preparations were being done in absolute secrecy, somehow the demons got wind of the plan," he paused. She waited.

"I don't remember much, it was so many ages back and I don't want to remember also. In a nutshell after marriage, we would have achieved supreme supernatural strength and powers. Preparations were underway for the marriage. Despite the preparations being done in utter secrecy the demons got whiff of it. Their vast machinery swung into action and I was abducted, tortured and killed."

Aishani stared at Adheesh horrified.

"Yes, I was tortured and killed but not before I had destroyed half of their army. But we were not together. We were not as strong as we should have been. They had hacked my body into small pieces and parts had been chewed and spat out. After that, killing you was comparatively easy. I don't know what they did with you or your body and I don't want to know," his hoarse breath came fast.

He kept quiet for sometime. "This is why when your Baba died, the elders panicked. We were not married, your father was not there to bless us, your training was incomplete and our lives would have been wasted again," he smiled wryly.

Ash sat down beside him and took his hands. "So in order to destroy these demons we had to be married," she mused wryly. "So much for falling in love and the elders approving it. In a way, even Guruji was desperate for us to get married. Not that we love each other any less after the revelations."

Adheesh took her in his arms and kissed her lightly. "We have no escape," he smiled. "We will always love each other from here to eternity." He then added in a flippant note, "We have to keep on loving each other if we have to destroy these demons. There is no other way," he smiled.

She smiled back, "Suits me fine."

Adheesh became serious, "In the earlier times, it was different. These fights would take place in the open with both parties being almost on neutral ground. Now in this age, we have to go to the enemy's lair that too without his knowledge and destroy him. Rumour has it that Dr Shambhu has developed a virus which after ingestion will turn human beings into Raktabeej kind of demons who will produce more demons of the same kind. Once this virus is unleashed our Earth will literally become hell and our race will be annihilated in no time."

Aishani was stupefied. "No," she breathed her anguish, "This can't happen Adheesh, we will destroy them before they destroy us."

"Yes Ash, we will. We have to be very careful. We have to outsmart every manoeuvre of theirs, outsmart them at every point and..." he paused searching for an appropriate sentence.

"And what Adheesh?" she asked impatiently.

"Ash the last killing has to be performed by you and you only. Nobody can kill Dr Shambhu and his assistant Veeju. It is only when they are struck by your hands with your special weapons will they finally die."

Her breath came out in a large sigh. "I know Adhee, I

have to do it. There is no question of not wanting to do it. You know I abhor bloodshed and would avoid it at any cost, but when I think of these demons and their senseless and merciless killings and torture, I know there is no option."

"Guruji has comprised a team for us, a team of the most experienced warriors and technicians. Of course, you don't have to worry about all that; that will be my department"

"Adhee the weapons which I have, will they match up to Dr Shambu's superior weapons and skills? I know I should not doubt myself, but why do I have this niggling feeling that there is some other great weapon also which I should be using."

Adheesh sighed, "There is something else you have to remember Ash," he paused.

Aishani turned towards him. Adheesh was not really looking at her. Was he avoiding looking at her? Why? Did he know something about their past births that she could not remember?

"Adheesh you have to tell me. First we will never hide anything from each other and secondly, we have to kill the rakshasas. Even the most insignificant information may become most useful at any part of the time."

Adheesh looked at her quizzically. Would she be able to bear what he was going to divulge to her? Would she be shocked or would she become more determined? In any case, he had to tell her. Everything depended on her. She would have to perform the ugliest act without which both the demons would not die. She would have to pay very heavily for that. He looked at her; she was waiting for him.

"Ash you know the story of Shumbh, Nishumbh, and

Raktabeej. Maa Kali had to drink the blood of every demon whom Maa Durga was killing. One drop of his blood which fell on the ground would produce hundreds of the same kind of demons. The only way Raktabeej was destroyed was by drinking each and every drop of his blood. There was no other way and there is still no other way."

Aishani stared at Adheesh, her heart palpitating.

"Does this mean that I will have to drink their blood?" she choked on her words. No, this couldn't be happening; she who couldn't see anybody bleeding had to do this! She couldn't say the words aloud or even think about them.

"No Ash, this is the twenty-first century, you don't have to drink the blood per se, but you will have to absorb their blood in your body and immediately take it out also so that it doesn't harm you. Ash I had told you that the powers of these demons have also diminished to such an extent that they are no longer capable of proliferating just by their drops of blood falling on the ground. Now they actually have to work on it. So Dr Shambhu now collects his and Veeju's blood in large containers and preserves them in his lab. We have to reach that sanctum and destroy those blood containers."

She looked at him for a long time. He somehow managed not to look at her in the eye.

"And how will we destroy these containers Adhee? The blood cannot be allowed to spill on the ground for obvious reasons. What are we going to do? Maa Kali is not here to drink the demons' blood," she mused, hinting that she knew that he knew.

Adheesh exhaled, "Ash you have guessed what will happen.

Our life is an uphill struggle full of dangerous challenges. Even though it is our destiny to free the Earth of these demons, we have ourselves chosen to live this life no matter what trials and travails we have to go through."

Aishani nodded, "Yes Adhee I know, I know I have to dispose of the venomous blood. I am not capable of drinking their blood, so what can be done?"

Adheesh exhaled, "Ash rest assured you will not be drinking their blood but what will happen will be no less traumatic for you and for me."

"Adhee you're scaring me. How do you know all this? Did Guruji tell you?"

Adheesh nodded, "Yes, in some parts Guruji was there and some parts I know myself. If you ask me how I really know all this—I just know. Maybe it's the memories of our past births."

Adheesh went on. He took her hands in his, "Ash we're in the twenty-first century. We cannot go about drinking anybody's blood. It's preposterous!" Then sheepishly, "Well not exactly that, but you'll have to put your hands over the plasma part of the blood wherein the blood will enter your body through osmosis," he said triumphantly. They both looked at each other for some time then burst out laughing. The whole thing was so ridiculous that there was nothing else to do except laugh.

"So then does the blood stay in me or is it expelled?"

"It is expelled rather it will be sucked out of you."

Aishani had a vague idea how this would be done. She had seen some of the blood-sucking creatures. Studying these creatures was also one of the subjects they studied. Aishani had almost always tried to close her eyes while studying these blood sucking slimy creatures. She shuddered. And now they would be sucking her blood. Well technically not her blood, it would be the blood of the monsters but it would be her body from which they would be sucking the blood.

"Trust me, Ash, I would gladly exchange places with you if that was possible. But only you can do it. You are the personification of Adi Shakti or Maa Durga, only you have the power to absorb the demon's blood in your body."

"What happens after the toxic blood is sucked out by these creatures? They can't be left out even in the puritan surroundings of the ashram. They will themselves turn into demons maybe more dangerous too. And how will it be possible that they suck out only the poisonous blood and not my blood too?"

"That is the beauty of the whole thing," Adheesh answered, "These creatures have been bred in such a way that the moment they gorge their bodies with the blood of the body they are preying on, they drop on the ground and die. As far as both yours and the demon's blood mixing together is concerned it will take about ten minutes for your body to get over its shock of being host to the tainted blood before both the bloods mingle into each other. By which time all the bad blood would have been sucked out of your body. These creatures have been bred very carefully. They have been given small doses of poisonous blood. So they now have a penchant or lust only for demon blood. When given an opportunity they will sift through any other liquid and suck only what they have been fed with."

Aishani closed her eyes, opened them and stuck out her chin. What had to happen would happen. The Earth would be rid of a couple of demons at least. "And Ash," he said hesitatingly.

She shuddered, "Yes Adheesh?"

"Before the…the blood transfusion—for want of a better word, we have to kill both of them, otherwise everything will be in vain. We will have to kill them before Operation Blood. The whole exercise will be in vain if these two demons escape."

Aishani closed her eyes again and took a deep breath.

"How?" she whispered.

"You will have to use the sword with which you have been practising for the last couple of years. There is nobody in the entire world who can match you in swordsmanship. It is supposed to be Maa Durga's sword. Amongst the many other weapons she had, she used this sword to slaughter the demons."

"For me to kill these two with the sword it has to be in a lonely place without any witnesses, how do we get them there Adhee?"

"Everything has been planned out Ash, all the planning and preparations have been completed; the only preparation which you will have to do is to make yourself mentally and emotionally focused to execute them."

The whole exercise was conducted with clock-like precision. Aishani had a hazy idea of the scientists' seminar. She also did not have much idea of how Ruby enticed the two demons one by one into the jungle, but she did have a vague idea that apsaras, apart from being mesmerisingly beautiful were intellectually very superior too. The conversation with Ruby must have been very stimulating for Dr Shambhu to follow her to the forest where Adheesh and Uday were waiting to ambush him.

What ensued was undisputedly a brutal fight between demons and humans. Veeju had also followed them. Aishani was camouflaged behind a bush, continually chanting the Durga mantra. Three of her loved ones were involved in the clash. She watched in amazement when Dr Shambhu and Veeju turned into demons and was horrified by their superior strength and prowess. First, they overpowered Uday. Heart hammering, Aishani watched them turn towards Adheesh. For a moment a picture of Adheesh being torn and cut into pieces flashed in front of her eyes. She did not know whether it was her imagination or an actual memory which had been triggered. Adheesh, her Adheesh, who always fought fearlessly and with acute precision was facing these demons squarely and dauntlessly. But she was not going to wait for the outcome. With her fury erupting like a volcano she bellowed Maa Durga's name and lunged out of the bush with her sword and slashed Dr Shambhu's head in one stroke. It happened so suddenly that both Adheesh and the demon Veeju became paralysed for a moment. But Aishani did not notice all this. Her chest heaving and her eyes turning red with hatred and fury, she turned towards Veeju and slashed his head too with one blow of her sword.She kept on panting for the next few minutes her rage showing no signs of dissipation.

Dr Shambhu's Laboratory

They had now reached the inside periphery of the Lab. This was a huge, very tall, isolated building. It had a totally decrepit look to it and it seemed that it was uninhabited. Its bricks had weakened and become loose and were slowly falling off in places so that if someone wanted they could peep inside. Not that there would have been anything to see, it had been abandoned for such a long time. It had now become home to bats and pigeons and spiders.

But Adheesh and his party knew differently. They knew that the building was deliberately made to look so derelict and it was so far away that even beggars and tramps would not be able to camp there. Nights were meant for their work and play, mostly play with killings, orgies of eating flesh, torturing and mutilating humans and other living beings like animals and birds, etc. There was no sound except for the sounds of the night and the nocturnal insects and animals. There weren't many people or scientists in the lab as Dr Shambhu liked to have few people around. The fewer people knew about the lab the lesser were the chances that any gory secret would be let out. The security staff was mainly crossbreeds of demons and ferocious animals. But where were they? Was this the state of the art laboratory? Or was this an illusion? They had all rubbed themselves with a mixture of mud and a special kind of oil which was given to them by Guruji. This was the smell of night and a bit of rotting vegetation also. Their clothes and bodies also blended with the early colours of dawn.

Everybody in the team knew that the demons have an extra strong sense of smell. Even with the camouflaging of their body odours, the demons would detect them after some time. Aishani did not have to worry about these things. Adheesh was with her and that was enough for her. He was conducting the whole operation; he had to ensure Aishani's safety and he had to make sure that the doctor and the Vaidya carrying the blood-sucking eels would be there at precisely the same time that Aishani would be going into a coma, induced by the blood of the demons.

Adheesh signalled to one of the team members to make a foray into one of the buildings. This person was dressed in torn clothes and looked emaciated giving the impression that he had lost his way and was moving in circles for the last few days without food and water. They watched in tense silence as this soldier went inside one of the buildings. After a ten minute long wait, he came out and made a casual gesture which meant that there was nothing and nobody there. He then checked the other three buildings with the same results. Uday came near to where Adheesh was standing, "We'll have to wait a bit more I think."

"I agree," said Adheesh. And so they waited. It was getting dark in this dense jungle too. Another hour and they would have to abandon today's mission. After an interminable wait, Adheesh, through the corner of his eyes, thought he saw a movement. There was nothing. Disappointed they all waited. After sometime there was another movement which they all noticed. Immediately alert, their eyes turned towards the swift movement. The movement had come from somewhere in the third building. There was a dark blurred swift movement near the third building but it was gone before they could get a proper glimpse of it. The building itself still had a deserted look to it. Of course, Adheesh thought; he berated himself.

These buildings were just gates to the main building or lab which was underground! The swift movements had to be of the demons who were returning from their sojourns. They entered the building, used the password, and went down to their bunkers or quarters or wherever they were supposed to go. This was almost like their Gurukul except that their Gurukul had more advanced magic. They waited for some more time even after the blurred movements had stopped, giving the creatures time to settle down to their routines or siestas. The third building seemed to be the entrance to the underground labs, the others were just decoys. Nevertheless, Adheesh's team spread around all the three buildings. Adheesh's personal team consisted of Aishani, Devnath and two physicians, one ayurvedic and the other allopathic. In addition to being doctors, they were both trained as warriors too. They were both required for Aishani when she would be ingesting the blood of the demons and when the blood sucking leeches would be sucking her blood and dropping down dead.

Each and every warrior was handpicked by Guruji. They excelled in the art of subterfuge and killing without mercy. It was either kill or be killed. Half of them entered the third building almost at the same time to an empty hall and rooms. There were four elevators, two each on the opposite walls of the hall. There were no buttons beside these lifts to operate them. Adheesh was ready for this. He put both his hands on the door of the lifts and recited a mantra. Sure enough, a green display of buttons appeared on the wall beside the lifts. They all went inside and went down. The different teams went in different lifts. Each of them pressed for the lowest level for that is where the blood laboratory should be according to their calculations.

They gave a gasp when they reached the lowest level. It was like a state of the art hospital and laboratory. Many of the rooms had glass doors and they could see inside. Everything was deserted. They had entered a broad and long corridor with closed rooms on both sides. The doors did not have any handles nor was there any fixture which could open them. Time was of the essence here. Sure they would crack the code for opening the door but they were racing against time. They looked around desperately.

"Bhaiya," It was Tejas. Adheesh looked at him questioningly.

"Bhaiya, there are very small circles on the wall above,

probably for air circulation. I can go through these holes and try to open the doors from the inside which should be easy."

Adheesh looked at the small holes up in the walls. They were very high up and very small. He looked at Tejas thoughtfully. He knew about Tejas' ability to stretch himself but could he risk it? There was no time. A decision had to be taken immediately. He looked at Aishani. She was looking very worried. He took his decision. Tejas was almost jumping with anticipation.

"Ok Tejas up you go," Adheesh hoisted Tejas upon his shoulders. Tejas stretched himself and caught the lower end of the circular hole. He swung himself on to the hole and lengthened himself almost like a very thick rope. Then with considerable effort, he wriggled his way inside the hole in the wall and within a minute disappeared from view. There was no sound of a scuffle or anybody's angry exclamation. What was happening? Tejas was the baby of their army. Nothing should happen to him. Aishani started praying to Maa Durga when suddenly one of the doors slid open. There was Tejas, perfectly elongated and sliding to the next door. They heaved a sigh of relief and rushed inside but not before Aishani placed a bottle of water in his hand.

There was not an iota of proof that this place was the killer place they had been sent to. Adheesh and Uday opened a couple of doors but didn't find anything incriminating there. These were like normal wards of any hospital excepting that none of the beds were occupied. Slowly they backed against the wall, their nerves tingling with nervous anticipation. They held their breath... Adheesh could now hear a rhythmic pounding beyond the wall. Slowly they crept near the wall from where the sound was coming. There was a small glass window in the wall. Adheesh and Uday peeped inside. There were some bizarre looking machines to which hundreds of tubes were attached. There were human looking demons attending to these tubes. They were sorting the tubes and rotating them. There was a sort of dark red liquid flowing from one tube to another and finally, the liquid was allowed to flow into one-litre bottles. A few demons were picking up the filled bottles and taking them to another room.

Suddenly all hell broke loose. They were attacked from all sides by ferocious screaming and shrieking demons. A fierce battle ensued. No way was a fair battle expected and no way did it happen. The demons just bore down upon them fiercely with no holds barred. Guruji's army was very different but no less. The added advantage was they were specifically trained to fight demons.

Adheesh who was keeping Aishani by his side was finding it increasingly difficult to do so. A fully charged Aishani was flying at the demons with full vigour and fury. Even a light stroke of hers was slaying more than four demons at one go. Adheesh was with her as she remembered her father's death. He came and stood in front of her blocking the demons from her line of fire. He gestured to Uday who immediately came in front of them with his team. Adheesh caught hold of Aishani and gestured to the doctors to follow them. The doctors were also valiantly fighting the demons. Adheesh was worried about their safety too. It was uppermost in his mind. Though they were fighting valiantly they were not bona fide warriors. They were doctors and medicine was what they excelled in.

Adheesh led them from the front with Devnath at their back. Aishani was flush with vigour and stamina, but she had come back to her senses when Adheesh pulled her away from the melee. They ran in the corridors peeping into every room trying to find the blood and the cloning lab. They ran the entire length of the corridors and checked every room but there was no sign of any laboratory. The bloodsucking eels were getting hungrier and more ferocious by the minute and the doctor carrying them was finding it difficult to hold them now. These eels were in a special bag with special linings and a special kind of liquid so that they could breathe and not escape.

"Adhee, this is the lab," Aishani whispered to him, "There must be another way to find it."

"Yes Ash, I know, let me try," Adheesh went to a wall, spread both his palms in the middle and chanted some mantras. These were similar to mantras which they chanted at the entrance of the Gurukul but very different in their incantation. Sure enough after two minutes of chanting of the mantra, the wall began shimmering and a doorway opened. They went inside quickly. The wall closed behind them. This was again a huge corridor with rooms on both sides. Here there was the lab they were looking for. Dr Shambhu wanted to keep this a secret from the demons also. The only people who could come inside this lab were Dr Shambhu and Veeju by a three-layered password which had been broken by Guruji's team and given to Adheesh.

The blood and cloning lab was exactly as they had envisioned it. There were one-litre bottles of dark blood kept neatly on the shelves. They were not as many as they had thought but enough to clone at least a hundred Veejus who would again start giving their blood. All these bottles were joined together by thin pipes so that whenever a bottle became empty the other would automatically replenish it. In essence, only the first bottle was used with blood flowing from the other bottles into it.

Aishani shuddered when she saw all this. The two doctors quickly went about their work professionally. Though the demon's blood was going to be transferred to Aishani's body through osmosis, still to make the process faster and smoother, the first doctor rubbed some sort of a coarse solution on Aishani's hands and arms. Time was the crucial factor here. Adheesh was sure that most of the demons did not know about this lab, nevertheless, a couple of them must have informed the other senior demons and they could make an appearance anytime with the most disastrous consequences. The leeches had to be swiftly placed on Aishani's hands and arms so that they could quickly suck up the demon blood.

The first doctor took Aishani's left hand, put it in a sort of a wide-mouthed bottle and placed it on the table where the demon's blood was placed. He then opened the lid of the bottle and put a pipe through it; he siphoned a little bit of the blood and then let it flow over Aishani's hand. They all watched her closely for any signs of blood poisoning or any other fatal sign but Aishani was totally calm and composed. Her hand shook when the first drop of demon blood fell over it but after that apart from her body becoming a bit darker, she seemed to be alright.

Very soon she had ingested the blood of half of the bottles. The doctor gently took out her hand and placed it on the table, then put her right hand in the bottle.

Vaidyaji was ready with his bloodsucking eels. He carefully placed the squirming and twisting hungry eels with their hundreds of sharp teeth over Aishani's hand and arm. The eels needed no help. They clung to Aishani and began sucking her blood. A wave of pain and revulsion passed through her. She could not even look at Adheesh; she was so preoccupied with her own revulsions. Even Devnath who had seen so many gory sights was repulsed and overwhelmed.

Very soon both her hands were covered with the eels with their round vicious faces. Both the doctors waited in suspense. Every second was like an eon. At last one eels let go of her hand and dropped on the floor with a splat. Soon the other eels also dropped down dead. Vaidyaji was ready with his special bag. He scooped each of the dead blood sucking eel and dropped them in the bag. Both the doctors were heavily covered with anti-venom materials. Though they knew what they were doing, they were totally in awe of Aishani who was undergoing the whole painful exercise. They knew she was not an ordinary person, but this seemed to be beyond their comprehension. At last, all the bottles were depleted and the transference was complete. Adheesh dare not look at Aishani for fear he would lose his nerve. She had become very quiet and very pale with blotches of dark skin all over her body.

"Hurry up now,"Adheesh ordered them. Turning to Devnath he said, "Take Aishani and the doctors outside and go to the Ashram immediately. Take her to Guruji quickly and place her in his care. She needs immediate medical attention. All the others will take care of themselves."

"And you Bhaiya? Are you not coming with us?" though Devnath understood the gravity of the situation, Adheesh was his first responsibility. The idea of leaving Adheesh behind was abhorrent to him.

Adheesh looked at Devnath very seriously, "We cannot leave this place intact like this with all its advanced and sophisticated machinery. In good hands, it would have made a quantum leap in science, but it cannot be left here in the hands of Dr Shambhu's cohorts. We have to do something about it. You go, and I'll follow you in some time. I'll come as fast as I can with Tejas."

"Ok Bhaiya," Devnath had no choice but to concur. For a brief minute, Adheesh put his hands over Aishani, then they left.

Aishani was in a comatose state now. She was not in her senses. The blood transfusion had taken a huge toll on her body and mind. Aishani was born of human parents but she was blessed by Gods. Guruji and the doctors had catered for this contingency too. They had brought along a makeshift stretcher with them on which they placed Aishani. They carried her to the special vehicle waiting for them.

They had gone only about a mile when they heard a huge explosion behind them. All of them knew what it was yet none of them paused or looked back to see the spectacle. As there was no doubt that a celestial weapon was used, they did not halt but continued towards the Gurukul. They had no doubt that the labs were destroyed beyond repairs. Only time would tell whether anything remained of Dr Shambhu and Veeju or not.

It had been almost two months now since Operation Blood. Aishani had assimilated their blood and the blood of the other demons in herself and the tainted blood had been sucked out from her by the blood-sucking eels which after filling their bellies with the demon blood had fallen down from her body and died. All the dead eels had been collected, put in a box and taken outside the jungle and burnt to cinders.

But it was Aishani that Adheesh was still most worried about. Though all the poisonous blood had been drained out of her body, she was now just a pale shadow of her earlier self. It seemed as if there was no life or zest for life left in her. As they were now married she was mostly in Adheesh's home.

Initially, Aishani was in Vidyadhar's hospital.Though even the immediate family did not know the cause of Aishani's illness, they could guess that this was no ordinary sickness. As such Kalpesh and Padma, Adheesh's uncle and aunt who were ayurvedic doctors, were working round the clock to find a solution for Aishani's illness. On instructions from these ayurvedic doctors, Geetika would also make delectable dishes which sadly Aishani wouldn't even look at.

"Didi, see I have made this special barley soup for you with lemon and coriander. You'll love it. Come on didi have a sip," she would cajole Aishani. Another time she brought aromatic broccoli pulao for her, but Aishani wouldn't even look at the food. She would listlessly pick at the food, and then leave it.

Ruby would come to visit her along with Jayant and her mother. But these visits would become more of social calls rather than probing visits to find out about her physical condition. No one could pinpoint exactly as to what was different in her behaviour but her own family knew that all was not well with her. Guruji had told them that it would take Aishani some time to recoup from the stress and travails of the whole operation.

Adheesh was at his wits end. This was not his sober but happy Ash. This was a different person altogether. Was she Aishani he wondered? Or had she turned into somebody else after ingesting the blood of the demons? Had a trace of demon blood been inadvertently left behind in her body? These questions were driving him crazy as he mulled over them. One day, he just packed their bags and took her to the ashram to meet with Guruji. Guruji had told them not to come to the Ashram as he would be very busy in a great *yagna* which would be performed for Aishani in the Ashram. This *havan* was meant to purge Aishani of all the poisons which had entered her body. Surely he would be free now, Adheesh surmised. He was a little puzzled too. How can a *havan* be performed without his and Aishani's physical presence in the ashram? Till now they had not been asked to give any feedback on Operation Blood. Sure Guruji knew everything but this was the first time that they were not allowed to meet him.

Adheesh could not see Aishani in this condition anymore. They had to go to Guruji to find a solution to Ash's changed behaviour. When they reached the Ashram everything was the same. Nothing had changed. The same salubrious climate, the same smiling people and it seemed as if Guruji was waiting for them. Then why did he get the impression that they were not welcome here for the time being? He shook his head. He and

Aishani had gone to hell and back with none being the wiser. It was they who had changed, not the others. The others did not even know that they had gone away and on such a monumental operation. They smiled at everyone as if nothing had happened.

They touched Guruji's feet with reverence. Guruji blessed them and they sat down on the mat near his feet. Guruji looked closely at Aishani. Adheesh understood immediately that Guruji knew everything about Aishani's condition. He did not seem too perturbed also. Then why did he not warn them earlier? He waited for Guruji to speak.

As if reading his thoughts Guruji answered, "Both of you were already burdened with the herculean task of taking on Shambhu and his cohorts. The ingestion of demon blood in Aishani's body and then the activities of the blood-sucking eels were too much even for both of you."

Guruji looked at Adheesh and understood the unasked questions in his eyes.

"There were two reasons for not allowing both of you in the ashram. To begin with, Aishani was not in a proper physical condition to be kept here. Your father's hospital was the best place for her to be, with the best care and treatment without any questions asked. The *havan* here is so potent that it requires a healthy person to participate in it. Aishani wouldn't have been able to bear it. Now that she is a bit stronger she can sit and perform in the *havan*. Without you beside her, she wouldn't have been able to survive."

Adheesh nodded. He looked at Aishani; his heart went out to her. She looked so pale, listless and indifferent. There was no escape for them in these things. Not that they wanted to escape but the repercussions were too big.

Guruji looked at Adheesh, "Don't worry beta, Aishani will be alright in some more time. The *Mahamrityunjay* mantra and *Yagya* are both going on simultaneously for her. I had deliberately not asked both of you to come here because I wanted Aishani to gain physical strength first, eating the right food and supplements and doing light exercises in your father's hospital. And she has been meditating also. All this has paid dividends. Aishani is now strong enough to heal with Mahamritunjay Yagya."

Adheesh heaved a sigh of relief. Guruji never gave false consolation. What followed was a whirl of pujas and *havans* for Aishani, many of the *havans* with Adheesh beside her. There were many *havans* which could be performed only when both husband and wife were present. Very soon Aishani's health started taking a turn for the better. He knew it was so when she turned to look at him and smiled. She took his hand in hers and the familiar sparks flew, though sparsely and for a very brief period.

Guruji

Aishani woke up startled and looked at the alarm clock. She had overslept. Today of all the days! Guruji had called them early for a special assignment. It was for a meeting of his senior teachers and his senior students. It was six months now since their last assignment. Their last mission of demolishing Dr Shambhu, Veeju and his laboratory had taken a severe toll on Aishani's physical and mental health and it had taken her a very long time to recoup.

But the demons, they were not going to rest; it wasn't just one species of demons, they were so many breeds. No sooner had they eliminated one kind than another sort would raise their ugly heads. The lesser of them were disposed off by their juniors or the interns still in the senior years of their training. But now Guruji had called all the senior leaders for this meeting. Must be something very serious, she mused, not duly worried. Things had always worked out for the best.

Guruji looked at them gravely. They were the best of the best. If they failed to face the stupendous onslaught that was going to strike them then nothing could save our dear Earth from certain carnage, mayhem, and destruction. Each of those present there, male or female, had a special superpower apart from being a warrior. Besides the gurus and students of the Gurukul, there were others who were not members of the Gurukul but worked for it from the outside; they were equally fierce and loyal to their cause. One of those included in the group was Devnath. There were other similar Gurukuls also spread all over the world that worked in utter secrecy for obvious reasons. She did not know much about any of them as Guruji had told them that it was for their own safety and security. This was the place she was born to be in and this was the place where she was the happiest. Among the secondary shield were her mother and Ruby's parents, equally fierce and protective. They were not in the active field, but had been warriors nevertheless, and were now looking after and protecting their families and children and making a place for themselves in the present day society.

Guruji looked at them solemnly. "In the coming week there will be one of the biggest attacks on all the Gurukuls of the world. Total annihilation of the human race has been planned by the demons and their ilk. They have planned to dispose of the Gurukuls first thus making it more convenient to destroy the human race thereafter. Rest assured I have faith in each of you. Like it is said, 'when the going gets tough, the tough get going', not necessarily by facing the enemy squarely but rather recognising and acknowledging the fact that at times the enemy is stronger. Forewarned is forearmed. What I want each of you to do right now is to go back and make plans on a war footing to counter the demons and protect the Gurukul. We will meet again tomorrow to go through your plans and choose the best and the most practical in order of priority."

"In case," Guruji paused for a moment, "In case any harm comes either to the Ashram or to me, Aishani and Adheesh will take charge of the whole situation till it becomes normal."

A surprised muted gasp went around the group. There was full consensus on Aishani and Adheesh but what could happen to Guruji? He was invincible.

They came home fully charged with the thought that they had to make a grand plan to thwart the demons. Though they had planned such strategies earlier also, this was the first time that they would be making it so independently. They spent almost the whole night making their plans, looking for new ideas and trying to incorporate new and old weapons in various places against the different kinds of demons in each of the *Panchtattvas*—Earth, Water, Air, Fire, and Space. The demons could hide and attack from anywhere.

The Gurukul and its inhabitants had to be prepared for any such eventuality. Devnath stood outside the door protecting them against the dark forces and ready to do any bidding. Aishani looked out of the window. The shadows of the trees and shrubs were dark, darker than the night itself. The shadows combined with their originals looked huge and grotesque. The tree, the shrubs along with their shadows moved silently like huge giants or was it like huge demons? She shook her head, but a premonition was setting in. What if their plan didn't work out? What if…? Oh! Why was she so doubtful? They had always won. Well, most of the time anyway. She blocked her negative thoughts and turned to Adheesh.

Adheesh and Aishani hammered ideas against each other the whole night and finally arrived at a sort of a blueprint. It now had to be shown to Guruji to get his approval. It was almost dawn now. Adheesh yawned, "Let's go to sleep now Ash, we have to be fresh to give our presentation tomorrow or rather today," he smiled ruefully. They went to bed without changing. They slept. Suddenly she was being chased by a huge shadow which looked like a tree. All of a sudden Adheesh came between her and the shadow. She watched mesmerised as the shadow killed Adheesh with one stroke of its branch. Startled she sat up on her bed. Heart heaving she looked at the other side of the bed. Adheesh was not there. He must have already woken up and was nowhere to be seen. Probably having his breakfast and waiting for her. She hurriedly got ready and rushed down. Adheesh was waiting for her at the breakfast table. She gave a sigh of relief.

"Sorry," she whispered and served breakfast for both of them and brought their plates to the table. A servant was bringing hot tea from the kitchen. Somehow they collided with each other, the food-laden plates and the hot tea fell on the floor. Adheesh was there in an instant helping Aishani and the maid to get up. Mortified the maid quickly went inside to get another pot of fresh tea. Aishani looked at her clothes with dismay.

"Are you hurt Ash?" he asked in concern.

"I'm alright Adhee, but I'll have to change my clothes again. You go Adhee, I'll follow you in a minute," then seeing Adheesh's undecided expression she said, "Ok then I'll just take a minute."

Aishani rushed up to her room, quickly changed and came down. They both reached the room at the entrance of the jungle with Devnath at their heels. Though Aishani sometimes did feel a bit hemmed in by Devnath's presence around them all the time, she had adjusted to the fact very well, so much so that sometimes he was almost invisible to her. They reached the wall. Adheesh quickly put his palms on the wall and mentally chanted the opening mantra. This had become second nature to both of them. They didn't even think that they were chanting any mantra. The door that was the wall would automatically open in their presence or so it seemed. But today there was no response. Surprised he looked at the wall then exerted more pressure from his palms and also verbally chanted the mantra. Nothing happened.

"This is not right Adhee," Aishani whispered, "maybe the mantra has been changed without our knowledge. Let me try."

Adheesh shifted back making place for her. Their eyes met for an instant. Devnath was now watching them closely. He could sense that something was not right but he could not gauge the extent as yet. Aishani had her palms spread over the wall and now they could hear her chanting the mantra. Nothing happened. Of course, they were aware of other ways of entering the Gurukul but may be a bit later. They now knew for sure that the Gurukul and its inhabitants were in grave danger. Guruji had warned them many times about such a contingency. He had also told them what to do when such a thing happened and that was to save themselves first.

Guruji had said, "There will be times when your whole world will have turned upside down as has recently happened with Aishani. Never lose faith in yourself and the people around you. As for me, I will always be around you to instruct and guide you. Sometimes because of my other commitments, I may not be there physically to guide you but rest assured I will always guide you one way or the other. When all escape routes fail, pray to, and invoke Garuda devta. You already know the Garuda mantra and how to invoke him. Be extra careful with Garuda devta. Tell him exactly where you want to go and request him to bring you back also when the time comes. Garuda devta is so fast that he surpasses sound and time too. Within the blink of an eye he can bring you back from a place from where you may not be able to come back on your own."

They had heard Guruji with complete attention and fully believed him too. Though why Guruji was telling them this now did not make much sense to them. But they also knew that Guruji never spoke flippantly about anything.

As of now things had become a tad serious but they were not alarmed. Both of them put their hands together on the wall and chanted the mantra together. After what seemed a long time the wall shimmered and finally opened reluctantly. Quickly all three of them went inside. What they saw inside took their breath away. As they slowly went inside the main campus, they halted as if someone had bound their feet with ropes. There was dust and black ash everywhere which had till now not settled down, which meant that it was a recent carnage. There were signs of violence and pandemonium everywhere. Their beautiful forest seemed to have been destroyed and burnt to cinders. Here and there they could see some dead animals and birds also burnt lying on the ground. All the beautiful cottages and buildings had been ruined and destroyed. They were just a ragged pile of debris. Their hearts broke. All these had been built and nurtured from centuries. They were gone just in the blink of an eye.

There was an eerie silence all around. The greenery had turned black for miles around. Their hearts in their mouths they ran towards the main buildings and stopped short. There were dead and mutilated bodies everywhere, blood still flowing from the bodies. The massacre had just taken place and the villains seemed to have gone but not before conveying their thrill of killing, the sick and evil joy of wanton violence and slaughter. The bodies of humans, animals, even birds had been mutilated after their deaths just for the pleasure of it. Some had been left half eaten also. It seemed by the ghostly silence that the demons had left, but they were not taking any chances. Adheesh covered Aishani and he himself was covered by Devnath. No way were they going to leave Aishani! There was no time for sentiment.

Sweat drenched their skins. They could hear their own hearts thumping loudly in their chests. Aishani's eyes hurt and throbbed as she looked at the mayhem in front of her. She could not close her eyes even if she wanted to. There was more to see and agonise over. Her nails dug into her fists, cramps flooded her stomach. They held each other's hands for sustenance. Raw fear washed all over them not for themselves but for their beautiful ashram and what was left of it. There was one thought that both were avoiding and that was going inside Guruji's hut.

A bird's cry made them look up. A couple of vultures were circling overhead. Vultures! They looked closely at the sky. There were more black specks swooping down from the sky. More vultures! What had happened? The whole Gurukul had been decimated. There were no signs of life anywhere. Where was Guruji? The thought struck them almost simultaneously. They ran towards Guruji's cottage. They were panting by the time they reached it. The door of the cottage had been plucked out of its hinges and thrown away at some distance. They paused, hands held together not wanting to go inside. They knew Guruji was invincible; nothing could happen to him, he had lived through the ages and centuries. But still, they did not want to go inside.

It was ultimately Devnath who after seeing the dilemma of his master and mistress went inside. Adheesh and Aishani had frozen, though Aishani was mentally chanting the Durga mantra. When Devnath did not come out for a long time they had no choice but to go in. With trepidation, they entered the cottage and stood stock-still. Guruji was lying on his mat very still with his eyes just a bit open. His throat had been very neatly sliced with a razor sharp knife. It looked as if it was just a small nick but quite a lot of blood had flown from his neck. Guruji's neck had been totally severed and he was dead.

It took them some time to assimilate the fact that Guruji was dead. No, this couldn't be happening! The shock paralysed them like icy, liquid metal. With shaking legs they walked towards where Guruji lay. Aishani's first impulse was to turn around and run back to the time when she had just got up from the bed. She did turn around, but the image of Guruji with his severed neck kept on playing on her brain again and again like a horror movie. She wanted to scream but that would wake Guruji up. She bit hard on her lower lip and tasted blood. Every step seemed to be weighed down by lead.

Aishani let out a jagged breath. Both of them went near Guruji. This couldn't be happening! Guruji was invincible! Guruji was the avatar of Lord Hanuman and was thus blessed by God himself to be there till eternity. Was this then the end of eternity? Was this the end of life on Earth and beyond too? If Guruji was dead then destroying life on Earth would be just child's play for the demons. At a closer look, it was not only Guruji's neck which was severed but his whole body had been mutilated. Horrified, they sat down beside his body in silence. They had turned into stone. Their minds had stopped working. How long they sat there they did not know. They were not interested if there were any more killings or destruction taking place outside.

Devnath stood mutely in respect of his master's loss and shock. But eventually, his sense of urgency for Adheesh and Aishani's survival made him restive. Though the Gurukul was destroyed beyond repair and abandoned too, now that Guruji was dead, still his sharp sixth sense was telling him that these were some faint signs of life somewhere and some invisible demoniac presence also. Leaving them inside the cottage he went outside. The vultures were still crying and hovering overhead. But they were not coming down.

Devnath thought for a moment. Of course! The vultures were not landing because there were signs of life here on the ground. He looked around but could not see any sort of life anywhere. But he could sense fading life signs. Something had to be done to save Adheesh, Aishani and the dying people around them but what? He racked his brains to think of an idea that would help them escape and, if possible, with the few barely living ones. There were no two ways about it that they had to escape but even with their powers Adheesh and Aishani would not be able to escape these super intelligent, cunning, powerful and merciless demons. They had to run and fast, faster than the speed of lightning, maybe faster than the speed of time too, to an absolutely safe and secure place where nobody would be able to find them unless they themselves desired. There was only one celestial being who was capable of performing such a great feat and that was Garuda devta, the king of birds and the steed of Bhagwan Vishnu. There was no other alternative.

Devnath knew that only Adheesh and Aishani could invoke the Garuda mantra and hail Garuda devta. Devnath thought hard. He had to break the reverie of his master and mistress and impress upon them the urgency of escaping from this massive destruction which could destroy them too at any moment. He went inside. Adheesh seemed to be coming out of his stupor and he had started looking here and there as if trying to find some escape route. His killer instinct had come to the fore. This was the steely warrior that Devnath had witnessed earlier and wanted to see now. Adheesh knew that he had to protect Aishani even if it meant backing down. Devnath heaved a hurried sigh of relief and went to Adheesh.

"We don't have to worry about Guruji. He has survived many such situations. Guruji's body has been destroyed not his soul. He must have gone and come back many times. He has the boon of staying alive for this world. I do not know how that will happen, but right now we have to save ourselves and the few others who may be still alive. The demons will be waiting for us at every nook and corner of the Earth. After Guruji, killing both of you is vital to their survival. We have to escape from here. We have to survive to avenge Guruji's death and to avenge the death of humanity. We have to summon Garuda devta. Only he can rescue us from this grave crisis."

Adheesh looked at his friend and guard for many years. Devnath had made Adheesh come to his senses. Now to wake Aishani from the numbness of her shock, he put his hands around her. She did not respond. Gently he shook her. She turned and looked at him blankly without any expression. Her eyes were red-rimmed though there were no tears in them.

"Ash," he whispered urgently, "We have to escape from here otherwise nothing will remain. You have to overcome your grief, save it for some other more opportune time. There are still some people alive though barely so; I have to go and round them up as fast as I can. Ash, are you listening?" he asked urgently.

She nodded. Aishani was familiar with Garuda devta as she had taken his permission and used the Garuda astra in killing the nagas who had killed her father. Maybe Garuda devta would listen to her entreaties faster than any of them, Adheesh mused.

"I will join you as soon as I collect these battered souls. In the meantime, you invoke Garuda devta and chant his mantra." Aishani acknowledged and began preparing for the Garuda mantra. Adheesh looked at her with respect and hurriedly left the cottage instantly followed by Devnath. Aishani never failed to surprise him. The vultures were still screaming in their raspy and shrill voices, but nonetheless only hovering and not coming down for their feed. They were flying high above in the skies, their black and white bony feathers beating excitedly waiting for the kill.

It was Devnath who led him to the still barely alive bodies. Together they carried these bodies near Guruji's cottage. Adheesh barely recognised any of them nor did he try to do so. Some of the demons could still be there to kill any leftover living beings. The vultures had almost disappeared and so had their screaming. But why? Then it suddenly dawned on him. Aishani's chanting of the Garuda mantra was affecting the atmosphere. The vultures had also heard this and got scared and had flown away. Garuda devta was the king of birds and the mount of Bhagwan Vishnu. It is said that he is so powerful that he can move heaven and hell by the mere flapping of his wings. A ray of hope entered Adheesh's heart. The shooing off of the vultures meant that Garuda devta had heard their prayers and was coming to them. Adheesh went inside the cottage sat down beside Aishani and began chanting with her. Slowly the sky began darkening and after some time became very dark. There was a high rise in the wind. The black ashes of the Gurukul had now spread everywhere in the air. Suddenly they heard someone calling them.

The call was so imperious that it cut through their concentration and ordered them to come out immediately. They looked at each other their hearts pounding. Their prayers had been answered, they were sure of that. And indeed it was so. As they came out of Guruji's cottage they saw a huge colossal bird. In fact, it wasn't even fully a bird. It was like a half bird like an eagle or kite and half man. Different parts of its body were of different colours ranging from emerald, golden yellow, black and white. It seemed to them to have three heads and four hands, but when they looked closely they could see only the man-bird. Its sharp eagle yellow eyes were looking sharply and cruelly at them but they knew that it was empathising with them and had come here to help them escape the carnage and whatever life was left here. Both of them along with Devnath folded their hands in obeisance to Garuda devta. There was no need to tell him anything; he already knew and he had seen the destruction of the Gurukul from miles alone.

"You can put all the living people on my back and yourselves too. You have to work fast. I can see some of the demons coming towards this side again," said Garuda devta. Whether he said it loudly or whether he conveyed it telepathically they did not know nor were they in a position to be curious about it.

Charged by his presence, Adheesh and Devnath set to work. Only Aishani stood there undecided. Garuda devta looked at her and understood. In a soft mellow voice, he addressed her, "I am the conveyer of the living to safety. We cannot take our dead with us, not even your Guruji. He knew exactly what was going to happen. If he chose this then it must be for the greater good. There can be so many reasons for his leaving you at this time. We can dwell on this later. You can come and sit on my back now."

Aishani had no choice but to do as she was told. Her heart, body, and mind were all scarred beyond belief. She knew that she would never be able to get over this horrifying annihilation and the mass murders.

As soon as everyone was aboard Garuda's back, he folded his legs and flew straight into the air. His back was huge. He gestured to them to balance themselves by holding on to his feathers. The almost dead were carefully laid on his back. Then with a huge cry, he flew into the sky. He flew faster than the wind. Everything was a blur to them. They flew so fast that there was no time to think. How long they flew they had no idea. They had lost so much, almost everything; it did not matter where they were going. They had no choice but to leave everything to Garuda devta.

And suddenly, it was over. Garuda devta landed gently over a vast piece of land surrounded by mountains on all sides. They got down and helped the other unconscious people gently on the ground.

"You are somewhere near Mount Kailash and sometime in the past. Don't worry; nobody will be able to discover you here because this place is invisible to all except God and a few devtas. There is fresh water and there are herbs and food. You know how to survive in less than this. After you have fortified and rehabilitated yourselves and become stronger you can call me again and I will take you back to the present. Heal yourself, heal your colleagues. There are enough herbs here to heal an army. Food and water are no problem. I will bring others who may have hidden and escaped the massacre."

With a shrill screech, Garuda devta flew high up in the air and disappeared.